Historical fiction
Roth 2025

Enemy on the Other Side

Caroline Allana Scott

Copyright © 2024 Caroline Allana Scott
All rights reserved (scott.caroline@hotmail.co.uk).
ISBN: 9798326179081

To all the brave pioneers of Spiritualism.

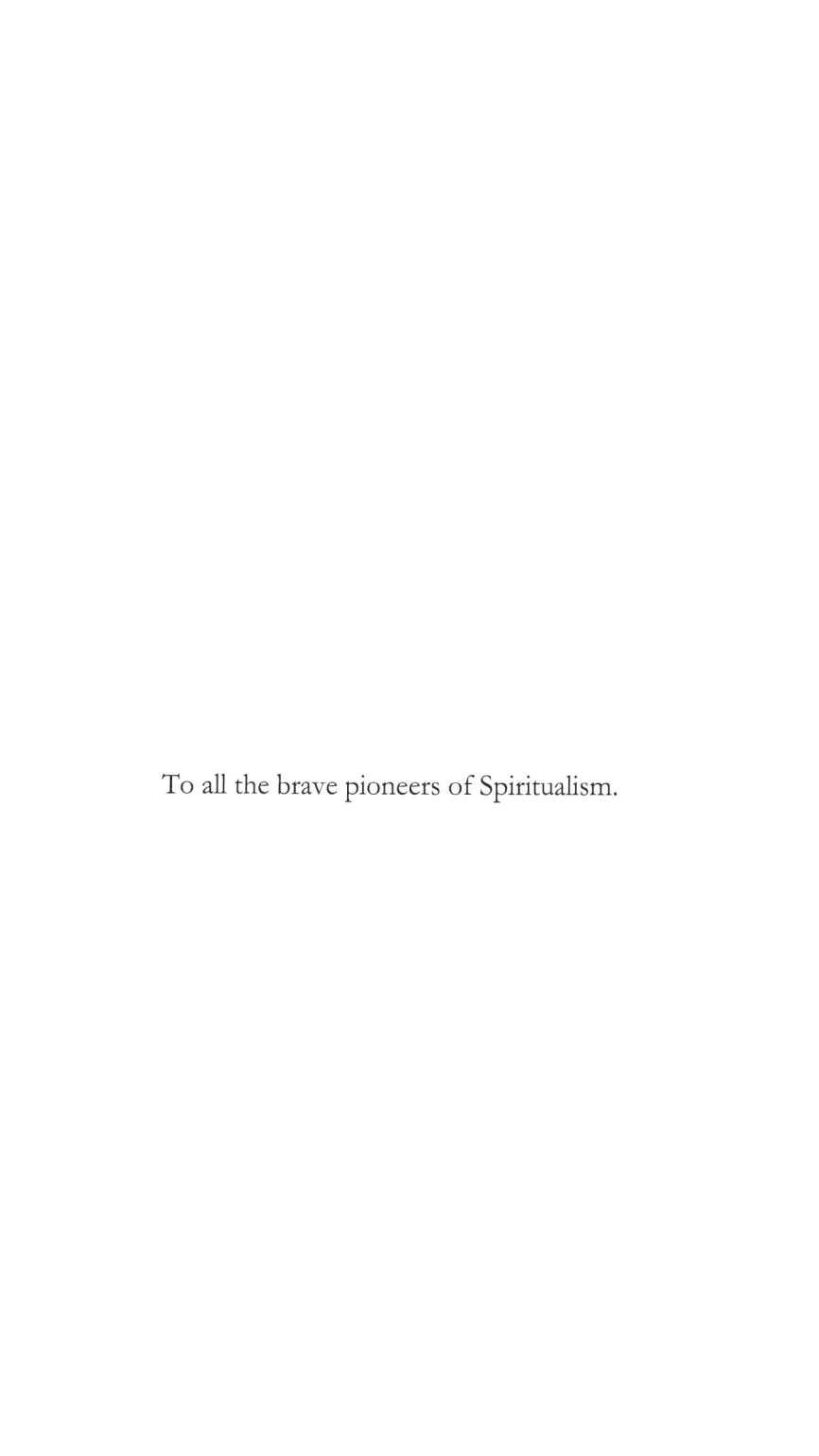

ACKNOWLEDGEMENTS

My heartfelt thanks to Dr Catherine McSporran of Glasgow University and everyone in the Garnethill Writers' Group.

1

Cairo, Egypt 1939

Bette

I'd been stuck in a taxi for the best part of two hours. The journey from the train station should have taken a quarter the time it took, but there'd been a few mechanical problems, and the driver had spent at least an hour with his head under the bonnet. Had I known it was a six-mile journey, and had I known the way, I'd have walked. My glasses had steamed up, my head was sore, and the traffic was getting on my nerves. But that wasn't the worst of it. My hands were beginning to twitch.

"Fucking dodo!" I yelled out the open window. *Control, Bette, control.* I shut my mouth tight and grabbed the seat. "Attagirl," I said quietly, after a moment or two when I finally descended from orbit.

The driver, who'd now stopped, was getting out the driver's seat. He'd ignored my outburst. Probably hadn't a clue in hell what was happening anyway. One of the things about being an American. No one abroad seems to understand you. There again, more likely he just wasn't interested. "Well, fuck that!" The words were out before I could stop them. "And fuck this!" I yelled, as my neck jerked. It hurt like hell. But there it was. The simple truth of the matter. Tourette's is the biggest fucking *dodo-ing* bastard of the lot.

Anyway, here I was at my destination. The driver was demanding money. Far too much. I tried to haggle, but it was no use. "Thanks for the ride," I said, slamming the passenger door shut, wondering if there really had been mechanical problems.

"Any time, Miss Tomato!" said the driver, escaping with half my funds.

I squeezed my lips tightly together. I'd already said enough for a fortnight. But the guy was a jerk, and it's not my fault I'm a redhead. Still, I had to agree. I probably wasn't a pretty sight. After a long, sticky journey, my short, wavy curls would, no doubt, be hanging over an over-heated and *very* sunburned face. Anyway, the dude was gone, and here I was standing at the bottom of a flight of marble steps leading to a block of apartments, wondering what the hell I'd got myself into. What indeed?

I work for a magazine: *Amber St Claire*. I'm based at the head office in Glasgow, Scotland. It's supposed to be a society magazine, but I have my doubts. One or two of our more enterprising reporters have managed to infiltrate the political lives of the rich and famous. Some of them infamous, and some of them able to give damned good information about nefarious goings-on in Europe, particularly in regards to the German Nazi Party.

But me? Ten years in Scotland, and never once had I been asked to venture from Glasgow. That was until about a month ago. My boss, Joe Bannerman, called me into his office one day. Told me he'd got wind that things were happening, and put me in touch with someone, who put me in touch with someone else. Then he got information that things were happening in Egypt. Well, I knew *that*. Things were *always* happening in Egypt. But *this* he said was different. Things were *really* happening in Egypt. Cairo in particular.

Unfortunately, given my track record (I'll go into that later), I'd decided that the mundane was good. Weddings and christenings suited me just fine. Local things that kept me out of bother. However, the way Joe was talking, it sounded like I just might be travelling. "So, what do you want *me* to do about it?" I'd asked.

"I want you to investigate," he'd said.

"Investigate?"

Now, Joe's from Yorkshire. Speaks his mind and loses his temper. It was a typically cold day in Glasgow, but already I could see the steam coming out his ears. When the colour in his cheeks began to turn a darker shade of puce, I realised he meant business. "Get information," he'd said slowly.

"How?"

"Infiltration."

So, he'd sent me on a course on the *dos and*

don'ts for private eyes in-the-making, but when it came to the rifle range, they'd decided not to issue me with a firearm. Joe hadn't seemed that bothered, so I took that as a plus. The job clearly couldn't be that dangerous.

"And where am I supposed to stay?" I'd then asked.

"With your brother."

"And what the hell do I tell him?"

"You're on holiday."

So, here I was standing outside a block of apartments. The top one belonged to my brother. I went in and climbed the stairs. I'd been there a couple of years ago, but one or two things on the landing had changed. A fancy great cabinet sat in a corner. That hadn't been there before. It was big enough to hide a dead body. Maybe even two.

When I reached the door, I stopped. It was slightly ajar. Now that was strange. I pushed it slowly open. Inside, it was cool, and there was an overriding smell of lavender, as if I'd just been whacked with a dish of potpourri. I looked up. Electric fans were spinning with the intensity of aircraft propellers. I sniffed the air. Another smell. Someone had been smoking a cigar, and my senses told me that someone was there. Someone who shouldn't be there.

To my left was the door leading into the master bedroom. Next to it was a table with a small bronze of the goddess Venus. How very apt for my brother. I picked Venus up, and pushing the bedroom door open, entered. A large bed sat in the centre of the room, but no one was there. I glanced across at another door leading into an ensuite bathroom. It was shut.

"Hello!" I called. No response.

I turned and left the bedroom, replacing the bronze on the table. But I was uneasy. Where the hell was Stephen? And why had he left the front door open? I decided to stay around a while. See if he turned up.

The rest of the apartment was open plan. Making my way over to a couch, I sat down and stretched my legs across a rug. I hadn't seen it before, and as I studied its bright colours, something shiny caught my eye. Bending over, I picked the thing up, and held it close to my eyes. It was a gold chain. Attached to it was a gold locket. But the locket wasn't alone. Also hanging from the chain were a gold cartouche pendant and a bronze swastika.

I caught the three pendants between my fingers, and held them up to the light. I could only make out some of the features. Two tiny stones were fitted into the locket: a diamond and an emerald.

I wiped my glasses. Something was inscribed on the cartouche pendant. It seemed to be some kind of hieroglyphics, but I'd have to check that out later.

I opened the locket with my nail, and a lock of hair fell out. I'd just turned the hair in my hand when I heard a noise. It came from the bedroom. I jumped, and shoving the hair back in, clipped the pendant shut. There was a crash, and the master bedroom door flew open. Two willowy figures tripped through, half naked.

Now it made sense. I was relieved I hadn't gone

into the bathroom. I knew the first figure. It was my brother, Stephen, the most eligible bachelor in Cairo and star of the Egyptian silver screen. "You left the door open," I said.

"Did I?" said Stephen, his blond hair hanging forward over his vivid blue eyes. "Didn't expect you quite so soon, I'm afraid. I thought you were coming tomorrow."

I glanced at the second figure. It was a woman. Her penetrating, violet eyes stared back, and I realised that she was the one smelling of lavender. She jabbed my brother in the ribs with her elbow. "Not a very good introduction," she said in a soft Irish brogue, her cheeks crimson with embarrassment. She was tall with dark hair, and very beautiful. "Sorry," she added with a smile that displayed a row of perfectly white teeth. She turned and made her way back into the bedroom with the speed of an uncoiling spring.

"Go and wait for me on the balcony," said Stephen.

Good idea.

The balcony was big and looked out on to an assortment of buildings, depicting different cultures and religions: minarets, spires and the familiar form of the synagogue of Ben Ezra. Further in the distance was the Nile, its banks adorned with palm trees. I studied the view, and for the first time since leaving Britain, reflected on the real reason for my being in Egypt. I'd been assigned a very unfortunate task, one that I kept questioning. I'd been sent in to investigate my brother, Stephen Milligan.

"Sorry about that," said Stephen. He'd put on a bathrobe, and now followed me on to the balcony carrying a glass of water. His foot knocked against a potted palm. "Whoops."

Yeah, whoops all right.

I pulled a chair out from under a metal table, and sat down. Two crystal champagne glasses rested on their side on top of the table, next to an empty champagne bottle. "Someone's been having a good time."

"Farida sends her apologies."

I smiled. I still couldn't get to grips with Stephen's accent, nor his turn of phrase. It was like he'd just walked out of a chapter of a Nancy Mitford novel. "I see the elocution classes paid off."

"Do I detect a hint of sarcasm?"

Now, that was Noel Coward to a tee. "You don't say!"

"And maybe *you* should invest in a few lessons. Dispense with that New York twang. You should have got rid of it a long time ago."

"Maybe I just don't want to!" I replied sharply. "Anyway, who's Farida?"

Stephen's eyes went to my hands. "I'd better take that," he said. I looked down and realised I was still holding the gold necklace.

"Does that mean it belongs to Farida?"

He didn't reply, but I didn't have time to ponder. I'd been given a job to do. I needed to get myself ready. Joe had made arrangements for me to meet my contact later on that day. It was time to kick ass.

*

I'd never been one to follow fashion trends, but had learned that in the world of espionage, image was everything.

"Where are you going?" asked Stephen, as I slipped on a pair of high heels.

"Secret admirer," I lied. I left the apartment and crossed into Kamal Pasha Street, where I was accosted by donkey boys. I wasn't used to high heels, and my feet were hurting like hell. I was to meet my contact at Shepheard's Hotel, the most famous hotel in Cairo. I'd been there before, but when I arrived this time, I noticed businessmen, mostly Europeans, networking on the veranda, which surrounded the entire building. They sat at tables, laden with bottles and glasses, and seemed to be consuming so much alcohol that I wondered how the hell anyone managed to strike a deal. Joe had told me it was a good place to blend. I didn't agree. Maybe for him it was. Not for me, though. Whatever. I still had a job to do.

I negotiated the front steps, and made my way into the very grand Entrance Hall, where I was met by the sound of an orchestra playing. I looked across at the Moorish Hall with its high arches and glass dome, and felt very much out of place. I turned towards the Grill Room, where Joe had arranged that I meet my contact. It was three o'clock exactly, and I was late.

The Grill Room was one of three restaurants. It was the least exclusive, and fortunately, the menu was in English. I stopped at the entrance. Loud chatter filled my ears. Men and women were jabbering on about nothing at all, until the sound of babbling was interrupted by the loud blast of a trumpet, and I realised that the orchestra in the lobby had managed to warm up, and a performance was about to begin.

I assumed the next tune was dedicated to all the supporters of Bing Crosby, for a small Egyptian in a tuxedo had just begun to croon his rendition of *The Very Thought of You.* The interpretation wasn't great. The singing was loud, and the man's voice wasn't the best.

I wandered in.

The Grill Room was smoky and I still hadn't identified my contact. That was until I finally clocked Joe in a corner reading *The Egyptian Gazette*. He was smoking a cigar. His face was florid, which made him look like a blushing pomegranate. It was then I noticed his hand on the bottle of whisky. It was a quarter way down. Great. Just what I needed. Drunk. I took a good look at him. His bulging jowls and corpulent neck had forced him to loosen his tie. He'd always had bad posture, and right now his portly belly sagged over his trouser belt.

I walked over. When he saw me, he raised a chubby hand and waved. As I got to the table, he removed his horn-rimmed spectacles and began to polish them with a dirty-looking handkerchief. "Good to see you, Bette," he said, looking me up and down. "Have a drink."

He didn't seem that bad, but he certainly wasn't going to let go of that bottle. So, deciding one of us had to remain sober, I was about to ask for lemonade, when I noticed afternoon tea on the menu. "How about afternoon tea?"

"I take it you don't give up your omnivorous habits for Lent," said Joe calling the waiter over and placing the order.

I didn't reply. A three-tiered plate arrived almost immediately. "So," I said, grabbing a slice of cake, "I take it you're my enigmatic contact?"

Joe rubbed his nose. "Don't eat too much. We're having dinner tonight."

"We are?"

"We're having dinner with a friend of your brother's. Omar O'Malley."

I almost spat the cake out. "Omar O'Malley? What kind of a name is that?"

"A very significant name. He's an important man. Very rich. Lives in a villa in the Muqattam Hills, not far from here. But more to the point, like Stephen, he has links with Egypt's fast-developing film industry. He's been producing a lot of its films."

"And that's a crime?"

"Not in itself. No. But it's a good cover. Unfortunately, we have reason to believe that O'Malley also has an affiliation with the German Nazi Party."

Mind boggling. The Nazis were cavorting with Tinseltown. "So, what you're saying is that money is being laundered to finance the Nazis?"

"And since the Egyptians have been doing their best to kick the British out of Egypt..."

"...then that opens the way for the Nazis," I finished.

"A can of worms, my dear. A can of worms."

"So, if this guy O'Malley has an affiliation with the Nazi Party, then you obviously think Stephen must have one too. Right?"

"Quite possibly. Things are happening in Germany. Very worrying things, and they're spreading to other parts of the world."

"Well, I know that."

"I don't think you do. You see, Bette, our dear friend Adolph Hitler is dabbling in a number of different things he shouldn't."

"That being?"

"Being, being the word. Or should I say, beings. In fact, energies, Bette. Dark and very negative energies."

I began to laugh. "Are you talking about ghosts?"

"It's not a laughing matter."

"Then what is it?"

"We're looking at the Etheric World, Bette."

"Etheric World?"

"The Spirit World. The place you go to when you pop your clogs."

"The Hereafter?" I paused and shook my head. "You mentioned dark energies. What do you mean?"

"Bad people, Bette. Bad people on the other side."

Other side? I couldn't decide if he meant the Nazis or bad spooks, and the fact he might mean both, just didn't bear thinking about. I narrowed my eyes. "Listen Joe, it's bad enough you got me to come out here. In fact, I only came to find out what the hell's going on, but now you've gone too far."

"You do realise Hitler is creating a special army?"

"You mean the SS?"

"I mean closely tied to the SS."

I didn't like the sound of this. A shiver ran up my spine, and my neck jerked. It hurt like hell. I gritted my teeth. "What's going on, Joe?"

"Things are happening here in Cairo. Things that we believe your brother and O'Malley are involved in. Things that we've yet to identify properly, but which we believe are a threat to our national security."

"And where's it all happening? Where in Cairo I mean?"

"We don't know. And that's why we've brought you out here. Your remit is to investigate O'Malley and question your brother."

"You do realise that that's not a very nice thing to make me do?"

"Question Stephen?"

"I think you mean *investigate* Stephen."

Joe took a deep breath. "We're not as bad as you think. We're prepared to give your brother the benefit of the doubt. It's quite possible he's been dragged into something against his will."

"We?" Joe had been talking in the plural for a while, and I now felt it was time to ask why. "You said *we*."

Joe's expression told me he'd been careless with his choice of words. It also indicated he'd no intention of explaining what he meant.

"Hitler is a very dangerous man," he said.

"So why did the people vote him in?"

"Promises. Political promises. Hopes of change for the country."

"Everyone makes promises."

"Not like him. He's a man with charisma. He can convince."

"So why hasn't anyone done anything about it?" I persisted. Joe didn't reply. "Can I take it from your silence, that someone *is* stepping in, apart from *yours truly*, I mean?"

"Look at Hitler's secret police and his other strange organisations," said Joe, still not answering any of my questions.

"Joe, do you belong to some kind of spy ring?" I asked.

He laughed. "The biggest spy ring in the world. The newspapers." He turned and called a waiter over, and ordered a lager.

"What about that?" I said, nodding towards the bottle of whisky.

"I'll keep that for later," he said smiling.

Later? My mind went back to our very strange conversation. Ghosts? Ghouls? And whatever the hell else there was. As for the dinner later that evening, heck! I looked at Joe's bottle of whisky. *To hell with sobriety*, I thought. I decided to join him. "Add a gin and tonic to that."

The drinks arrived. I took a couple of gulps, and was pleased to feel the gin act quickly. But Joe still hadn't answered all my questions.

"Let's be constructive here," he said after a moment. "Let's try and see what's really going on."

"What exactly do you want me to do?"

"I want you to write a double-page spread on Cairo's film industry. I want you to ask questions and find out what's going on. I want you to blend in like a chameleon."

Chameleon? What did he want me to do? Carry around pots of paint?

He stared at my blank expression. "Let me get to the point. You're still a very junior reporter, so be thankful for every window of opportunity. You're not here to disport yourself. You're here to work. I want you to fraternise with the enemy. Flirt with O'Malley. Kiss his arse. Quite frankly, I don't care what you do. Use your discretion, but please don't tell me you haven't the gumption to have a bash at it."

"Nope." I wanted to say more, but Joe wasn't in the mood for debate. Willingly agreeing to incriminate my brother wasn't a very charitable thing to do, even if Joe had suggested Stephen might not know what was going on. I remembered the woman I'd seen with Stephen, the one with the Irish accent. Did she have anything to do with O'Malley? Things were not looking good. What the heck had Stephen walked into? What the hell had I walked into?

A bang outside startled me. A bomb was my first thought, but it wasn't. It was followed by a series of smaller explosions, like the sporadic firing of a gun. Then there was cheering and rejoicing. Fireworks. Someone was celebrating, but it certainly wasn't me. It was time to hit the road.

2

Central Police Office, Glasgow

Jessie

"Get yer filthy hands aff me, ye scrawny-looking bitch!"

Bitch, Jessie MacTaggart didn't mind. But *scrawny*? That hurt. Jessie hadn't been scrawny for at least five years. She was still slim, but had put on a few pounds over the years owing to her mother's good cooking.

"Come back here, Clara MacNab!"

"Piss aff y'auld boot!"

MacNab was a shoplifter. She stank of alcohol, and had been caught red-handed by the owner of a small tobacco shop. He'd made a citizen's arrest until Jessie arrived to do the necessary. The police station was just round the corner. Unfortunately for Jessie, MacNab had slipped the cuffs and done a runner. The fact they were only a matter of yards from the police station didn't seem to matter, for Jessie had still been forced to spring into action.

I'm getting too old for this, she thought, as she hoisted up her skirt and followed MacNab, who for some strange reason was running in the right direction. Where was backup when you needed it?

In the end it didn't matter. Jessie didn't know if it was coincidence, or just good timing, but as they neared the entrance of the station, a tall skinny man stepped out. *Great! My prisoner escapes, and it's in full view of Detective Inspector MacLeod!*

MacLeod was from Lewis. He hated the drink, and the fumes from MacNab's breath had probably already found their way up his nostrils.

"MacNab!" he called, sticking his right foot out.

MacNab flew over his leg. "Bastard!" she screamed as she hit the ground. "Fuck's sake! I've nae teeth left!"

Jessie's first thought was that this could, in fact, be true. The girl's mouth had struck the pavement, and was now dripping blood.

"Get up!" said Jessie. The girl didn't move. "Get up!"

"Fuck aff!"

"I suggest you control your prisoner, Constable MacTaggart," said MacLeod.

"Get up before he kicks your arse!" hissed Jessie, pulling MacNab to her feet. The girl didn't resist. She appeared to be in too much pain. A stream of blood was flowing down her chin.

"What's she in for?" asked MacLeod.

"Shoplifting."

"Well, I suggest you add resisting arrest and breach of the peace to that."

"And I'm getting *you* done for assault!" screamed MacNab. "I want a lawyer!"

"MacTaggart! In here!"

Jessie rolled her eyes. What now? For some reason Detective Inspector MacLeod had decided that it was time for the CID to integrate with uniform. Not only that, he was doing the unimaginable. He was speaking to the WPCs, the female police officers, who were a separate unit altogether.

Jessie knocked on his door. "Sir?" she said, entering the office.

"Sit down." Jessie complied. MacLeod looked her up and down. "How long's that you've been in the Force?"

"Ten years, sir."

"Pleased?"

"Sir?"

"Happy to be a police woman?"

"Of course, sir."

"Daresay you've got the war to thank for that."

"I was a child during the war."

"You know what I mean."

Jessie raised a brow. She knew exactly what he meant. During the war, the men had gone to fight, so women had been recruited to fill the spaces, and once open, the door had never quite shut. "Can't say we do much more than we do at home, though," she said, referring to the distinct lack of opportunities in the women's unit. "Looking after children and all that."

"Didn't think you had children."

"No, but I have brothers and sisters."

"You still live with your parents?"

"I do now."

"You must be nearly thirty?"

"Thirty-one next month, sir."

"Really? And no husband on the horizon?"

"I'm a widow, sir. Have been for five years."

"Oh." MacLeod had the grace to blush.

"Is there a problem, sir?"

MacLeod took a sharp intake of breath. "The Chief Constable's not happy," he said.

"I suppose that goes with the territory," said Jessie.

"That's as may be, but tell me, what do you know about a girl called Elizabeth Kipper, aka Bette Milligan? She's an American."

Jessie raised a brow once more. "Well, I know her as Bette Milligan."

"An associate of MacNab's?"

"As a matter of fact, yes," said Jessie, surprised. "In the past, though."

"Then it's very fortuitous MacNab was lifted today," said MacLeod. "In a manner of speaking," he added, a smirk across his face. "And Milligan," he continued, "was she ever in bother?"

"Aye, but that was a long time ago when she was a young teenager. I'd just started with the Force."

"So, you had dealings with her, then?"

"Aye. Both girls were about thirteen when I met them. Clara's from Glasgow, but Bette came over from America. They were a very bad influence on each other."

"And what about Bette's family?"

"Local, sir. Here in Glasgow. Bette's father's an alcoholic, so she was sent as a baby to live in America. Never met the mother, but I think she died."

"Anyone else?"

"One brother. Stephen. He's a lot older than Bette. Spent time in America too."

"Both women the same age?"

"Aye."

"So that makes them what?"

"Twenty-three, sir."

"So, Bette's been back in Scotland for ten years?"

"Aye."

"Any previous?"

"A couple of juvenile convictions for shoplifting, but that's all. She's done well now, despite her problem."

"Problem?"

Jessie smiled. "Tourette's, sir."

"Tourette's?"

"Tourette's syndrome, sir. She can't control what she says. Usually, it's offensive words. They just spill out."

MacLeod grunted. "Then half the police force has it!"

"Involuntary."

"That's what I mean."

Jessie smiled. "Bette scared the custody sergeant, one night."

"Really?"

"Not something you easily forget. She and Clara were brought in after shoplifting one Friday. They had to spend the weekend in custody. Two o'clock Saturday morning and Clara shouts for help. Seems that Bette was shouting in her sleep. When she finally woke up, her whole body was twitching and she was shouting abuse. The custody sergeant thought she'd been possessed by the devil."

"The devil?"

"Anyway. It didn't do her any harm. In fact, it did her a lot of good. She and Clara parted company, and Bette went on to get a job with a magazine."

"What?"

"*Amber St Claire.*"

"Is this a joke?"

"Not at all. She started out as a tea girl, then made her way up. She's a reporter now. I think it was a contact. Something to do with her father and an old friend of his."

"How on earth do you know all this? It's not in any of the reports."

"She told me round about the time she got the job with the magazine. Called in to speak to me."

"And why would she do that?"

"I didn't laugh at her, sir. She wanted me to see she'd turned a new leaf, even if her friend hadn't. I was pleased for her and there was no need for me to write this up. She hadn't committed a crime."

"What's her father doing now?"

"He's still in Glasgow."

"And who is the contact?"

"Can't remember his name, but he runs *Amber St Claire*. I think he owns it as well."

"I see," said MacLeod, as the pieces fell together.

"It's also when Stephen, the brother, came back into the picture. It was quite funny really. Bette was so proud. That's how I remember. She told me that after the war, Stephen returned to Britain and joined the British Army. He was shipped off to the Suez Canal in Egypt, but had a medical discharge. A heart condition. Anyway, he decided to stay on in Cairo. Learned Arabic. A short time later, he became just about the most famous actor in Egypt."

"An actor?"

"Yes, but out there her brother's known as Angel."

"Funny I've never heard of him."

"That's because you don't live in Egypt, sir."

"No, and never will."

"So, what's all this got to do with Clara MacNab, if you don't mind my asking, sir?"

"When Clara and Bette were hanging around together, was there an aunt on the scene?"

"Bette's aunt?"

"No. Clara's aunt."

"Don't remember seeing one," said Jessie.

"Probably kept out the way." MacLeod paused. "She belongs to that funny church in Holland Street. You know, the spooky one."

"The Spiritualist Church round the corner?"

"The very one. Ellen Fairbairn's her name. Mrs Ellen Fairbairn, and she's a medium." MacLeod began to tap his desk with his fingertips.

"Sir?"

"The Chief Constable has a problem."

Jessie smiled. "Because she talks to the dead?"

"Ellen Fairbairn has become something of a worry. She knows things she's not supposed to know about. In fact, things very few are supposed to know about."

"If she's a medium…?" began Jessie.

"…or a fraud."

"What happened?"

"The Chief Constable's wife went to one of the services the other week, and it seems that Mrs Fairbairn was telling the congregation things they shouldn't know."

Jessie smiled again. "Strictly speaking, it wouldn't be Mrs Fairbairn. It would be whoever she brought through."

MacLeod narrowed his eyes. "I take it you've been to a service?"

Jessie swallowed hard. "I lost my husband five years ago, so yes, I've been to a few of the services, and the name Ellen Fairbairn does ring a bell now, only I didn't know she had anything to do with Clara MacNab."

"And have the dead spoken to you?" smirked MacLeod.

"I have a very open mind, sir."

"Well, just you keep your mind as open as you like. But remember this. The world's going to hell in a basket, and this woman is not helping." MacLeod stopped tapping his fingers. "Mrs Fairbairn, I am led to believe, told the Chief Constable's wife that one of her husband's colleagues has information."

Jessie was intrigued. "Sir?"

"Information concerning army intelligence. A top-secret operation. Operation MPRS. When the Chief Constable heard this, he liaised with an acquaintance he has at MPRS. The acquaintance at MPRS, I am led to believe, went a clear shade of puce."

"Can't someone have a quiet word with Mrs Fairbairn?"

"God damn it! The woman is a spy! She must have been giving out information to members of the congregation. And mark my words, if you go back, which I assure you, you will, you'll see a few empty seats. Other spies on their way back to Nazi Germany ready to upset the applecart!"

"Isn't that a bit far-fetched?"

"Forgive my ignorance, Constable. But I'd say that talking to the dead is rather more unlikely. What's more, the woman was spouting out random names, and one of them just happened to be Bette Milligan. So, you see why I'm interested, and the Chief Constable is quite rightly upset?"

"You mean it might start another war?"

"I want you to keep a vigilant eye on MacNab, an eye on Ellen Fairbairn and an eye on Elizabeth Kipper."

"Bette Milligan, sir."

"Whatever the hell her name is!" MacLeod paused. "I just want you to use your feminine skills and wiles and extract as much information as you can about what's going on. We already have a good idea, but just need things confirmed."

Bollocks, thought Jessie. They hadn't a clue what was going on.

3

Spiritualist Church, Glasgow

Jessie

"I know who you are," said Ellen Fairbairn. "And I know why you're here."

Great, thought Jessie, *busted before I've even started.* She studied the elderly woman sitting opposite her. Mrs Fairbairn had grey hair, parted in the middle, which was neatly drawn back over her ears into a loose bun. Light wrinkles scattered themselves across her round face, the top ones melting into large brown, intelligent eyes. She had a short, plump body, and her swollen ankles hung over sensible brown shoes. Jessie guessed she was around sixty and could have been anyone's granny.

"You're here to talk about Clara MacNab," continued Mrs Fairbairn. "I heard she'd been arrested for shoplifting."

Jessie's wondered what she meant by 'heard'.

"Psychically, or, through the grapevine?" she asked, her eyes descending Mrs Fairbairn's white blouse and brown pleated skirt. They stopped at the woman's hands, which rested on her lap. The knuckles were inflamed with arthritis.

Mrs Fairbairn smiled. "We're not as bad as all that." Her smile was wide, and reminded Jessie of the *Cheshire Cat* in Lewis Carroll's *Alice's Adventures in Wonderland*. "So, what can I do for you?" she asked.

Jessie wasn't sure now. Her cover had been blown, so she'd have to think on her feet. "Do you see much of Clara?"

"Not anymore," replied Mrs Fairbairn, her eyes becoming sad. The smile, nonetheless, remained.

This has to be the Cheshire Cat, thought Jessie. When Mrs Fairbairn's smile relaxed a little, Jessie decided it must be the expression reserved to bring comfort to the bereaved. Jessie stared and wondered if Mrs Fairbairn, like the character in the book, could disappear at a whim, leaving behind nothing but that smile. In fact, was she even real? Or, was she one of those ghosts with whom she was supposed to communicate?

"Clara doesn't come near me," continued Mrs Fairbairn. "I've tried to help, but she's not interested."

"You're her aunt, aren't you?" said Jessie.

"No." Mrs Fairbairn paused and the smile disappeared. Jessie was glad. It made her look like an ordinary granny again. "Clara is my best friend's daughter. Or, was, depending, of course, on how you look at it."

"Best friend?" repeated Jessie. MacLeod hadn't mentioned anything about a best friend.

"Helen MacNab. Only she's in Spirit."

Helen and Ellen? That had to be confusing. "I take it *in Spirit* means she's dead?"

Mrs Fairbairn nodded. "Sad case of like mother, like daughter, I'm afraid. When the drink takes over, there's very little you can do."

"Bette Milligan seemed to escape," said Jessie, hedging her bets. "Do you know Bette Milligan?"

"Personal responsibility," said Mrs Fairbairn. "And yes, I know Bette. Not well, but I know her."

"Because of Clara?"

Mrs Fairbairn nodded. "We all have choice. That's why we're here. We have to learn to take the correct path."

"Maybe Clara didn't have the same choices as Bette. I hear she's a reporter for a society magazine."

Mrs Fairbairn smiled. "*Amber St Claire*," she said. "Very up-market. And by the way, Clara *did* have a choice. When they took Bette on, they offered to teach Clara to read and write."

"That was rather philanthropic of them."

"Well, Clara didn't take the opportunity. She decided to follow her own path. The wrong one, I might add."

"You're right there."

"I think you're here for a reason," said Mrs Fairbairn.

"I came for a private reading."

"Not just that. But I daresay a police officer is entitled to speak to her discarnate loved ones."

"The dead ones?"

"Aye. The dead ones. And don't pretend to be hard. You've a heart as soft as a marshmallow."

"Really?" Jessie felt her face tighten. "You'll have to clue me in a bit here. I don't know how this thing of yours works."

"Oh, I think you do."

"I'm not a religious person, Mrs Fairbairn."

"No. But I think you're a spiritual one."

Jessie squinted her eyes. "So, what do you believe in?"

"Me? I believe in energy. Some call it God. But most of all, I believe in helping our fellow man."

"And woman?"

"Everyone. I believe we must do our best here on earth, so when we pass over to the other side, we're in a better position to evolve."

"You mean life after death? Doesn't that apply to most religions?"

"But you forget one thing, Jessie. The reason you're here."

Jessie frowned. "I'm here for a private reading," she said.

"Exactly. You're here to speak to the dead."

4

The Desert, Egypt

Bentley

The horse raced across the soft sand. Captain Bentley Ford-Jenkins clung to the animal's back as he rode with a vengeance.

Bentley was Australian, but attached to the British Army. He'd done well in his career, albeit he was still a relatively young man. Forty-five to be precise. And everything he'd achieved had been down to one man: his boss, a colonel, who had started his career in army intelligence then moved on to other more secret things. The colonel had been the first to recognise all of Bentley's skills: educational and mediumistic.

They'd met in Australia, and it hadn't taken the colonel long to whip Bentley away from his native country, and get him to sign up for the British Army. He'd then got him a place at Glasgow University, where Bentley had got his medical degree, all paid for by the army of course. Bentley had first served in the British Intelligence Corps, and had later been transferred to his current position with MPRS, a little-known section, affiliated to the British Army, so he could put his particular skills to good use. But the pressures of the job were now clearly taking their toll.

The animal charged on, its hooves leaving their mark on the surface. Bentley laughed into the silence. Nothing, except tiny granules of sand flying into the air, like a mass of messy powder. Freedom engulfed Bentley, as the heat of the sun seared his face. He continued at speed, his cheeks aflame with excitement.

Ahead were rows of rocks, large, heavy and still, giving the impression they were secured by roots well into the sand.

Maybe they were.

As he rode, a piercing shriek drew his attention to the sky. A bird of prey circled the sand. It had the wingspan of an eagle and the speed of a hawk. The creature scrutinised him, clearly identifying him as potential fodder. Nothing was going to get rid of that bird, as it continued to surf through the clouds.

Bentley licked his lips. He would have killed for a beer. He turned to his right, and examined the familiar triangular shapes. The great pyramids of Giza: truly the best evidence of antiquity. Ancient structures, created long ago, with remarkable mathematical precision.

He shut his eyes and felt his body relax. He knew

the calm feeling wouldn't last for ever. Soon the sense of peace would be replaced by the call of duty and another unpleasant task. But not yet. Still time to savour every moment of freedom.

Then it happened.

He felt his spirit rise gently from his physical body.

Not now!

Not when he was riding a bloody horse!

Unfortunately, his spirit wasn't listening. It had a mind of its own. Bentley felt himself float upwards into the sky. It was like time no longer existed, at least not on the same dimension as the earth world. He found himself drifting over rivers and hills, and his mind began to buzz when his finely attuned sensibilities connected with the universal energy.

But therein lay the problem. Just as his spirit could detect joy, it could also pick up pain, which at that moment was travelling at considerable speed through a tangle of electromagnetic fields and connecting with his own.

Bentley floated towards a castle. He was immediately struck by a sense of foreboding. He knew where he was. Wewelsburg Castle, the headquarters of the German SS, at its head, a very dangerous man: Heinrich Himmler.

Himmler was one of Adolph Hitler's most devout followers, who spent days in the castle, dreaming of ways to take over the world. He had already turned the building into a medieval fortress, and a place of what he deemed to be spiritual communion. But that in itself was a lie. There was nothing spiritual about the place. It was ungodly and sinister, and any communications achieved there, were certainly of a very dangerous nature.

The castle had become a treasure house. Jewels, suits of armour, shields, swords, fine tapestries, solid oak furniture, priceless carpets and heavily brocaded curtains adorned the place. For a country that had suffered, there were parts that seemed to be doing pretty damned well.

Bentley's spirit glided through a turret. It tickled like a mild electric shock. He filtered downwards through a floor, and landed opposite a large oak door. All the rooms were named after famous German rulers, and Bentley knew that this one was the portal leading into Hitler's very own chambers: the Barbarossa room.

He was about to glide through the door, when he stopped. The atoms of his spirit body were too fine to be perceived by human senses, but that did not guarantee he was invisible to all. Just as he could see both worlds, there was always someone else with that ability, and it was not inconceivable that Heinrich Himmler just might be one of these.

Bentley could not take the chance. He remained rooted to the spot, until without warning, a voice boomed from within.

"So, tell me, General Himmler, what have you discovered?" Bentley shivered as the voice of Hitler invaded his space.

"First, my Fuhrer," said Himmler, "can I just say what a pleasure it is to be summoned to speak."

Hitler's voice became impatient. "Tell me about the energies."

"They lie deep within the earth," responded Himmler.

"I mean the other ones! I refer to the *young* energies, the energies of youth and eternity. Susceptible and amenable energies we can work with."

"Of course, my Fuhrer. We are making progress."

"Progress is not enough! We must master them so we can use them."

"Will you join us in circle?"

"Have you reached a conclusion?"

Himmler sighed. "Not as yet."

"So, you sit for hours pursuing magic?"

"Valuable hours!" cried Himmler.

"But hours we cannot afford to waste. You must continue with your work, and when you know the answer, then you may invite me."

"That would be my greatest pleasure."

"I am a thinking man, General, and must apply myself to everything."

"Scientific developments? Another war?"

"I demand vengeance!" hissed Hitler. "Two million Germans fell during the last war. Our nation was dishonoured and it will not happen again."

"We are progressing, my Fuhrer. We are examining every avenue."

"Then work on! The words *impossible* and *never* are *not* in my vocabulary."

"Nor mine, my Fuhrer."

"Mind over matter..."

Mind over matter? Pondered Bentley, as the voices became distant. That certainly applied, but only in the sense that neither man minded what he did, and the sacrifice of millions of people certainly wouldn't matter.

As for the *energies of youth*, that wasn't good. Not good at all. Bentley's mind was so deep in conjecture, that when the stallion stumbled and reared, he wasn't prepared. He gasped, as the etheric joined the physical, and flying into the air, he hit the ground, and blacked out.

5

Spiritualist Church, Glasgow

Jessie

"I have a young man here," said Mrs Fairbairn. "Went long before his time."

Jessie swallowed hard, and felt her face tighten. "Plenty young men went before their time," she said. "There was a war on twenty years ago."

Mrs Fairbairn smiled. "This man didn't die in the war. He says his name is Charlie."

Jessie's body stiffened. *Steady girl*, she thought. *There's a lot of Charlies out there, and if you don't watch your step, you'll be right there amongst them.*

It was obvious Mrs Fairbairn had been doing her homework. After all, she'd clearly known she was a police officer.

"He's saying Natural Philosophy to me, and he's laughing."

"Really?"

"He says he's your husband."

Jessie narrowed her eyes. It would have been easy enough for Mrs Fairbairn to check out her family situation and discover that Charlie MacTaggart had indeed been her husband, so she wasn't going to fall for that. "My husband?"

"Don't be shy, Jessie," said Mrs Fairbairn. "Charlie's here."

Jessie took a sharp intake of breath. "I need evidence," she whispered.

"He taught Natural Philosophy. Physics."

Easy enough to find that out, thought Jessie.

"And he still does, Jessie." Mrs Fairbairn smiled again. "Relax. I'm not trying to trick you. Keep an open mind and listen."

Keep an open mind? On the one hand, Jessie wanted more than anything to believe Charlie was there, but she also had a job to do. And that job was to prove that the woman speaking to her was nothing more than a fraudster and a spy.

"He adored physics," Jessie said after a moment, deciding that animosity would achieve nothing.

"He says he drove you mad with his theories."

"Yes, he did."

"He says it's amazing. He's talking about energy. He says we're all living in a world of electromagnetic energy fields."

Well, either this woman was some kind of secret physicist, or Charlie really was there. "Would he care to elaborate?" she smiled.

"He's talking about the law of conservation of energy."

Jessie shook her head. "Tell Charlie, I didn't understand this before, and I don't understand it now."

"Quantum Physics: atoms, molecules, particles."

"Charlie, stop!"

Mrs Fairbairn smiled. "He's glad you acknowledge his presence. He's telling you to think hard."

"I'm not sure what to think."

"Universal energy."

"What?" Jessie stared hard at Mrs Fairbairn. Something strange was going on. Her eyes were beginning to shut. But not only that. She was beginning to look like Charlie. Was she imagining it? "What's happening to your face, Mrs Fairbairn?" Jessie's voice was urgent.

"Transfiguration," came Charlie's calm voice from somewhere behind her.

"Charlie?" gasped Jessie, spinning round. Her eyes scanned the room, but there was no one there.

"It's a mask," continued the invisible voice, emanating from the middle of the room. "A spirit mask. Exact same features as our dearly departed, and replicated on the medium's face. All made of living energy. Different compositions, and it's used to remind you we're still here."

Jessie swallowed hard. "I don't understand any of this."

"It's simple, Jessie. We're all energy. Energy that moves and changes. We ebb and flow like the sea!"

"Now, I'm totally lost."

"Lost at sea!" laughed Charlie. "Then let's go back to basics, Jessie. We *all* have a spirit body. That's why

I'm still here. Take a look at the scientists: Born, Planck and the wonderful Lord Kelvin. We only have to examine their first Law of Thermodynamics, and you'll see *how* that's possible. Energy cannot be created or destroyed. It can only change form."

"Lord Kelvin? Who on earth is Lord Kelvin?"

"William Thomson. Mathematical physicist and engineer, and strictly speaking, earth has nothing to do with it. He's been here in the Spirit World since 1907. Did great work at Glasgow University. Fine Scotsman. A bit like myself!"

Jessie was growing exasperated. "*What* exactly are you trying to tell me, Charlie?"

"I'm telling you that when my physical body died, the energy transformed. My spirit took over, and I've been with you ever since."

"So why can't I see you, Charlie?"

"We're on different vibrations. Frequencies, if you like."

"Like the wireless?"

"Exactly! Oh Jessie! Just think about it! I always knew everything was energy, but I didn't realise the depth of it until I went to Spirit."

Jessie turned back towards Mrs Fairbairn and squinted. The wrinkles had gone, and it really looked like Charlie. But surely the mask explanation wasn't possible. It had to be her mind. It had to be playing tricks. "You're a clever woman, Mrs Fairbairn," she said. "I don't know how you're doing it, but you really managed to draw me in."

The voice spoke again. "It's not Mrs Fairbairn. It's me, Charlie."

Damn it! Even the voice was like Charlie's. Jessie turned round again. Still no one. How the hell would she explain this to MacLeod? *Play along, Jessie. Play along,* she told herself. "So where exactly are you, Charlie?"

"Right here, in front of you."

Jessie held out her hands. "Here?" she whispered.

"I'm still here, Jessie, and I'm holding your hands."

Jessie gulped. "I can't feel you."

"It doesn't matter, my darling. Our two worlds still interpenetrate, and I'm blending with Mrs Fairbairn's energy to communicate with you."

This was getting hard. It wasn't just a question of playing along now. Jessie felt she was in a bubble with Mrs Fairbairn, and a force was tugging at her heart, reminding her of unfinished business: something she hadn't thought about in a long time. She wanted answers. In fact, she *needed* answers. "Why did you make me go that night, Charlie?"

"The night I died?"

"It was only a family dinner."

"It was your mother's birthday."

"I should have realised it was serious."

"How could you?"

"Indigestion?"

"It felt worse than that, but I didn't want you to know. I didn't want you to miss the dinner."

"You made me go."

"Yes. I made you go."

"Then you left me."

"I *died*, Jessie. I *died*."

"You were on the couch, Charlie."

"I know. I was there. And now I'm here. I haven't gone."

"You were bolt upright, stiff as a..."

"As a corpse?"

Jessie shut her eyes. "I thought you were pretending."

"I tried to tell you, but you couldn't hear me."

"Your eyes were open and glazed. They were just staring, and your face was grey. You were like an empty shell."

"I'd died in the night, Jessie, and it was very quick. I felt no pain."

"You died when I was out enjoying myself."

"It doesn't matter."

"A massive heart attack."

"It doesn't matter, Jessie."

"Five years," whispered Jessie, "and it doesn't get any better."

"It will."

Suddenly Mrs Fairbairn spoke and Jessie spun around. Charlie's face had gone.

"He's laughing now, Jessie," said Mrs Fairbairn, opening her eyes. "He was like you, a non-believer, but now he's amazed with everything. He's just said: "*Who would have guessed I'd be talking to you like this?*" Jessie shut her eyes tight, but was unable to suppress a tear. It dripped down her cheek. "He's very proud of you, Jessie."

Jessie shivered and wiped her face with the back of her hand. "Is he OK?" she asked.

"He is now."

"Now?"

"He didn't know where he was to begin with, but he does now. He wants to help you, Jessie."

"Help me? How?"

"He says there are people who are trying to manipulate energy for their own purposes. He wants you to understand the dangers, and the upset that could be caused by fighting the laws of nature and physics. He wants you to know we're all connected, whether we like it or not, and damage affects us all."

"Is he talking about politics?" asked Jessie.

"He's telling you to open your mind. If you can understand that life goes on and you can connect with your loved ones, then it really does help your life here."

"It sounds too good to be true," said Jessie.

"Remember the physics, he's saying. You have to understand that there are things in the universe that our human minds can't even begin to comprehend."

Jessie sighed. "I suppose so."

"He's examining everything here, and on the other side. And he's telling you to remember one very important thing: energy cannot be created or destroyed, and since we are energy, we cannot die."

6

Cairo, Egypt

Bette

Joe had arranged an evening out. We would be eating at Shepheard's in the most exclusive of the restaurants. This, of course, meant formal dress. I anticipated meeting some very interesting people.

As I entered the restaurant, I was greeted by the sound of just about every language known to man. I looked around, and my eyes followed the height of columns, which reached as far as the painted ceiling. I scanned the room until I clocked Joe's bald head. Stephen and an older man were sitting next to him.

"Bette," said Joe, as I approached their table, "I'd like to introduce you to Omar O'Malley." Joe turned to O'Malley. "Bette is a colleague from *Amber St Claire*. She's also Stephen's sister."

"How do you do," said the older man, holding out his hand. He remained seated, as did everyone else.

I took hold of the hand, and felt its iron grip. "How do you do?" I responded, prising my hand away. He was a strange-looking guy with a grey moustache and a head of salt and pepper wiry hair. He looked in his mid-sixties. Tall and well-built, he reminded me of an old university professor. He also had a very distinct Irish accent.

"Omar's daughter will be joining us soon," said Joe.

I had a good idea who that would be.

Farida arrived ten minutes later, and as she walked through the door and across the dining room's green carpet, she stunned the diners into silence. She was wearing purple velvet, covered in chiffon that rustled as she moved. What was more, she was wearing the gold chain and the pendants.

I wondered for a moment whether O'Malley knew his daughter was having nooky with his best friend. I'd no doubt find out.

Stephen, who was dressed in a white dinner jacket, got to his feet, as did the others, until Farida sat down. A waiter, wearing white gloves, appeared at our table, and when Joe ordered a bottle of champagne, I decided to peruse the menu, until I realised the damned thing was in French.

"Not used to the foreign lingo, eh, Bette?" said Stephen.

"Nope."

"If you turn it over, you'll get it in English."

He was right. "I'll have the soup, the sole and the roast lamb," I said, looking across at Joe, whose face was grim and ruddy. A spot had begun to emerge on the tip of his nose. He'd obviously been to the barbershop, for what scant hair he had remaining, had been cropped, and his head now looked like a ball of beetroot.

"Dig in!" said Joe, when the food arrived.

I didn't need to be told. I'd already made a mental note to order the cheese board.

Farida was sitting across from me. She'd been talking to Stephen for a while, but turned her head for a moment and saw me staring. She winked.

"So, what do you do?" I asked her.

"I'm a student."

"Really? Whereabouts?"

"Trinity College."

"There's a Trinity College in Cairo?"

"No. Dublin."

"Dublin, as in Southern Ireland?"

"The very one," she said, smiling.

"I did not expect that," I said.

"Not many people do."

"And what are you studying?"

"Engineering."

"No kidding!" I laughed.

"I'm not," she said. "I'm going into third year."

I wanted to ask her what she was doing in Cairo, but O'Malley interrupted. "So," he said, "you're interested in the Egyptian film industry. What do you want to know?"

I opened my mouth to speak, then shut it again. My right hand twitched, so I shoved it under the table. *Not now, Bette. Not the time nor place. Control the hand.* The twitching stopped, but I still had a problem: what the hell *did* I want to know?

"Joe, could I get a glass of water, please," I asked in an effort to think.

"Here," he said, shoving a jug and empty glass in my direction.

I took my time filling the glass using my left hand. Didn't trust the right. "Well, I suppose I want to know how it's developed over the years, and how it actually affects the lives of the ordinary Egyptian people."

That sounded good enough.

O'Malley smiled. "How does the cinema affect the people?" he repeated. "Pretty much the same as all over the world. It doesn't give them wealth, but it provides a means for escapism."

"Escapism?"

"The freedom to pretend that the world is a better place."

"A better place?" I was beginning to sound like a parrot, but I couldn't stop myself.

"A fairer place, where we can forget our troubles."

"Yes," I said, "I suppose in this day and age it's quite nice to forget what's really going on."

"That being?"

"The actions of certain countries," I said.

"Ah," said O'Malley. "Power games."

"Not exactly games."

"Indeed not. So, why don't we look at the British occupation of Egypt?"

"That's in the past."

"Except that little part called the Suez Canal," said O'Malley, his eyes fixed on my face.

"Well, I suppose..." I got no further.

O'Malley leaned back in his chair, still watching me closely. I didn't conceal my astonishment on hearing his subsequent words.

"You do know," he said, leaning forward and positioning himself like a jaguar about to pounce, "that a country's most valuable resource is its children?"

"Pardon me?"

O'Malley paused and smiled, just as a string of violins went into action. The after-dinner ball in the Pharaonic Hall was about to begin, and the moment was lost.

After the meal, Joe, who'd booked in at Shepheard's, took Stephen to the bar for a nightcap. Farida left with her father, and I went back to Stephen's place to work out what to do next.

Joe needed the nitty-gritty. He liked his reporters to dig up dirt, but dirt that was for *his* eyes only. As far as my assignment was concerned, that was *definitely* for his eyes only. Any mention of the Nazis, and I'd have been out on my ass. It was all down to tactics, and since O'Malley seemed aware that Stephen and Farida were an item, I decided to construct a good old-fashioned love story that would hopefully conform to *Amber St Claire's* high-class standards.

When Stephen returned around midnight, he told me Joe wanted to see me the following day. Since I wasn't allowed in the Long Bar (men only) I was to meet him on the veranda. I wrote through the night, and found him the following afternoon sitting on a rattan chair behind a table, positioned next to a potted palm, sipping a gin and tonic.

"Here," I said, putting the article in front of him, and sitting down.

Joe glanced down at it. "*True love always finds a way*," he began to read aloud. He turned the page. "*Never ignore the needs of the heart. With the softest of whispers, love will always find its master. When Angel met his own angel. Soul mates can never be divided.*" He looked up and smirked. "Yes, well at least the readers will like it."

Better than a rebuff, I thought. I decided to chance my arm. "Enough for a drink?"

"I suppose so. What do you want?"

"Same as you. Gin and tonic."

Joe summoned a waiter, placed my order, then turned back to face me. "I'm going to stay here for a while," he said, sliding the article back across the table in my direction. "I don't see any need to read it all. I trust it's a good enough account of sentimental drivel."

Typical! I thought. "So, what now?"

"I want you to go back to Glasgow. Hand in your material, put your feet up, and I'll get back in touch with you when I need to."

I watched Joe closely as he spoke. "I don't wish to presume," I said, "but when are you going to pay me?"

"Remuneration will depend on the success of your article."

"And how do I get back without any money?"

Joe frowned and took out his wallet. "Well, given the circumstances, I can give you something." He slid half a dozen Egyptian pound notes across the table towards me. "But remember, we keep a tight budget, so try and show a bit of initiative. There's a clever girl." He paused. "Anyway, your fare's already been paid."

"Really?" Something wasn't right. "Tell me what's going on Joe? First you push me into an investigation, and then you shove me out of it. It doesn't make sense."

Joe didn't reply. When he swallowed the rest of his drink, and turned to order another, I knew he was finished with me. I picked up my article, then the cash, and left.

I bumped into Farida the following day. My conversation with Joe had so disillusioned me that I'd downed a few more gin and tonics and crashed out. Now I was sitting on the veranda of Shepheard's Hotel, hung over from the night before. It was then a loud boom startled me. It resonated like the sound of a gong.

I looked up, and saw a vehicle driving slowly along Kamal Pasha Street. It was a green four-door Ford V8, badly in need of attention. I wondered, at first, if its exhaust had been replaced with an explosive device, until I realised it had just backfired. The noise evoked an angry response from bystanders, and a small monkey that had been sitting in the corner, chewing an apple, jumped with fright and screeched at the top of its voice.

The vehicle pulled in, and stopped.

I was just wondering who the driver was, when a woman got out with an air of verve and vitality. It was Stephen's girlfriend, Farida. She saw me and came over to join me.

"Beer please," she called out to a waiter. She sat down. "Might sound like a bomb," she said, "but goes like one too when she wants. Any time you want to borrow the old girl, she's at your disposal."

"Thanks," I said, wondering whether or not that was a good idea.

"I was actually looking for you," she said when her beer arrived. "I have a photo."

"Photo?"

She dipped her hand into her bag and withdrew a glossy print of herself, my brother and Omar O'Malley. "I thought you might like it as a nice little keepsake. Something personal for yourself."

"Thanks," I said, making a mental note to hand it in with my article.

Farida was chatty, and told me all about her studies in Ireland. "Stephen and I meet from time to time when I'm studying in Dublin. He comes over. But I spend the vacations in Cairo."

The relationship seemed to have been going on for a while. "How did you and Stephen meet?"

"Through my father."

I found it strange that Stephen hadn't mentioned her before. "When was that?"

"Oh, a good while back," she said, remaining vague. She continued to chatter. "If you're interested at all in Egyptian archaeology, I'll take you round the sights. They're excellent."

"So, I've heard. But I've got to go home soon."

She seemed surprised. "Really? I thought you were here for a while?"

So did I, I wanted to say, but didn't. "Sun's too hot," I mumbled, instead.

"My father has a great interest in archaeology," she continued to enlighten me. "He's financed quite a number of expeditions." My ears pricked up, but I didn't say anything. "You've the temples and the tombs. Then there are the mosaics, the pillars and the pylons."

And so, she continued.

She seemed to have an encyclopaedic knowledge of everything there was to know in Egypt, but I'd stopped listening. I was still hung over, and my head was spinning like a top. I heard her mention something about archaic rites and executions, but it was no use.

"You also have the Hanging Church, where Copts go to worship, and the mosques."

By then I was wasted.

My eyelids began to open and shut like an overworked concertina.

"Tired?"

I jumped with fright. My neck jerked. It hurt like hell. "Fucking dodo!" I shouted, looking into her amused eyes. I felt my face flush. "Sorry. I have a problem."

"I think you do," she agreed, playing with the pendants on the chain round her neck.

"Sorry," I repeated. "I haven't recovered from last

night. I had an unfortunate meeting with my boss and then had a drink or two to drown my sorrows."

She smiled warmly and ordered me a strong Turkish coffee. It arrived promptly. "Drink that," she said, still playing with the chain round her neck.

"Your necklace is very interesting," I said. "But what's with the swastika? Isn't that a bit strange?"

"Ah!" she sighed. "Not what you think. It's actually used to represent wealth and good fortune."

"Then why do the Nazis have it?"

"They've adapted it for their own purposes. But this has nothing to do with them. My father was given it when he was excavating in Iran a number of years ago."

Now that was interesting.

I didn't probe any further. I was too tired. We talked for another half hour, and then I made myself scarce, and got ready to return to Britain.

7

British Military Hospital (BMH), Alexandria

Bentley

"For God's sake, Bentley!"

Bentley kept his eyes shut. He didn't want to open them. When eventually he did, he found himself looking into the bespectacled face of Colonel Joe Bannerman. "Joe," he said. This was one face that would never appear in a beauty pageant. The man had a pug nose, and tiny blood-shot eyes, and without the aid of lenses, he was as blind as a bat.

At one time, Joe had had the constitution of an oak tree, and his thick neck and broad shoulders had been likened to those of a buffalo. Over the years, however, fat had replaced muscle. Now he had the physique of a balloon, and hadn't had a waistline for the past ten years. He was definitely looking the worse for wear, and it would take more than one coat of paint to lick that body back into shape.

Bentley studied Joe's deprecating glare. His thin moustache stood out predominantly. Years of heavy drinking and riotous living had created the uniqueness of the man's battered expression, and his rubber-like features, at that moment in time, reminded Bentley of a ventriloquist's dummy.

"Take a seat, Joe," whispered Bentley.

"You're a total nutcase!" Joe's voice grew louder, and he began to bombard Bentley with a battery of questions and impolite observations.

"Thank you," said Bentley.

"Firstly, you didn't have the authority to ride the animal, and secondly, they had to bring you back on a stretcher!"

"You'll forgive me if I say I don't remember."

"How many times do I have to bail you out, you stupid bloody Australian? Do you think MPRS is insured against stupidity? We thought we'd lost you!" He paused. "By rights, you should be dead. Didn't know whether to call a priest, or a bloody witch doctor!"

"Like I said," repeated Bentley, "take a seat." Joe was wittering on about nothing, and Bentley wished his boss would simply stop talking.

"Can't you do anything right?" rebuked Joe, with the ferocity of a terrier gnawing at a bone. "At the very least, you're going to end up on crutches, and then you'll be no bloody use to anyone!"

Bentley shook his head. A nurse was parading behind Joe, tending to other patients, so he supposed he was in hospital. A clock on the wall said three o'clock. Since it was still daylight, it had to be afternoon. Bentley wondered how much time had passed. He knew he hadn't shaved in a while and that his chin would be as rough as sandpaper. He tried to raise his left hand, but was incapable of doing so. Then looking further down his body, he realised it wasn't good. The plaster cast on his left arm told him why. He grunted loudly, as for the first time, pain registered in his brain.

8

Back to Britain

Bette

Joe sent me back by ship. No valediction. I simply vamoosed. My cabin was well in keeping with his efforts to maintain a *tight* budget, for the space was insufficient to accommodate much more than a bed, a pillow and a blanket.

I spent most of the voyage on deck with a queasy stomach, looking out at the hazy horizon. I waited patiently for the first sign of a quay, whiling away the time by searching for coastlines and harbours, and thinking about my father, Jim, back in Glasgow.

Fortunately, the weather was good, and when we eventually drew closer to the British shore, I could see outlines of tiny people. Gradually these took on the shape of full-grown men, working away at Southampton Docks. I smiled. At long last. Dry land. I left the ship, and clutching my suitcase, made my way to the train.

The carriage was draughty. Someone had left a newspaper on the seat opposite, open at a page discussing the collapse of the world economy. I decided not to read it, and instead, looked out the window. The train pulled out, passing a small beach surrounded by cliffs, until finally we entered countryside.

After a bit, we stopped at a station, and I leaned back in my seat. A woman wearing a brown fur coat and matching hat got into the carriage. Picking up the newspaper, she sat down opposite me. *Rich-looking dame*, I thought.

"Morning," she said, flipping through the pages.

She looked around twenty-eight. Maybe older. Heavy makeup and good skin. "Morning," I replied.

"It's all been something of a slow recovery," she said, after a moment, placing the paper on her lap.

"The economy?"

"Yes." She paused and stared at me.

"Yeah, well, that's politicians for you."

"You're American?"

"Yeah."

"Where abouts?"

"Where abouts what?"

"Which part of America are you from?"

"Long Island."

"Ah, New York. I've been there. Lovely place. Lovely weather."

"Yeah, in the summer."

She smiled, and turned her attention back to the newspaper.

After a while the train stopped at a station. I shut my eyes and pretended to sleep. We remained stationary for about ten minutes. When the train started up again, I peered through half-closed lids, and when satisfied the dame had lost interest in me, opened them and stared out the window.

We crossed a bridge. I glanced down at a murky-looking river, where ducks, moorhens and coots navigated between boats, tugs and barges. On one side of the river, was a large factory. Steam and smoke belched from its chimneys, whilst effluent and toxic chemicals were discharged into the water.

"You'd think they'd do something about that," said the woman.

"Pardon me?"

"Pollution. I know iron has to be extracted from its ore, but this is ridiculous."

"Whadda, ya mean?"

"Total carelessness, and refineries may well have a lot to answer for in the future."

"Really?" My head was beginning to hurt.

"In fact, if pollution continues, in years to come there will be considerable damage caused by the release of chemicals into the atmosphere." She had a point, but the subject was way out of my range of interest. "However, there *is* a problem."

"Problem?"

"Well, what's the most important? Industrial progress, or a healthy environment? Especially at a time there might actually be a war."

I didn't reply. Too many people were suggesting the possibility of another war, and I didn't like the sound of it. I shut my eyes and went to sleep.

I'd been sleeping for what felt like an hour. When I woke, the dame was staring at me. I felt hot, and it wasn't the weather. My right hand began to twitch and it took every ounce of effort to stop my neck from jerking. *Control, Bette, control*. I turned my attention back to the window. Anglers fished in a river. I clocked a couple of trout squirming and fidgeting in one of the nets, and knew exactly how they felt. But it wasn't just that. I could see the dame's reflection in the glass, and she was still looking at me. *Control, Bette, control.*

Streams and marshes appeared in the woodland margins. Hills with steep inclines popped up in the distance, outlining moors, heaths and woods. Lanes, trails and turnstiles sprang up, followed by ditches and parcels of land, decorated with flowers and hedges that stretched for miles against a background of magnificent hills.

And still the dame stared.

Fallow fields were replaced by acres of land, where farmers husked their grain and ploughed the soil. We passed trees, where birds sat in branches, well defined against the rich blue sky.

After that, I couldn't tell you.

My eyes were fixed on the glass and I was watching Miss Nosy Parker. She smiled as if to tell me she knew what I was doing, and then as suddenly as she'd started to stare, she stopped, relaxed back into her seat and shut her eyes. I continued to watch her in the glass. Her muscles relaxed. I listened to her breathing, until its steady rhythm suggested she just might be asleep.

I leaned back in my seat as we passed more pasture and woodland, and ventured into deep valleys and verdant vales. But my eyes were heavy. A couple of blinks and I was asleep. When I woke up, the dame had gone, but the funny thing was, a little voice in my head kept telling me I'd be meeting her again in the very near future.

My father was an alcoholic, and had been for many years. I called him Jim. It was easier. I'd not met him till I was thirteen, and as far as I was concerned, he was just another old geezer, but one with a difference: I had the unfortunate pleasure of living with him.

Jim's flat was above the butcher's shop in Byres Road. His drinking made him prone to disappearing for weeks on end, going on binges, and returning when the drink ran out, so I didn't even know if he'd be at home. I had a key to the flat, and as I made my way up to the second floor, where he lived, I half-hoped he wasn't there.

Inside, I was immediately struck by the smell of cabbage and onions. I went into the kitchen. The budgie was sitting quietly in its cage, its wings spread out, looking like a nifty hooker doing a burlesque routine at the Moulin Rouge. The fish wasn't any better. It was going round in circles, trying to avoid a mini-version of the Great Barrier Reef.

"Hi," I said to them, before turning and making my way to the living room. The place seemed shittier than usual. Well, so long as the electricity was still connected, what did it matter? I sat down, and removed my shoes. I was feeling despondent. Not in the mood to move. But there were things to do. Getting to my feet, I left the room and made my way across to Jim's bedroom.

I knocked on the door and went straight in. The first thing I saw was a body ensconced in a bed in the corner. So, he *was* there. His upper torso was propped up on a couple of pillows, and I could see his face. His beard was white. So was his hair. Deep lines and wrinkles framed his face, and his eyes were shut. As I stared, a gentle growl crept from his throat, followed by a series of snorts that ricocheted around the room. They sounded like the temperamental pipes and boiler, and I was reminded of the paradox that this grumpy, yet frail, old geriatric had once been a handsome young man. It must have been one hell of a heavy night. I closed the door, and left him to sleep it off.

I'd been back for more than a fortnight, and there had been no word from Joe, but at least he was out of my hair. As for the home front, well, that was a big fat zilch. Jim was in one of his deep, dark moods that could go on for weeks. I'd learned from experience that avoiding him was the best course of action.

Since we hadn't really spoken, I'd not had a chance to tell him about Stephen and his new girlfriend, far less show him a copy of my article. I could, of course, have made the first move, but I didn't want to.

So, here I was, in the John, staring at my face in the mirror. I started to examine the blackheads on the tip of my nose. Some had turned into spots, and when I tilted my head backwards, I realised one or two of the intrepid little fuckers had actually gone up a nostril. I rued the day I'd reached puberty.

And then just as I thought the day couldn't get any worse, Joe telephoned.

He arrived the next day. Why, I didn't know, and I wasn't about to ask. It was evening, and the sun was setting. He appeared, humming *The Lambeth Walk*, and the first thing he did was raid the drinks cabinet, and help himself to a double whisky. "Tell your father to get up. I'll meet him in the back yard."

What the hell was going on?

I shook Jim awake and passed on the message. Jim grunted behind my retreating back. Time to put my training as a spy into practice. I made my way to the kitchen. Since the flat was two up, the window was a good vantage point to spy on the yard below.

I planted myself on a stool behind one of the tobacco-stained curtains, and opening the window an inch, peered out. The yard was full of junk. Kids' toys and unloved garbage. It hadn't been touched in months. It only took a moment to clock Joe's hulk of a figure standing outside. It was as if he waited with the anticipation of a black widow spider.

I'd only been to the office twice since my return to Glasgow. Once to deposit my article, and once to collect a printed copy of the magazine, which I'd just put down on the kitchen table. I heard Jim's footsteps descend the close stairs. The back door squeaked open. Jim eventually appeared in the backyard. He hobbled towards Joe, like a toddler learning to walk, and stumbled. For a second, I thought he was going to fall. So did Joe.

"Careful, Jim," said Joe, his voice even louder than earlier. "The yard's starting to look like a building site. Can't have you falling over. Maybe we should go inside and have a hot toddy."

Jim looked at the double whisky, which was still in Joe's hand. "I'd prefer to stay out here," he returned, dryly.

"As you wish," muttered Joe, taking a huge gulp of his drink.

There was a silence as both men stared at one another. "Well, well, well," said Jim, after a moment.

"Well, well, well, indeed," replied Joe.

Never mind the 'wells', I thought. *Get on with the business!*

Jim took a step towards Joe, and pointed his finger at him. "You and I have known each other for nearly ten years," he said.

"As long as that?"

Jim's finger was inches from Joe's nose. "We've shared secrets."

"We have that."

"And we know more about the world than the average human being could even begin to imagine."

"We do that," agreed Joe, taking a step back.

Good on you, Jim! I thought. *Scare him!*

"What's more," growled Jim, "we both know there's still something going on." Joe made no comment and Jim seemed ready to explode. "I've been a bad bastard in my time," he said. "A stupid, bad bastard. But I do read the newspapers."

I crinkled my brow and wondered where this was leading.

"I've even read a couple of your magazines," he continued. "I've noted the sentimental drivel it produces about our happy society."

My mind went into overdrive. *Careful Jim. That's my writing you're talking about!*

Jim continued his attack. "Really, Joe, there are standards to maintain."

"You know as well as I do," affirmed Joe, taking another step back, "that the public would rather be happy than be informed of the miserable facts."

Jim's face darkened. "I know that the politicians certainly don't want them knowing anything."

"So, the magazine's doing a public service," said Joe. "We don't want the public to know our politicians are panicking like hell, do we now?"

"And so am I, Joe. So am I."

"And why would that be, Jim?"

"Why on earth are you endangering the life of my daughter by placing her in a dangerous environment at a dangerous time to write a pathetic article about the Egyptian cinema?" Jim's face darkened further as he spoke, and the tone of his voice rose high. "For pity's sake, Joe! What's wrong with you?"

My right hand twitched, so I sat on it. The twitching stopped. Yeah. Keep the hand there. Best under a butt cheek. I leaned further forward towards the open window.

"What can you mean?" murmured Joe, his face impassive.

This served to anger Jim even further. He took another step toward Joe. They were inches apart. He glared into Joe's face. "I haven't been much of a father, but I still have children."

"I'd hardly call them children," replied Joe, glaring back.

My hand began to twitch under my butt. *Never mind staring him down! Punch him, Jim! Punch him!*

But Jim wasn't interested in a physical showdown. Instead, he shook his head and turned away.

You missed the opportunity!

"Stephen can look after himself," resumed Jim, his back still to Joe. "But Bette…"

"Bette?"

Me?

"She's had a difficult life."

Understatement of the fucking year!

"And that would be *whose* fault?"

"I'm not going into that, Joe. All I want to ask is: what are you trying to do?"

"What do you mean?" said Joe, clearly taunting him.

You know what he means! Tell him, Joe! Tell me! Tell us both what's going on!

"Do you want to finish her off?" continued Jim.

Finish me off? This was getting serious.

"I think you're exaggerating."

"You really think that?" said Jim, his tone unexpectedly demure.

"The girl can look after herself."

You're right there, but you still need to tell me what's going on.

"You're sure about that?" said Jim.

Joe took a deep breath. "Stop worrying, Jim. It won't be for long. In any case, best to get her working before she marries and starts a family. You'll be hearing the patter of tiny feet soon enough. You know what women are like. All they really want is a husband and children."

What? My mind was racing. I didn't know which was worse. Being finished off, or being impregnated by an overbearing husband.

"You believe that?" said Jim.

"Give her a break. A chance to prove herself."

Jim looked bemused. "Prove herself?"

Joe frowned. "Why not?"

"You know as well as I do, that we're on the brink of another war. There's enough local gossip here in Glasgow to write about if you want to give her something to do."

Joe shrugged. "But you have to agree that this is far more interesting."

What? The film industry, or getting my brains blown out?

Jim's eyes narrowed. "Tell me, Joe, what's your real motive?"

Yeah, Joe! What's your real motive?

"Look, Jim. We have to look after ourselves."

"And I'm trying to look after my daughter. Bette's my responsibility!"

Joe narrowed his eyes. "Wasn't always."

"Well, she is now."

Good to hear!

"For heaven's sake, Jim! Stop taking it all so personally. It's a bloody good opportunity for your girl."

"Don't you mean for yourself?"

Yeah, Jim! You got that in one!

"I'm sending her back in," said Joe. She's going to be very useful."

Jim's body stiffened. "Useful to whom? You?"

"The British."

Doing what exactly?

Jim began to laugh raucously. "Joe! I was a reporter myself. I know the score. Never away from the blood and gore."

"That's because there was a war on, Jim."

"And there's every likelihood there'll be another!"

"Jim, she's twenty-three."

Jim rubbed his face then clasped his hands together. "She's a child," he said. "She's spent her life in trouble! Don't put her back there!"

"It's a unique opportunity for her."

"You're not thinking, Joe. You're not thinking. What happens if Egypt decides to side with the Nazis in the event of another war? If she's stuck out there, what then?"

"No. *You* think it through, Jim. Egypt has the option of supporting Britain in the event of another war, and I happen to believe that is exactly what will happen."

"And so, you think everything will be all right?"

Joe folded his arms. "You won't be convinced, will you?"

Jim stared stonily into his face. "No, I won't."

"Then you're going to make it very hard for yourself."

The conversation seemed to be going round in circles. So was my head. There was a mission, but no one was making it clear. There was also the possibility my life might be in danger, and that was being made even less clear.

"Listen Joe," said Jim. "We can go on and on about the possibility of war for as long as we like, however, I was never so totally out of my drunk little mind as not to remember what else we talked about. We both know about the Dead Army."

My body jumped and my neck jarred. My hand would have gone into uncontrollable spasms had I not been sitting on it. I leaned further forward and whacked my head on the window glass. "Shit!" I drew myself back, but no one had heard me.

"Jim, it has to be dealt with," said Joe. "It has to be taken very seriously." He broke off abruptly. A cat had appeared, and was sauntering sleepily around his legs. Joe tried to kick it away, but lost his footing. The cat meowed loudly, and shot away into the bushes. Joe regained his balance just as an overhead bird deposited a white missile on top of his head.

Jim stared at the mess on Joe's head and began to smile. The smile widened and he began to laugh loudly. He continued to laugh, not stopping. He laughed until I thought he would never stop.

I looked across at the magazine on the table. It was opened at the middle pages. I jumped down from the stool and stared at the article I'd written.

Next to it was the photograph of Stephen and Farida, posing with the infamous Omar O'Malley. Still not sure whether the photo was for me or the public, I didn't care. I knew there wouldn't be a better opportunity. I grabbed the magazine, and skipped down the stairs, out the backdoor, and into the yard.

Jim and Joe seemed surprised to see me. Too bad. I pressed my copy of *Amber St Claire* into Jim's hands. "A bit of light reading," I said. "It'll tell you what your kids are up to, since you haven't actually asked."

Jim kept hold of the magazine, and looked at the photograph. He seemed confused. I turned to Joe, who was looking up at the sky and cursing, totally disinterested in my article. Didn't even give it a glance. I didn't care. The mess on his head had started to drip down his cheek. "Guess ornithology's just not your thing," I muttered, turning away, and making my way back into the building.

Things were definitely becoming complicated. I'd been sent in to spy on Stephen: for his own good, of course. And now here I was finding out that somewhere along the line, Jim had also been up to things. As for the Dead Army, well, I'd no idea what that was. Suffice it to say, the mere thought of it sent a shiver up my back.

What was going on? What was Joe up to? What was Jim up to?

Well, there was one thing for sure: the Kipper household was quite aptly named, for there sure as hell was something very fishy going on.

9

Central Police Office, Glasgow

Jessie

DI MacLeod shook his head. "World's going to hell in a basket, and all you can come up with is this gobbledygook!"

Jessie gritted her teeth. "I'm telling you what she said, sir."

"Well, it doesn't make sense."

"Actually sir, if you really think about it, some of it does make quite a lot of sense."

MacLeod brought his hand down hard on his desk.

"Are you trying to tell me *that's* not solid?"

"Natural Philosophy, sir."

"MacTaggart! Shut up!"

Jessie closed her mouth, then opened it again. "You can't dispute proven science sir."

"Proven?"

"It seems energy can't be destroyed. It can only

change form: and that's a fact. That's what Lord Kelvin says."

"Bugger Kelvin!"

"Lord Kelvin, sir. And you shouldn't really say that. I think he has a point."

"Really?"

"Yes, sir. You see there's consciousness and mind. They're all part of our spirit. That's what Charlie told me."

"Charlie?"

"My husband."

"You said he was dead."

"He is."

MacLeod thumped the desk again. "I don't know if you're playing with me, MacTaggart."

"Not at all, sir. I've spoken to Charlie a couple of times, and it's all really very informative."

"So, inform me," said MacLeod, his face turning red.

"Well. Charlie says it's all about energy, and he says we don't use enough of our mind."

"I could have told you that! No one uses their brain!"

"No, sir. He doesn't mean the *brain*. He means our consciousness. Haven't you ever wondered where inspiration comes from?"

"I'm afraid I don't see enough of it. Not in this job."

"Charlie says we should learn to use our mind properly."

"You're going off at a tangent, MacTaggart."

"Not really. You see, our brain and mind are two

different things. Our brain is a physical organ. It's in our head. But the mind is all round our physical body. That's why we feel things all over. It's the mind working. And when we die, our brain decays with our physical body, but our mind, which is consciousness, or, our spirit, if you like, lives on."

"Really?"

"And we have to learn what we've chosen to learn before we can go back to the Spirit World. Only thing is, we might not have learned what we set out to learn in the first place."

MacLeod narrowed his eyes. "In that case it'll take a long time for most of us," he said.

Jessie ignored his sarcasm. "Charlie says it does. Even he's got a long way to go."

"And he should know."

Jessie smiled wryly. "Better than us!"

"MacTaggart, this is getting too weird for me. I don't know how people who claim to talk to the dead do it, or *if* they do it! And I don't really care. All I know is I've got a job to do, and so have you. The Chief Constable wants that woman Fairbairn off the street, and if that's what *he* wants, that's what *I* want. So, get out there. Find evidence to link her with the Nazis. If you can't do that, *find* a crime. Any crime. Find out if she's part of a Glasgow gang. Nazi spy, or gangster! I don't care what it takes. Just get her off the street." MacLeod paused. "And the same goes for Milligan."

"Bette?"

"I've already told you, MacTaggart! Fairbairn mentioned her name when she brought up Operation

MPRS."

"But I don't really see what they've done wrong."

"Then maybe you should get that *mind* of yours working, MacTaggart!"

"My mind?"

"The one you're so adamant is different from your *brain*." MacLeod made a fist with his right hand and thumped his stomach. "*That's* where I feel it, MacTaggart. Only I call it a gut feeling." He paused. "Remember the gangs here?"

"Aye."

"The racketeering! The reign of terror!"

"Aye."

"The Shanley Boys, the Brigton Boys, the Carlton Entry Boys, the Billy Boys, the Derry Boys, the Kent Star, the Norman Conks!"

"The Cheeky Forty?"

"Aye! Laugh at me, young lady! Laugh at me!"

"Sir, the woman happens to believe in something different."

"Ah, but does she *really* think something different?"

"You *really* think she's a spy?"

"It's not for me to think, and it's not for you to think. It's what the Chief Constable thinks."

10

Jim's Flat, Glasgow

Bette

"Quite noisy here, isn't it?" said Joe, settling into his third glass of whisky.

"I can suggest a couple of hotels," I began, wondering just how *tightly* they'd fit into his budget. He was going to be staying with us for a week, and I wasn't relishing the prospect.

"No need. I'm perfectly comfortable here," he replied, sombrely. My eyes were fixed on his double chin. He'd always been fat, but now he was beginning to resemble a clapped-out version of a prehistoric monster. But that wasn't all. I knew from experience he could be as deadly as a shark, and any day now I expected a fin to grow out of his back. "And how about serving up some of that red jelly I saw in the kitchen," he continued. "Spot of cream on the top wouldn't go amiss."

"Yeah, Joe."

I went into the kitchen and switched on the wireless. A soprano was singing her heart out, so I switched it off. I was tired. I wasn't sleeping properly, and to make things worse, I still couldn't get hold of coffee. The Brits didn't understand the fundamentals. The pitiful pot of tea from that afternoon just hadn't done the trick. What was more, things were bothering me, and at the top of the list was the question: when was Joe going to pay me?"

"Ah! Let's have a look!" came Joe's voice. I looked up, and realised he'd followed me into the kitchen. "Death by spoon!"

"Pardon me?"

I looked down to see what I was doing, and realised I was thumping the jelly I'd made the night before. I'd smacked it into a mush.

"I take it it's already dead," he said. "You really don't have to finish the job with a spoon."

I was reminded at once that Joe's patter was only bearable in small doses. "You don't say."

"Will we be having dinner?" he asked. "Or are you going to skive off and reduce us to a bowl of cornflakes?" I didn't reply. "You know I'm staying a week", he continued, "so, let's try and have a good time." He paused, and going into his back pocket, withdrew his wallet. He opened it, and I half expected the moths to come flying out. As if reading my mind, he closed it again, and burrowing into his other pockets, withdrew a couple of coins. He examined them, before tossing them on to the kitchen table, where they began to spin, like dancers attempting to do pirouettes with stiff feet. "Extra wages," he said. "I've decided you're taking extended leave here in Glasgow."

I looked down at the coins. They were spinning fast, but my head was spinning faster. It was obvious my extra wages wouldn't last me a week. Typically, Joe. But it was more than that. I'd heard him tell Jim he was sending me back in, but now he was giving me extended leave. It didn't make sense. What was he up to?

As luck would have it, Joe only stayed two more days. A back molar had begun to annoy him, so he had to go to his dentist in London to get it out. He told me to stay put in Glasgow, and he'd go directly from London to Cairo. I was pleased. Good things had to be savoured. Joe had just wafted away like a bad smell.

I took out the coins Joe had tossed at me. They didn't amount to much. Certainly not enough for shopping. I needed more. I tiptoed into Jim's room and found him in bed sleeping. His jacket was hanging behind the door, so I delved into one of the pockets and managed to appropriate a pound.

I was about to leave the room when I clocked Jim's old bread bag from the war, shoved in a corner. Its single strap meant I could walk around town, hands-free. I grabbed it, and throwing it over my shoulder, hit the road.

Byres Road had a variety of shops situated within sandstone tenement buildings. I passed the Curler's pub, and went into a teashop. A chatty waitress showed me to a table and took my order.

"Any chance of a coffee?" I asked.

"Not here, hen. Tea and buns."

"Guess tea'll have to do." As I spoke, my eyes strayed towards a trolley full of cakes, and stopped at the chocolate brownies. "And a couple of those."

I finished the tea and brownies, then paid the cheque with one of Joe's coins, and took the change.

Where now?

It was too early to load myself down with food shopping, so I tossed a coin. 'Heads' for the Botanic Gardens, 'tails' for Kelvingrove Park. 'Tails' it was. I stayed in the park for about an hour, but when I clocked two blasts from the past, I decided it was time to move.

Constable Jessie MacTaggart, in full uniform, and Ellen Fairbairn. Strange combination. They were sitting on a bench next to a fountain, deep in conversation. Jessie was all right. She'd been good to me. She'd helped me out when I'd had problems with the cops during my teenage years. Helped put me on the straight and narrow. As for Ellen Fairbairn, well to be truthful, I didn't know her that well. All I knew was she'd been friends with the mother of an old associate of mine, Clara MacNab. And as far as I knew, Clara was still bad news.

I returned to Byres Road and bought a pile of groceries. By the time I'd finished, I was hot and in need of something cool. My prayers were answered. Just as I stopped at one of the corners, I saw an ice-cream cart. Unfortunately, it was surrounded by screaming kids with the same idea. Only one thing for it. I went up to the group, twitched my hands and rolled my eyes. The kids scarpered, and suddenly I was first in the queue.

"Hey, whadda ya know," I said to the ice-cream vendor. "Two free hands for two of your best cones!"

I continued along Byers Road with my merchandise and stopped at a newsagent's shop. I went in, and ran my eyes along a row of magazines on a rack in front of the counter, where a sales clerk was filing her nails. I finally found what I was looking for: *Amber St Claire.*

"I'm in that," I pouted. The girl behind the counter looked back at me. She clearly didn't care. "*Amber St Claire.* I'll take a copy," I said, and held out an ice cream.

She put down the nail file, and extracted a coin from my sticky hand, and stared. When I opened my mouth, she understood, and reaching over to pick up a copy, placed the magazine between my teeth. Then it was home time before the ice-cream melted.

On the way, I began to drool. *Fuck it!* I thought. By the time I got in, everything would be liquid: and that included the magazine. I decided to apply some acrobatics and got the magazine from my mouth to under my arm, without dropping the cone.

When I arrived home, I ran up the close stairs. "Jim!" I called. "Want some ice-cream?" There was no reply. I was surprised to see that the front door was open. "Jim!" I called again. Still no reply. I went into the flat and searched the rooms. He wasn't in any of them. Where the hell was he? "Hey, Jim, where are you?" I let the magazine drop on to the floor from under my pit, and went back out the front door. "Are you out the back?"

I made to go down the close stairs, but a noise on the landing above stalled me. "Jim? Is that you?" Still no response. I began to climb the stairs and stopped on the landing. Jim was leaning out the close window, vomiting. "What's going on?" It was obvious he'd been drinking. The landing smelled of whisky and urine. Slowly he turned and wiped his mouth. "What are you doing?" I asked.

Jim took a step towards me. "You really have no idea what's going on, do you?" he said.

"I can see you've just spilled your guts. You'll have to cut down on the booze, Jim!"

"Bugger the booze!"

"So, stop drinking!"

Jim shook his head. "You really don't get it."

"Come on. Is it because I took a pound?"

"Bugger the pound!"

"You'll not be saying that at dinner time."

"You really don't, do you?" His words were beginning to slur.

"Let's not fight, Jim."

"Too late! Too late!"

"What are you talking about?" I glanced at the ice-cream cones, still in my hands, and tried to keep my tone level. Now was *not* a good time for twitching, either major or minor.

"Did you know that someone once told me I had the mind, the organisation and the ability to do great work?" growled Jim.

His question disarmed me. I shook my head. No

doubt about it. He'd finally flipped. The years of drinking had gone and pickled his brain. I walked up to him, and noticed for the first time a pile of ripped up paper by his feet. "What's that?"

"Torn paper."

"I can see that. What's it doing there?"

"I was trying to throw it out the window."

"What for?" One of the pieces fluttered towards me as I spoke. It was a head. In fact, it looked very much like Stephen's head. Then I twigged. "It's the magazine. You've just torn up my article. You've torn it up," I repeated. "Why did you do that?"

"Because you just don't get it."

"I get that I spend an entire night writing it, and even if you don't like it, that's no reason to destroy it."

"Destroy? You don't know the meaning of the word."

I sighed loudly. What was the point? At least I had another copy. I turned and went back down the stairs, then stopped. Why? Then, again, why not? I wasn't the greatest reporter in the world, and certainly not the greatest writer, but that wasn't any reason to tear up my article.

Suddenly my right hand twitched, and I nearly lost the cone. "Fucking dodo!" I yelled, turning back to the stairs, just as Jim appeared at the top. He grasped hold of the banister. "Get back on the landing," I cried. "You're going to fall."

But Jim continued to cling to the banister. After a moment, he began to make his way down the stairs. "It's too late!" he hissed.

I opened my mouth to speak, but couldn't. I stared. Jim's frenzied expression became fixed, and his body rigid. There was a pause, and then a silence, as he flew heavily through the air and landed at my feet, closely followed by two melting ice-cream cones.

Jim never opened his eyes again. He lay in his casket on the kitchen table with a broken neck, a broken hip and a shattered nose. I sat with him in silence, shrouded in darkness, and as I breathed in the soporific effect of the room's atmosphere, I began to reflect.

Jim had never credited young women with financial sense, so his estate, which consisted of the tenement flat and an unexpectedly healthy bank balance, was to be left in trust for me. As matters stood, I wasn't allowed to touch a penny until my thirtieth birthday, when both the property and money would be given to me outright. To Stephen he left nothing, not out of malice, but simply because he didn't need anything.

That was all well and good.

Unfortunately, it meant one thing: Joe still figured in my life.

11

Central Police Office, Glasgow

Jessie

"You were seen in the park with Mrs Fairbairn," said Detective Inspector MacLeod. He was sitting in his office behind a pile of tiresome-looking paperwork. Jessie was seated in front of the assortment of green and pink files, which inadvertently obscured MacLeod's view of her. She noticed a particularly bulky manila envelope balancing on the top.

"Sir?"

"Coincidence or planned?" said MacLeod, shifting his chair with force, causing the envelope to wobble. He fixed his eyes on Jessie's calm face.

Jessie smiled and leaned forward to reposition the envelope. "Actually, that was one of the things we were talking about."

"Coincidences?"

"Synchronicity. It's called synchronicity." Jessie sat

back in her seat. "Things happen for a reason, but for the record, it *was* a coincidence."

MacLeod's body stiffened. "You can call it what you like. I just want to know what Fairbairn is up to."

Jessie frowned. She knew she was about to upset MacLeod. "Well," she said, "we were discussing the soul." She paused for a moment for a reaction. There was none, except a very blank face. "And I'm afraid we were talking about angels."

The blank face changed to one of astonishment. MacLeod shook his head. "I wouldn't go broadcasting that one. In fact, I absolutely forbid it. I'm not having the police force turned into a laughing stock."

"I'm not talking about winged creatures," continued Jessie, refraining from smiling.

"No? You mean they use engine power? No, wait a minute. They sit on unicorns!"

Jessie's face remained impassive. She wanted to laugh, but didn't dare. "I don't think they need engines, sir."

"I'm being facetious, MacTaggart!"

"Yes, sir." Jessie rubbed her face to stifle a giggle. "But it doesn't matter anyway. You see, Charlie doesn't believe in them, either."

MacLeod's face was grim. "Well, I'm glad to hear that."

Jessie felt her mouth twitch again. "Not with wings, anyway, sir. He says flies have wings. Angels are actually highly evolved spirits. They're much further up the ladder."

MacLeod pushed the paperwork to one side and leaned forward. He looked closely into Jessie's eyes.

"To be honest, MacTaggart," he said, "if the Chief Constable wasn't breathing so heavily down my neck, I'd tell you to take a couple of days off work to rest your head."

"Sir?"

MacLeod sat back. "So," he said slowly, carefully articulating each word, "if you know so much about angels, tell me what Mrs Fairbairn is saying about the greatest one of all: Bette Milligan. Especially now her father is dead."

"Sir?"

"Have you actually managed to find out anything of use to me," he clarified, "like *why* Bette has an alias?"

"Yes, sir. The foster parents in America were a Mr and Mrs Milligan."

"Foster parents?" MacLeod sat back, causing the chair to scrape against the floor. "So, no legal adoption?"

"No."

MacLeod smiled. His eyes began to wander the room, then fixed themselves on Jessie's face. "So," he said. "Jim Kipper was still the legal father." He paused to consider this. "So, why did Bette change her name? In fact, why did Stephen change his name?"

Jessie had a very good idea why that might be. "Well sir, does anyone want to be named after a fish?"

MacLeod clearly didn't find this funny. "Be that as it may," he snapped, "but I suggest you take cognisance of this: if Jim Kipper was the legal father, then his children are the legal inheritors. I call that motive!"

"You think Bette killed her father?"

MacLeod smiled. "Well, what do *you* think?"

"No, sir. If you're looking at inheritance, I happen to know that won't work."

"No?"

"Because there's a trust. And although Bette is the sole beneficiary, she won't get anything until she's thirty."

"And you know that how?"

"A line of enquiry. I happened upon the information."

"Ah! But killing him would certainly stop him spending any more of his money."

"He lived in a shabby flat, above the butcher's shop in Byres Road, sir. Not exactly a big spender."

"Greed, MacTaggart! Greed! What's more it's been reported that Miss Milligan's been in Egypt, and now she's back in Scotland. What was she doing in Egypt? And why is she back?"

"I know she's in Scotland, sir. I saw her when I was in the park with Mrs Fairbairn. She appeared, but when she saw us, she disappeared."

MacLeod smiled smugly. "Which only goes to prove a point."

"Sir?"

"A murderer fleeing from the police!"

Jessie shook her head. "I think it's more to do with the fact she's embarrassed about her past."

MacLeod raised a brow. "Really? Well, I happen to think she's up to no good." He pulled a report out of one the drawers in his desk. "Do you know what this is?"

Jessie glanced at his hand, in which, was a sheet of paper. "No, sir."

"This," he said, shaking the paper in her direction, "is an accidental death report. It details the death of James Kipper. The *accidental* death, I might add. Only I don't happen to believe it *was* accidental. Read it. You'll see it's really not as cut and dried as people seem to think."

Jessie leaned over the files on the desk and took the report. She cast her eyes down the pages. "You really think Bette Milligan pushed her father down the stairs?" she said. "But why?"

"Well, I can think of quite a few reasons, and all connected to Mrs Fairbairn!"

"You mean a Nazi association?"

"Some kind of association. Think about it, MacTaggart! Think about it. Bette Milligan and Ellen Fairbairn go back a long way. If it's *not* a Nazi association, which the Chief Constable happens to believe it *is*, then it *has* to be a criminal association. Take Clara MacNab, *she's* not changed. So, why should Bette Milligan have changed?" MacLeod paused. "As far as I'm concerned, once a criminal, always a criminal."

Jessie was confused. She'd already treated MacLeod's earlier reference to gangsters with little more than a pinch of salt. "So, what you're saying, sir, is that if there *isn't* a Nazi association, then there *must* be a criminal association. If Ellen Fairbairn and Bette Milligan are *not* Nazi spies, then they have to be gangsters?"

MacLeod looked smug. "Ever wondered where Bette Milligan *really* came from?"

"Like I told you, she was fostered out to a family in New York. Her own dad couldn't cope, then when he could, a sympathetic friend made arrangements to have her returned."

MacLeod shook his head. "Glasgow to New York, and back again? Don't you find that strange? And that's supposing it *was* Glasgow in the first place."

Jessie shook her head. "I really don't know, sir."

"And do you honestly think an old drunk wanted the responsibility of an awkward teenager?"

Jessie hadn't considered this. "You mean she was forced back on him?"

"Who exactly are the Milligans?" said MacLeod slowly.

"Irish immigrants." Jessie paused. "Are you saying Bette's involved with Irish-American gangsters *and* the Nazis?"

Macleod narrowed his eyes. "Then there's another minor detail. The IRA have been collaborating with the Nazis since 1937."

Jessie shook her head. "Wait a minute, sir. You're now saying there might be an association between Bette, the Irish-American mobsters, the Nazis *and* the IRA?"

"I see your *mind* is finally beginning to work," said MacLeod, his tone dry.

"But why would any of these organisations want to kill Bette's father? And why would Ellen Fairbairn have anything to do with the IRA? She's Scottish, *not* Irish."

"A theory, MacTaggart. A theory. And as for Jim Kipper, he might have been a drunk, but that didn't stop him uncovering things he wasn't supposed to."

Jessie was incredulous. "You think Bette's father found something out, and Bette was ordered to kill him?"

MacLeod's right eye began to twitch. "Why did Jim Kipper give up custody of his children in the first place?"

"Lost his wife. Like I said, he couldn't cope."

"You believe that?"

"Yes, I do, sir. And Bette's changed over the years. She's done well for herself. She's left her past behind her."

"Well, I'll be keeping my eye on that girl!" MacLeod thumped the desk, and as he did so, the envelope wobbled again, this time tumbling to the ground, and landing inches from Jessie's feet.

Jessie moved her legs and retrieved the envelope, which was already opened. She glanced inside and took out the contents: a copy of *Amber St Claire* and a photograph. Her eyes remained fixed on the photograph. It was Bette Milligan. "Where did you get that?"

MacLeod opened a drawer and produced a 35mm Ansco Memo Miniature spy camera. "Take my word for it. We'll soon be pursuing a new line of enquiry, and it won't be long before we can add *that* mugshot to our rogues' gallery. As far as I'm concerned, enquiries are, most certainly, *not* complete."

12

British Military Hospital (BMH), Alexandria

Bentley

Bentley had been confined to hospital for seven weeks, in accordance with Joe's very specific instructions. He'd just swallowed a spoonful of medicine that left an annoying aftertaste in his mouth. His head was hurting, and he longed for a dose of belladonna to put him out his misery.

He glanced around the ward. There were five other beds. Only one was occupied, and the person was sleeping. "How's the arm?" whispered a voice in his left ear.

It was the nurse who'd been responsible for his care for the past three weeks, and had replaced the assortment of grumpy-looking women who'd attended to him at the beginning. This one was British, and very soft-spoken, with a tone of voice that made him think of a purring kitten. She had hazel eyes and brown hair.

"The arm's fine," replied Bentley, smiling.

Just the medicine, he thought.

Bentley had a penchant for brunettes, and this one was a beaut. He'd already made enquiries about her, and one of the doctors had informed him that her name was Jacqueline Brown. She was twenty-nine years of age, and had served in India for the Queen Alexandra's Imperial Nursing Service. She had come to Egypt the previous month.

"What about the leg?" she asked, folding down the sheets and rolling up the right leg of his pyjamas.

When Bentley had fallen from his horse, he'd broken his left arm, and had been knocked out cold. His right leg had been exposed and badly burned by the sun. A group of British soldiers had found him, half dead, when they'd been out on a training exercise.

"Buggered!" he responded, referring to his leg.

Nurse Brown raised a brow and began to apply ointment. Bentley watched the supple movement of her fingers as they touched his flesh, her fingertips moving almost imperceptibly. She completed the job and took his pulse. Bentley looked up at her clear skin, and admired her slim neck, until quite unexpectedly, a button fell from her blouse and a chain popped out. Hanging from it was a sapphire ring.

"Nice ring," said Bentley. Nurse Brown drew away. *Sore point*, he thought. She turned to leave the room, but paused, and stepped aside, as a visitor came in.

"Stop upsetting the staff!" came Joe's booming

voice, as he entered the ward. "At the very least, try and conduct yourself with a modicum of decorum."

Bentley observed Nurse Brown smile as she left the room. "I'm not upsetting anyone. Everything's just fine and dandy!"

"I'm actually wondering if you're right in the head!"

Bentley frowned. "And why would that be?"

"You're a twit!"

"Thank you, Joe."

"Best place to keep you is locked up in the kennels! Even then you'd probably do something stupid to the bloody dogs!"

Bentley exhaled loudly. *Bugger the kennels!* He thought. His back was sore, and he longed for something decent to drink. He hated hospitals, and he particularly hated hard metal beds and coarse army blankets, with their rough texture that irritated the skin. "Anyway," he said, "what are you doing here? I thought you were in London."

Joe ignored the question and sat down on the edge of the bed. "Any drink in the house?"

"Plenty," replied Bentley. "Just happens to be water. It's in the jug over there. Help yourself, and you can refill my cup whilst you're at it. I've got a mouth like the bottom of a cocky's cage!"

"I assume that means you're thirsty," said Joe, getting up. He filled two cups and placed them on the trolley next to Bentley, then sat back down on the bed.

"Make yourself comfortable," said Bentley, dryly.

"Anything I can get you?" asked Joe. He took off

his glasses and proceeded to polish them with a handkerchief, before placing them back on his nose.

Bentley cast his eyes towards a vase on the windowsill, which contained a collection of wilting specimens. "How about a fresh bunch of flowers?"

"Compliments of MPRS," said Joe. "Don't tell me we don't care."

Just then, Nurse Brown returned with Bentley's breakfast. She placed it on the trolley with the cups of water, and rested her eyes on Joe. Bentley smiled. Nurses weren't shy about coming forward.

Joe got to his feet. "You can contact me at the usual place," he said, as he left.

"And where might that be? London? Cairo? Or, maybe somewhere else?" Bentley shouted after him.

"Try London!" came Joe's distant voice, as he marched away down the corridor.

"Better hope they don't start charging you for overuse of military aircraft!" shouted Bentley. There was no reply. Bentley turned back to the food. He eyed up the fried eggs on his plate. "Not bad for a change," he commented, looking up at Nurse Brown's very pretty face. "Although a single red rose would have added a nice touch to it."

Nurse Brown fixed her eyes on his face. "Enjoy your meal," she said.

"Service with a smile."

"Always."

"Twist my arm and I might ask you out on a date!"

"Is that a fact?"

"Only make it my right arm. My left one is somewhat indisposed."

"I'll think about it," was the response, but the expression on her face indicated she would probably rather have twisted his neck. She left the room.

Bentley began to eat. The eggs slid easily down his throat. They were good for a change, but he missed steak. That was his favourite. Steak washed down with a good red wine. Hell! Even a spot of the amber fluid would have done. Yes, a bottle of Tooheys Flag Ale would have done just nicely.

He sighed. He was losing his touch with the ladies. Strewth! It wasn't as if he'd asked her to marry him. Still, there was no point in fretting. He finished the eggs, then lay back against the pillows, shut his eyes, and tried to relax.

"That plaster comes off tomorrow." He hadn't noticed Nurse Brown return to the ward. He knew that could only mean one thing.

A few days later he found out why. Joe rang him. "Get your togs together, and no shoddy excuses! You're out of there. You have a mission."

Two days later, Bentley was flying to London. It was all familiar ground. He'd learned his trade the hard way. Make a mistake and you'd be forced to do it right the next time. If you didn't, there would be consequences.

Bentley let his thoughts wander. More than anything, he wanted to retire. The Military Psychical Research Section was a very exacting part of Army Intelligence. He'd served with MPRS as an agent for most of his career, but now it was time to quit. He was ready to go, and the only thing standing between him and a good pension was another war.

And that was the problem.

Things weren't looking good. The world was in a precarious state. There was a threat of war looming, and things were coming to a head. There had been plenty talks between countries as they tried to negotiate their differences, but loyalties were flying all over the place.

That in itself was bad enough. Unfortunately, Bentley was aware of something else. Something that not even the politicians knew about, and this was where Bentley's services were very much required.

13

Jim's Flat, Glasgow

Bette

"Cup of tea would be nice," said Joe, who'd somehow managed to magic himself back to Glasgow. He stood in the doorway, filling the space like a bumbling yeti, only this particular yeti was just out the barbershop. Joe's head was shorn, his face puce with the heat, and one of his lapels was sticking up. When I let him in, he was hobbling.

Good, I thought. *Gout.* "Nice jacket," I said, taking him into the kitchen and putting the kettle on.

"Weak tea in a porcelain cup with a spot of sugar would do just nicely."

"I'm sure it would," I said, dryly, my back to him. When the kettle boiled, I filled the teapot, and pouring him a cup, dolloped three large teaspoons of sugar into it.

"Sorry about your father," he said.

"Thank you," I replied, turning to face him. I wondered just how true that was, and handed him the cup of very sweet tea, before sitting down opposite him.

"At least you've got somewhere to stay, even if, technically, it isn't your flat yet." He paused. "I suppose we could still call it Jim's flat." He smiled. "Tell you what, we'll hold a party here on your thirtieth birthday, when it's yours outright, and you can do what you like with it." He winked. "That's if you'll let us, of course."

Yup, that was the *real* Joe. "Who gives a fuck what it's called?" I snorted.

"We went back a long way, you know. Me and Jim, that is."

"Yeah." I leaned forward and stared into his eyes. "Funny you've never told me *all* the details, though."

"Ah! The details! Well, here's one: I've a new assignment for you." He sipped his tea and made a face.

"The tea lady?"

"Not if you make tea like this," he said, laying the cup down on the table. "Certainly not! No! You're going to return to Cairo and write another article on the film industry."

My mouth opened, and I gawped at him: "You have to be joking?"

"Indeed, not." He got up, and pouring the tea down the sink, got himself another.

"I think I'd rather make the tea."

"Lost your nerve, Special Agent Milligan?" he said, returning to his seat.

"Special Agent?" What the hell was that about?

"Can't take the pressure?" He took a sip of tea. "Lovely," he said.

"Pressure?" I gasped, as a clear picture of Jim falling down the stairs leapt into my mind. "You obviously don't know what happened to my first article."

"It was published in the magazine."

"I know it was published in the magazine, but you don't know what *happened* to it."

"To be honest, I never actually read it," he said, taking another sip of tea.

"Well," I said slowly, leaning further across the table, my elbows fixed on its surface. "Jim did. He read it, tore it up, then fell down the stairs! Oh! And one more minor detail: he did all that after puking out a window!"

Joe looked surprised. He scratched his chin. "Didn't know that. I'll have a quick read of it when I get the time."

"You'd better do just that," I said, sitting back.

"Doesn't change the situation, though. You're still writing another article."

The man's mad, I thought.

"So, I'll run you through a few pointers. You remember Omar O'Malley?"

"Yup."

"Well, we now *know* he's actively involved with Hitler's special army. The one I mentioned before. The one that's there to supplement the existing German national army and Hitler's SS."

"What kind of special army?" I asked,

remembering his conversation with Jim. "It wouldn't have anything to do with the Dead Army, would it?"

For a second, Joe looked shocked. He quickly composed himself. "Don't know where you got that from," he said.

But I wasn't finished. If I wasn't going to get the truth from him, I was still prepared to set the cat amongst the pigeons. "And you're still saying: *we*."

"Semantics," he hastily responded.

Crap, I thought, but I wasn't going to push the issue. I badly wanted to know what was going on, but knew I'd have to bide my time. If Joe didn't want to tell me, he wouldn't tell me. What was more, he didn't like questions: not ones he didn't ask, anyway.

Joe leaned forward and looked me straight in the eye. "It's been brought to my attention that the Nazis are using an Egyptian tomb somewhere in the desert to train a special army, but its exact location is still unknown."

"Have you tried Mars?" I suggested.

"Your detail is to locate this tomb," he continued, ignoring my comment. "And to do that, you need to go back to Egypt and take up your role as a simple reporter."

Simple was the word. Joe clearly wasn't joking. Problem was, he had me where he wanted. As usual, he wasn't being truthful. And going back to his conversation with Jim, I wasn't sure if I was supposed to be dealing with the living or the dead.

"You'll be travelling by ship."

No surprise there, I thought.

"And you'll be making contact with an agent from

an organisation called MPRS."

"MPRS?" I repeated.

"And a word of advice. Keep your mouth shut. Don't ask questions and don't give opinions: and above all, don't discuss personal matters. The agent in charge of you doesn't like it. You're there to learn, so, go with the flow."

In charge of me? Go with the flow? Don't discuss the case? Personal matters? What was this? Some kind of crazy training exercise for rookies? I was about to ask, but Joe got up and left the room. I stayed put. I was getting confused. If all this had something to do with intelligence matters, and international espionage, then why was Joe involved?

And then another thought. A far more worrying one: why was I involved?

14

En route to Egypt

Bette

I packed a bag and left the fish and budgie with one of the neighbours. I knew it was serious when Joe sent me to France in a military plane all the way to Marseille. After that I caught the boat to Alexandria.

Joe had given me a box of goodies, which included a torch, a camera and a thick file. The latter contained information telling me what to do, and what not to do during the course of the investigation. It included a reminder to keep my mouth shut, listen and learn, and above all, not to discuss personal business.

There was also a section giving up-to-date information on Cairo's film industry. Attached to that was a report giving the name of the agent from MPRS: a Captain Bentley Ford-Jenkins. Clipped to that was a mugshot. The face that stared out at me wasn't smiling.

My eyes scanned the pages. Still no explanation of what MPRS was. I read on. Captain Ford-Jenkins was to make contact with me at some point aboard our ship, *La Belle Femme,* or, *The Gorgeous Dolly Bird*, as Joe had written in the notes.

I clocked Ford-Jenkins the next morning in the restaurant. He was sitting at a table across from me. He glanced over at me, then turned his attention to a menu.

After a moment he got up, and walked in my direction. I was about to shove out my hand and introduce myself, but he ignored me, and walked straight past. Not even a perfunctory nod of the head. I wondered if his offhand manner was a prerequisite for MPRS.

There was no doubt about it: he and Joe were definitely tarred with the same brush.

Bentley

Bentley sat quietly in his cabin and thought about his new partner, Bette. Joe had warned him that she had one or two unfortunate traits. He was right. She had a face like a dropped pie, and her hair was on the brighter side of carrot. Not only that: he'd wager she could waggle those ears. Joe had claimed there was a deficiency in suitable candidates for the assignment, and that he didn't have a photograph of his new partner. Bentley now understood why.

But it was her skills in surveillance that troubled him. *Kangaroos loose in the top paddock,* he thought.

She clearly hadn't a clue what she was doing, and that made her very, very dangerous. What the bloody hell was Joe up to? There had to be an explanation, but the only one Bentley could come up with, wasn't very pleasing.

Joe had wanted Bentley to pass on his skills to other agents, but Bentley didn't have the patience to teach, and had told Joe so on numerous occasions. Now he could only assume that the bastard had tricked him, and he'd walked right into it, like a lamb to the slaughter. Joe was as cunning as a dunny rat, and it was becoming clear that the job ahead was about to become little more than a matter of nursing the baby.

Joe had told him that the new agent, who was female, was posing as a reporter with the magazine *Amber St Claire*, which had been set up a while back by MPRS to let agents in to do undercover work, and to-date, the new agent knew nothing about the Dead Army. Joe had finished by saying that she came from a very unfortunate background.

What the hell! His hadn't been much better. For a start, he and his mother had never seen eye to eye; but to really understand why, you had to review the life of his Great Great Aunt Thelma: or, was it three Greats? He was never quite sure.

Thelma was from his father's side of the family, of course. Born in Moffat, Scotland, she'd been accused of being a witch, invoking the services of unwelcome entities. She'd been tried and found guilty, but rather than condemn her to death, the court had decided that she should be transported. So, she'd been shipped off to Australia.

But the *gift* had continued on down the line.

When he was ten, Bentley had seen the ghost of a woman. He'd described her to his father, who'd said that in all probability it was Thelma. His mother had been less forthcoming. He'd tried to raise the subject, but she had refused to discuss it.

When he was twelve, he'd woken up in the middle of the night, and started to see his room fill with grey mist, only, it wasn't mist, his father had later explained, it was a substance called ectoplasm.

"What's that?" Bentley had asked.

His father had sat him down with the same expression he'd had when explaining the biological facts of life. At the time, Bentley hadn't been sure which was worse.

"Well, Bentley," his father had said, "ectoplasm is living energy. It's a very interesting substance."

Interesting? Bentley had barely been able to pronounce it. "Where does it come from?"

"Well, it usually comes from a medium and sitters during a séance," his father had continued.

"What's a medium?" Bentley had then asked, his expression blank.

"In this context, Bentley, a medium is a person," his father had explained, patiently.

But it still hadn't made sense. "Why are they called mediums?"

"Because they're used to communicate."

"And what's a séance?" Bentley had pressed.

"A séance is a circle of people wanting to communicate."

"Why do they do that?"

"To speak to their loved ones."

This had seemed crazy. "Can't they just go and visit them?" he'd asked.

"No. Because it's the ones that are dead. They want to communicate with the Spirit World. Thelma's in the Spirit World."

Now that had been something of a revelation. "You mean I could speak to her if I wanted?"

"Well, if *she* wanted to. If it was the right thing to do. But usually anyone who wants to speak to their loved ones has to go to a medium, because it's the medium who knows what to do. They use *clairvoyance* to see what normal humans can't see, or *clairaudience* to hear. Some use *clairsentience*: they feel. And that's how they communicate with the Spirit World. It's called mental mediumship."

It *was* mental! And this had started to excite Bentley. "So why do you need ectoplasm?"

"That's for physical mediumship: materialisation. Things that humans *can* see."

Bentley had scratched his head. Just when things seemed to be getting simpler, he'd become confused again. "What does that mean?"

"Well, it's another way for a medium to act as a channel for the spirits."

"I thought the Channel was a bit of sea?"

"Yes, Bentley, but in this case, the channel is the medium, not the sea. But like the sea, it's the bit that joins two different parts."

"What do you mean?"

"Well, the Channel, the sea, I mean, joins France

and Britain. The medium joins the Spirit World and the physical world."

"And we're in the physical world?"

"Yes, Bentley, yes! And those in the Spirit World can produce another substance. Don't ask me to explain that. But the mixture of what *they* produce and what *we* produce allows lots of things to happen. It could result in ectoplasm coming out the medium's nose."

"Like snot?"

"It's a different substance, Bentley, and it can also come out of other parts of the human body."

This had made Bentley laugh. "The bum?"

"Yes, the bum," his father had acceded.

Bentley had then remembered the ectoplasm in his room. Where had that come from? Out his nose? Or, out his bum? Had the Spirit World been using his body to create this strange mixture? "Am I a medium?" he'd finally asked.

"Yes, son, I think you are." His father had then paused and looked at him pensively. "Just one thing. Best not to tell your mother."

And that had been Bentley's first conversation about mediumship. He'd begun to have very vivid dreams, and from there, things had developed further. The net of ectoplasm, surrounding him at night, had become dotted with small black spots, clearly visible against the surface of his white walls and white furniture. Were they dreams? At first, he'd thought they might be, until over time the spots had grown larger and had begun to move around, diving within the mesh of ectoplasm.

"Thelma," said his father, when he enquired. "She's trying to make contact."

But spots? Some the size of footballs. Some black, some grey, some solid and some hazy. Some were shooting through the air, and others across the floor, but all of them towards him. Bentley had grown understandably alarmed.

"Is she trying to play football?" he'd asked.

"Don't know," his father had said. "But she certainly wants to play."

Bentley then began to keep a notebook of his experiences, and hid it at the back of his wardrobe. That was until the day of reckoning.

When he turned fifteen, his mother, a devout Christian, who thought that speaking to the dead was a cardinal sin, found the notebook. One witch in the family was more than enough. Convinced that Bentley was damned, and in need of salvation, she showed the book to the authorities. They, in turn, became concerned about the impact his behaviour might have on his peers, and so he was suspended from school and locked up for a year.

His punishment included hard work in a tin mine. But over the months he developed firm biceps and soon realised that brawn and brains were a great combination. Not one to normally show his true feelings, he made an exception, and when he was eventually released, he gifted his mother a tin mug, as a token of his appreciation.

But the experiences had never gone, and nor had the dreams. He shook his head, as his mind went back to Bette. If he got through this, it would be little more than a remarkable achievement. He'd have to work out an effective strategy to handle her. But it wasn't looking good, and he had a feeling in his gut that this preliminary encounter was little more than a prelude to disaster.

Bette

I was angry. Why was my contact ignoring me? I hadn't seen him all day, and when I went to dinner that evening, there was still no sign of him. A waiter came to my table and handed me the wine list. I perused it for a while, until finally deciding that MPRS would probably be paying the bill, I ordered a bottle of *Chateau Paveil de Luze*, and drank the lot.

Bentley

Bentley wasn't hungry. He lay on top of the bed covers in his cabin and yawned. He looked at his watch, as he recalled his last conversation with Joe Bannerman. "*Britain might be neutral at the moment,*" Joe had said, "*but there's definitely talk of war.*"

Bentley's eyes began to nip. He shut them tight, and laid his palms across his lids. He watched the colours as they appeared before him: purple, black and plenty, plenty sparkling dots of energy. When the colours developed into images, he found himself stepping out of thick vegetation, towards a clearing...

German East Africa, 1914

Bentley advanced through trees, and out on to open grassland. After a moment, he stopped. A number of hundred yards ahead was a male lion, basking in the sun. As Bentley stared, an unexpected sound filled the air. The lion sprang to its feet, but was struck by a fast-travelling spear. Bentley continued to watch, as a small group of tall, slender figures emerged from woodland.

The Maasai.

A young warrior stepped forward, and made for the lion, which was now dead. He withdrew the spear from its chest and held it up into the heat of the day. Pride crossed the young man's face as he cried out to the Supreme Being and the spirits of his ancestors.

Suddenly a blast of machine gunfire exploded in the air, and the young warrior collapsed on top of the lion. Another barrage threw the remaining Maasai to the ground, and Bentley found himself running back into the foliage, and hiding behind a tree.

When the firing ceased, a platoon of soldiers appeared. Bentley remained hidden, and observed one of the soldiers advance towards the dead warrior. He rolled the lion over with his boot. Bentley moved his foot and a twig snapped. The soldier lifted his head. It was Baron Heinrich von Kosch. But how did Bentley know that?

"Halt!" cried von Kosch. "Come out of there with

your hands up!"

Bentley made to move, but his eyes sprang open. It was another dream.

15

Egypt

Bette

We were due to disembark in a few hours, and my contact still hadn't introduced himself to me. I made my way to the restaurant for the last time, and decided to have a go at the continental breakfast. Croissants and coffee. That would do just nicely. I spread a thick layer of jam on the pastry, and dipping it into my coffee, began to reflect.

I'd finished reading the file, so making a mental note of all possible suspects, I began to review the evidence. Hitler was creating a special army. I had an idea that this was the Dead Army that Jim had referred to, although I still hadn't a clue what that was. The file also said the special army had links to the German national army and the SS. Furthermore, I'd discovered that Omar O'Malley was at the top of the list of suspects.

Unfortunately, this created another problem:

where did Jim and Stephen come in?

Jim had definitely known about the Dead Army, but since he was dead, there wasn't much more I could do in that department.

Then there was Stephen, who, of course, was being investigated 'for his own good'. Joe had already said he might have links to the Nazis, so if he did, what did *he* know about the Dead Army?

As for Farida, I couldn't make my mind up about her, but I wished she'd stop wearing that goddam necklace.

However, it didn't end there.

My notes specified the additional presence of two other individuals: a Mr and Mrs Campbell, whom I'd yet to meet. I knew that no one could be discounted, and was beginning to wonder if I should add Captain Bentley Ford-Jenkins to the list, when he unexpectedly appeared.

"G'day," he said in an Australian drawl.

"Hi," I replied.

"Can I join you?" He sat down before I answered. "Not much meat there," he commented, eying the croissant. He called over a waiter. "Steak, and make it as bloody as hell."

My stomach turned. "For breakfast?"

"Best meal of the day!" he replied, cheerfully.

"So, Captain Ford-Jenkins, we finally meet," I said, when his breakfast arrived.

"Yes, I suppose we do," he replied.

So, here he was, and here I was, and I hadn't a clue what was going to happen next. He began to eat.

"Did Joe give you a file as well?" I asked. "Do we

need to compare notes?"

"No need," said Ford-Jenkins, his mouth full. "It's all in my noodle." He pointed to his head with his fork.

Yeah! And what else was in his *noodle*? The way things appeared to be, I was *definitely* putting him on my list of suspects. "Good," I said. "Then I can pick your brain any time."

For a second, he stopped chewing. Perfect. A proper reaction. A reaction that indicated picking his brain was the last thing he wanted. I dunked another croissant into my coffee. "Who's paying for all this, anyway?" I asked.

"Joe has his contacts."

"MPRS per chance? Whatever that means."

Ford-Jenkins began to laugh. "He hasn't told you?"

This was getting annoying. "He hasn't told me what?" I laid down my croissant, and glared.

Ford-Jenkins laughed again. "You'll find out in due course."

This was crazy. Why was no one telling me anything? They wanted me to investigate, well, Joe wanted me to investigate, but not one bastard would give me the facts. I'd have given up there and then if it hadn't been for the fact *I* was probably Stephen's only salvation. Then, of course, there was one other important factor to consider: I needed my job.

When we finally docked in Alexandria a few hours later, I was none the wiser. As I stepped on to dry land, I looked around. "Not very pretty, is it?" I said, surprised. "What's that great monstrosity over there?" I was pointing to a pillar in the distance. It stood out amongst some ruins.

"Pompey's Pillar," said Ford-Jenkins, absently. He paused. "Look, I need to stay here for a couple of days. You get the train to Cairo, and I'll meet you there."

"Why?"

"I've business to attend to."

This wasn't sounding good. "So, where will you be staying if I need to get in touch?" I asked.

"I've booked in here at the San Stefano."

The San Stefano? I'd read about it. Plenty gambling, wining and dining, by all accounts. "OK. So, when you *eventually* come to Cairo, where will you be staying?"

"Probably Shepheard's," he replied.

"Probably?"

"Strewth" he gasped, turning to look at me. "Do you always ask heaps of questions?"

I met his gaze. "Don't you want to know where I'll be staying?"

"Joe's already told me. You'll be at the villa and I'll be at Shepheard's."

Well, the good Captain Bentley Ford-Jenkins had got that one wrong. But who was I to correct Bentley Boy? Let the fucking dodo find out for himself. At least I'd discovered how to push his buttons, and that was going to be very useful. The guy had a short fuse, and the heat probably wasn't helping.

It was the beginning of August, and temperatures were very high. When the train arrived in Cairo, it was no different. I knew that Farida spent a lot of time at Stephen's apartment in Garden City, so I decided to stop off at a bazaar to buy flowers in case she was there.

It was then I clocked the woman.

She was a smart-looking platinum blonde, dressed from head to toe in red, and was already at the flower stall, haggling over a bunch of red roses. She stood out. Here was a dame who got what she wanted, and how right my observation would prove to be.

I didn't know it then, but she was going to bounce back into my life in the not-too-distant future, just like the broad on the train.

Farida's car was parked outside Stephen's apartment. "You've just missed him," she said, letting me in. "He's gone to the film studios with my father. I'll cook us something to eat if you like."

"Wouldn't mind." I was starving.

"How about a fry-up with a few muffins?"

"Really?"

"Well, the Egyptian equivalent."

"So, no bacon?"

"No bacon." As she cooked, we exchanged polite platitudes, and nothing more. "Tea or coffee?"

"Coffee, please."

"So, what brings you back to Cairo?"

"Joe wants me to write another article on the Egyptian cinema."

"Super!" she said. "You'll need to come and stay at the villa. That way you can pick my father's brain."

*

I'd hoped the villa would be accessible by car. Whether or not that was the case, I soon found myself astride a donkey, both feet controlled by stirrups, climbing higher and higher into the Muqattam hills.

Stephen had stayed on in Garden City because he was working on a film, but O'Malley had decided to return to the villa the day before. So here I was, on a scabby-looking creature, following Farida, who had her own ride. A small Egyptian walked on ahead. I'd never been on a donkey before, and as I rode on, my main concern became the distinct lack of a footbrake.

Very soon we left the foothills. As we climbed higher, I observed windmills in the distance, perched on peaks. Further up, I kept a vigilant eye on the rocks, searching for fissures, hollows and any other irregularities on the ground that might cause an accident. But I was tired, and for a split second I snoozed, only waking when I nearly fell off. My neck jerked and my right hand began to twitch. *Control, Bette, control.* The twitching stopped.

When the villa came into view, I felt better. It was a long building: two storeys high. As we got closer, we reached a gravel path that divided an expanse of rich-looking grass set in front of the building. About a dozen Georgian windows gleamed in the sunlight.

Joe had warned me that the villa was very much out of the way. O'Malley had got Farida to design a pump to draw water up from the Nile, which explained why the grass was so green. The walls were of beige stone, presumably limestone from the hills, and were covered in ivy.

I turned my attention towards the main entrance. There was a large brown Georgian door inside a stone porch that protruded from the body of the building. The whole setup reminded me of a stately home. Suddenly the door opened, and there stood Omar O'Malley.

"Father," said Farida, dismounting. She went over to O'Malley and hugged him.

"The intrepid reporter returns," said O'Malley, turning towards me. Is this work or pleasure?"

I swallowed hard. *Let the charade begin*, I thought. "Bit of both," I replied. "I'm here to write another article on your cinema, but I'm going to take every opportunity to relax."

"And this is just the place to do it," said Farida, slipping her arm through her father's. "There was no time to show her the sights on her last visit, so I insist on doing it this time round." As she spoke, she fiddled with the pendants round her neck.

Goddam necklace!

There was nothing much to do that afternoon, but as we walked past the kitchen, I stopped and looked in. A large fan spun crazily on the ceiling over a fire that burned inside a large black cast-iron cooking range. The heat was overwhelming. Copper pots hung from the range, and as I glanced down, I observed a couple of bones lying on the floor. They were big bones, and they'd been well gnawed, so I assumed there had to be dogs in the villa: either that, or someone in the household had very strange eating habits.

I was taken to my room and left to settle in. A

cream and pink patterned rug led to a large double bed, its headboard, mahogany. A cream quilt covered the large mattress. I bounced on top of the bed, and lay my head against the pillow. When I shut my eyes, I began to doze.

It was the sound of a gong that awoke me, and I soon realised it was seven o'clock in the evening. Where had the day gone? I jumped up, and hurried to the dining room. As I stepped inside, I stopped short. Two great mutts ran towards me. One was a Doberman, and the other looked like a mongrel. They leapt up and licked my face, but soon lost interest, and made their way to the head of a highly polished table, where O'Malley was seated. They planted themselves at his feet.

O'Malley pointed to a chair on his right, where a place had been set at the table. I wandered over, and as I did so, looked around. It was an interesting setup. The walls were covered with dark brown wooden panelling. A grey stone fireplace was built into one of the walls, and a metal fireguard sat in front of it. There was no fire, and given the brightness of the metal, and the shine of the stone, probably never had been. A couple of electric candelabras were built into the panelled walls on either side of the fireplace, and these burned with bright intensity, giving light to the entire room.

"Good evening," said O'Malley, as I sat down. "I hope you rested well."

"Certainly did," I replied glancing down towards the other end of the table, where another place was set.

"Farida is often late," said O'Malley, noticing my scrutiny.

"Nice place you have here," I said, turning to him.

"We aim to please."

I bet you do, I thought, glancing away, afraid O'Malley might read my mind.

Seemed he did, for as I examined the expensive looking rug that almost covered the entire floor, he coughed.

"Farida particularly likes the Persian variety," he said, "and you'll notice the deep blue in the fabric matches the silk stripes on the seats of the chairs."

I hadn't noticed the colour of the seats, so I lifted a butt, and looked down. Blue and cream silk stripes. *Should have changed my pants*, I thought.

"I hope you enjoy your visit here," said O'Malley.

I didn't get a chance to answer, for it was at that point that an old man, wearing a black jacket, entered the room. He must have been in his seventies. He was skinny, and his white hair was ruffled. As he approached O'Malley, I realised that he was the waiter.

Great.

The waiter was a septuagenarian with one foot in the grave. All he needed to do now was have a heart attack, or trip over the foot of a chair. Yeah. A couple of missed heartbeats, and we'd be wearing dinner. I watched as he balanced a tray in his right hand, and hoped the food would survive its journey to the table. It did, and so did two bottles of expensive-looking red wine.

It was at that moment that Farida entered the room. "Sorry," she said. "Didn't hear the gong." She sat down to join us.

The table was full of Egyptian delights. I helped myself to a kebab. The lamb was delicious. So was the *Kebda Eskandarani*, although the spices mixed in with the liver were a bit on the strong side, and I hoped they wouldn't play havoc with my bowels. The *Umm Ali*, raisin cake soaked in milk, was predictably yummy.

When our waiter left the room, O'Malley turned to me. "Mr Campbell is something of a jack-of-all-trades." So that identified the waiter. "Mrs Campbell, his wife, is my cook."

"She's good," I said, assuming that sometime in the past, Campbell had managed to purloin a young Egyptian girl. No doubt she was now as old and decrepit as her husband.

"Yes, she is," agreed O'Malley. "I met her on a visit to Scotland, and fell in love with her cooking."

"Really?" I hadn't expected that. An elderly Scottish woman cooking Egyptian food? But hey! What the hell!

"Anyway, don't let me stop you enjoying yourself," continued O'Malley. "I have business to attend to, but please stay and have more wine." He got up and left the room, closely followed by the two dogs.

The following day, O'Malley showed me round some of his estate. After a couple of hours, we stood at the edge of the hills, and studied the activities of the people down below.

"We get our fruit and vegetables locally," he said, pointing down towards matchstick-sized carts being pulled by tired-looking matchstick donkeys.

I squinted my eyes. "Bit of a trek, isn't it? Why not grow your own, what with the water pump and all that?"

"Are you a *frequent* visitor to Egypt?"

The change of subject and question disarmed me.

"Pardon me?"

"We seem to be meeting at quite regular intervals."

I paused, uncomfortable. "Not really."

By my count, this was only our second meeting, but I wasn't sure if he was assessing things, or simply passing comment. Fortunately, the lunch gong went off, and my mind went on to better things.

I followed O'Malley back to the villa. Once inside, he paused outside a small room. "I use this as my office," he said. I glanced in. In the middle of the room was a large, shiny mahogany desk, its surface decorated with green leather. A typewriter was perched on top of it, surrounded by papers. My eyes scanned the room, and I clocked Mr Campbell, sitting in one of the corners.

He looked up. "Hello hen."

That was the first time I'd heard him speak. His voice was hoarse and rough, and he was missing two front teeth. I couldn't decide if it was down to tooth decay, or if someone had taken a swing at him. Whatever, I was steadily forming the opinion that he might well be a jack-of-all-trades, but he would probably also prove to be something of a jack-in-the-box: no matter how many times you would try to shut the lid, he would just keep popping up.

16

Hotel San Stefano, Alexandria

Bentley

Another bad night.

In fact, it had been so bad, Bentley had decided to stay on at the San Stefano a couple more days, for a bit of peace and quiet. He'd been certain that good food and a spot of gambling would do the trick, but the dream that had started on the ship had followed him to his hotel room in Alexandria, and simply wouldn't go away.

He'd discovered over the years that his father also had the *gift*, and had studied the philosophy behind it all, in order to pass on his knowledge to Bentley, who in turn had bombarded his father with questions: questions his father very often just couldn't answer.

When he was seventeen, Bentley's mother died, and his father began to work with him, helping him to develop his clairvoyant and clairaudient skills.

"Do you think Mother will come to visit us?" Bentley had once asked.

"I very much doubt it," his father had replied, and indeed, she had not.

Bentley had then learned his own spiritual language through signs and symbols sent from the Spirit World. "Why do they use cryptic symbols?" he'd asked his father.

"Because the Spirit World doesn't communicate like we do. They don't need to speak. They think. That's why our own thoughts are so important. Thought is living energy, and it really can affect the balance of the laws of nature and physics."

And that was the problem. It only took one person with evil thoughts, evil intentions and evil actions to upset the balance of the world, and that person was Adolph Hitler.

Hitler thrived on hate.

His ethos created an effusion of blame and destruction: a very negative and combustible mixture. He blamed the Jews and he blamed the treaties of the last war, so much so, that his resentment rendered him merciless and greedy. He wanted what he didn't have, and he didn't care how he got it.

Bentley felt himself sink into a deep meditative state.

After a moment, the sound of machine guns crackled in his mind, piercing his skull with the intensity of flying shards of glass. He put his hands to his ears, as he felt himself being transported once again to another time...

German East Africa, 1914

Gunshots blasted, and the ground appeared to shake, as if Bentley had just walked into an earthquake.

"Lay down your arms, and come out of there with your hands up!" screamed a voice.

It was the German soldier from before. Bentley raised his head, and found himself staring at a pistol in the man's hand. It was pointed directly at him. The man wasn't old, but his gaunt face and prominent cheekbones made him look like a starving child.

Bentley felt his body stiffen. How strange. A German soldier, but the dream language was English. Slowly, Bentley lifted his arms, and moved forward, in compliance with the order. Unarmed and ill prepared, he found himself facing a row of bayonets. He flexed his wrists. He knew the man's name was Baron Heinrich von Kosch, but that didn't stop him wondering whether he was facing a unit of soldiers, or armed insurgents.

"What on earth!" exclaimed von Kosch, a wicked grin crossing his face. He lowered his pistol, and put it back into its holster. "Why didn't you say it was you?"

Bentley's eyes shot open. He was wide awake now, and back in his room at the San Stefano. After a moment, his lids started to become heavy. He fought to keep them open, but they finally closed. Almost at once he returned to the dream, only to find that time had moved on...

"We must hurry," cried von Kosch, as he led Bentley and the soldiers forward. They were jogging across open grassland. "We are beginning to lose light."

Bentley felt his pace quicken. Far ahead was a great wide river, its gentle flow hemmed in by miles and miles of sun-scorched grass. Bentley could see a group of wild elephants in the distance, some drinking, others walking slowly into the heat of the day, their ears flapping, and their trunks picking at tough vegetation. When they reached a group of small oval huts, made of tree branches and mud, Bentley realised that they'd arrived at the Maasai settlement.

Suddenly, a sense of foreboding struck him, and his mouth filled with a horrible taste. The entire village was engulfed in silence. Where were the women and children? His question was soon answered as he moved past the huts, and his eyes rested on what looked like a great pile of rubbish. He advanced, then stopped in his tracks, as a small dark hand caught his attention at the bottom of the pile. It was gripping the horn of an emaciated looking cow.

Now he understood.

The pile was comprised of stiff corpses and bright clothing, all covered in dried blood. Human corpses and dead cattle.

What did this mean?

It appeared that not only had the warriors been murdered, so too had the womenfolk and their offspring. The tribe and cattle had been shot like game, and the sight of such butchery warned Bentley that he should be very wary of his new-found friend.

A cry caused Bentley to turn.

A young woman was crouched between two small trees, devastation inscribed across her face. She wasn't dressed like the Maasai. She wore a long white European dress, and on her head was a pith helmet.

None of it made sense.

Her face was shadowed by the helmet, but still Bentley noticed the glow of her features, as perspiration shone on her ebony skin in the light of the bright sun. She was lovely, even as she glared, imperturbably, into the pugnacious face of Heinrich von Kosch, who turned abruptly towards her.

"What is your name?" he demanded.

The young woman swallowed hard, and raised her hand to a gold locket, hanging from a chain around her neck. Fixed to the locket was a diamond and an emerald, which sparkled in the sun. "My name?" she said in a low voice, its soft Welsh lilt, unexpected.

"Yes! Your name!" said von Kosch.

"My name is Marisol."

"Well, Marisol, get up. You are coming with us."

She was tall, and walked with grace, and when two soldiers stepped forward and grabbed her wrists, she raised her head, and walked with determination.

When, finally, they reached a wood of rubber trees, Bentley somehow knew they'd arrived at von Kosch's rubber plantation.

But why was it all so familiar?

Bentley had never been there, and yet nothing was strange. They reached a bungalow constructed of stucco. A thatched roof overhung the white walls. Bentley stopped at the bottom of steps, leading to a door. He turned, and glanced across a green lawn, set amongst trees, before turning back to the bungalow, where a rose garden opened up at the foot of its veranda. Bentley climbed the half dozen steps. As he made to enter the building, his head suddenly felt faint, and everything darkened.

Bentley woke up with a start and was disappointed to see he was back in his room at the San Stefano.

What the bloody hell was going on?

Surely the dream wasn't finished?

Welcome to Tanganyika. German territory, said a voice in his head.

Bentley knew it was von Kosch. He shut his eyes tight, and prayed for more information...

"What happened?" demanded Bentley. He was lying in a bed in what seemed to be a familiar room. Von Kosch was standing next to him, smoking a cigarette.

"You passed out from exhaustion," said von Kosch, placing his cigarette into Bentley's mouth.

Bentley inhaled deeply, and let his eyes stray across the room. Dark shutters concealed the outside light, and an oil lamp provided the only illumination.

He removed the cigarette from his lips, and exhaled smoke, before turning his attention to the surrounding walls.

His eyes continued to scan the room, and stopped at a large astrological chart, drawn on an enormous piece of parchment paper. At the top, was an

Egyptian eye. It was the eye of Horus. The chart engulfed the entire part of the wall. It was time to ask questions.

"Why did you kill them?"

At first, von Kosch said nothing. He wandered over to the window and sat on a chair. "I take it you refer to the Maasai?" Bentley's silence confirmed this. Von Kosch narrowed his eyes. "Never doubt the power of the astrological charts," he said.

"The charts?" repeated Bentley. "The charts told you to kill?"

"Unfortunately, in times of war, certain actions become necessary."

"I see."

"Don't let yourself be fooled. These people were scouts for the British. They were spying on my men."

"Your charts told you this?"

Von Kosch got to his feet. "You are tired from your ordeal," he said. "Tiredness can make a man say foolish things. I will excuse you on this occasion."

Bentley remained silent. He was tired, but what was more important was that although it seemed he had trusted this man at one time, he didn't trust him now: and he certainly didn't wish to exacerbate the situation any further. He wondered what hidden force governed this person, allowing him to enforce his own special law. Best to agree with him, for the moment anyway.

"You're right," he said.

"I am always right," said von Kosch.

Bentley very much doubted this, but knew he must bide his time. He still needed information. "What about the woman?" he asked. As he spoke, a wave of emotion engulfed him. Strange, but interesting, and something he had not anticipated.

"She is a nurse. Welsh mother, and father from the Dominican Republic. Both deceased." Von Kosch paused. "She does not conform to my idea of a woman, but she works hard, and if kept in hand, may prove invaluable to us."

Bentley wanted to ask more, but the dream was fading. His head had begun to whirl, and a familiar whoosh passed through his physical brain, the sign he was returning. When he opened his eyes, he was back in his room at the San Stefano.

17

Shepheard's Hotel, Cairo

Bette

O'Malley had told me the villa didn't have a telephone, and since I knew Bentley would be travelling from Alexandria to Shepheard's Hotel, I decided to take an impromptu trip into the city, and pay him a visit.

As an excuse, I told Farida that I wanted to get some photo shots of Shepheard's Hotel. When she said she'd like to see Stephen, it was suggested we travel together.

We commandeered a couple of donkeys, and when she dropped me off at Shepheard's, she made her way to Garden City, taking both donkeys with her: riding one and leading the other. I wondered for a moment where she would take them. Maybe Garden City had a donkey parking lot? Now that would be something useful to know.

I made my way to reception, only to be told that Bentley hadn't even arrived.

Still, not one to brood, I decided to make the best of things. Stephen had felt sorry for me and given me a wad of dough. In view of my assignment – to investigate him – that had only made me feel worse than ever, so to cheer myself up, I'd decided to sit for a while on the veranda at Shepheard's, and partake of a gin or two. Not only could I rest my feet, I could dull my guilt, and watch the comings and goings of everyone.

When I finished my first double, I ordered another, then another. Mistake. Halfway through, I conked out.

Bentley

Bentley made for the steps leading up to Shepheard's Hotel. The first thing to greet him was the slumped form of the American. She was asleep at one of the tables, head back, and mouth wide open. There were three glasses next to her. Two were empty, the other half-full, which suggested she just might be drunk.

He was about to wake her up, when he changed his mind. She was bad enough sober, so what the hell was she like drunk? No. That was something he couldn't cope with.

He went to the desk and registered.

"Ah," said the clerk. "A young American woman was looking for you."

"Cheers," said Bentley. He paused. "She's out there sleeping." He nodded his head in the direction of the veranda. "Do us a favour, mate, keep an eye on her. Can't wake her up."

The clerk smiled. "Room 490," he said, handing Bentley a key. "Fourth floor."

Bentley took the stairs to his room. He unlocked the door and went in. The room seemed comfortable enough, but his mind was too fixed on other things to consider this further.

It was strange the way things were evolving, and there was one thing in particular. The vision of the drunk American had reminded him of this. Normally he didn't drink to excess for that interfered with his concentration, but of late, he'd found himself becoming increasingly fond of the taste and effects of alcohol.

He made his way over to a set of French doors, and stepping out on to a balcony, looked across at the Muqattam Hills and the great stretch of eastern desert, beyond. He then cast his eyes downwards towards the noise directly below, where hotel guests were drinking. He wondered if the American was still there, or if she'd even woken up.

There was a knock on the door.

Bentley made his way over to it, and opening it, came face to face with Joe Bannerman, who was carrying a crate of beer.

Bentley smiled. "See you've brought a few coldies, mate. A spot of the good old amber fluid. Glad you've got your priorities right."

"It's good for my rheumatism!" said Joe, stepping into the room.

Bentley helped himself to a bottle, and opened it

with his teeth. "So, what's happening?" he said, taking a swig.

"Apart from the fact you've left your partner in crime snoring on the veranda?"

So, she *was* still there. "And do *you* like drunk women?"

"Take your point," said Joe, laying the crate on the floor. "Anyway. Don't worry. I've booked her a room here for the night. It'll be dark soon. I've also taken her money. Lots of it, I might add," he said, producing a wad of notes. "Can't have her getting mugged."

Bentley whistled. "She'll go off like a frog in a sock when she wakes up!"

"No, she won't," said Joe, helping himself to a beer. "She'll be more embarrassed. Anyway, I've left a note telling her where to find us and the money."

Bentley made a face. "Well, you can let her in when she comes to the door."

"No problem." Joe sat down. "So, are you fit?"

"Fit for what?"

"Fit for work." Joe delved into his top pocket. "Do you happen to have a pen?"

"Should do," said Bentley. He found one in his shirt pocket. "Thinking of writing a journal?"

"They say that the pen is mightier than the sword."

Bentley handed the pen to his boss. "I take it there have been developments?"

"There have indeed."

Bentley smiled. "Good. Are you getting any of the other agencies involved?"

"Not at this stage. At the moment, it's still *our*

investigation. Our agent is in the process of putting together a report. It's a tricky subject."

"Paranormal activities usually are," agreed Bentley.

"We'll have to wait until she hands in the official report."

Bentley's heart began to race, and he felt the blood drain from his face. "She?" he repeated. "Surely not my new partner?"

Joe began to laugh. "No, not Bette. Someone else."

"Strewth! That made the old ticker go!"

"Never mind that. We've got work to do. Ready to start?"

Bentley paused, but for once, he felt he really couldn't be bothered. "Put the pen away, Joe," he said. "I'm not in the mood for dreaming just now. Let's just relax, and have a drink."

"If you say so. But you'd better go and wake your partner in crime, and tell her to join us."

"Not on your bloody nelly!"

18

The Villa, Muqattam Hills

Bette

I got back to the villa the following day, sore head, dry mouth and totally humiliated. I'd woken up the previous evening to find myself on the veranda at Shepheard's Hotel, a note from Joe pinned to my shirt, informing me that he and Bentley were in room 490 with a crate of beer, and would I care to join them, and continue the party I'd clearly already started? Then there was the PTO: *You're booked into room 491, and don't worry about your money, we have it.*

I'd climbed the stairs, two at a time, to reclaim my funds. I'd then knocked on the door, which had been opened by Joe, who was holding my money and a key to room 491. I'd grabbed the money and key, and stomped off to my room.

The next morning, I'd signed out without telling

them, and gone straight to Stephen's apartment, but there was no one in. I'd then gone round the back. Stables with two donkeys. "Whadda, ya know!" I'd muttered, as I'd grabbed the nearest one, and set off.

So, here I was, back at the villa, sore ass, tired, fed up and none the wiser. When I discovered that everyone was out, I felt abandoned. Then I reviewed the situation. No better opportunity to dig around for clues. First, I made for the dining room, in the hope that some kind person had left me something to eat. They hadn't, so I decided to go upstairs.

I'd just started making my way up a narrow back staircase, when quite unexpectedly, I was pushed against the wall by a flying body, as it tumbled forward, like a whale breaching the waves. Flabby limbs bounced against the stairs, like an inflatable beach ball, until the person finally landed at the foot of the staircase. It was a woman, who appeared to be somewhere in her mid-fifties. When she groaned, and started to move, I approached her.

"You, OK?" I asked, kneeling down at her side.

She was clearly agitated, and paid no attention to me. She tried to sit up. Now, I knew there were easier ways to go down the stairs, so my assumption was she'd either fallen, or been shoved.

I started to help her up, and observed a large gash above her right eye, and a graze down her cheek. "Are you hurt?"

She turned her head, and noticed me properly for the first time. She began to stare at me. Weird. It was as if she'd just seen a ghost. "No," she said, after a moment, affecting a smile.

"It looks serious," I said. And it did. What was more, her face was becoming whiter by the second.

"I just fell," she said. She had a Scottish accent, and although her words were soft and polite, her tone was adamant.

"At least let me help you up the stairs." I was concerned, but my attempts to help were clearly unwelcome.

She looked up at me, and appeared to grow increasingly confused, until she finally acquiesced. "Give me a hand, then."

I hoisted her up, and slinging her right arm across my shoulders, I attempted to haul her back up the stairs.

She looked at me, and smiled serenely. "No, hen," she said. "I'll break your back." She balanced herself, and allowed me to lead her up the stairs. "But it was very thoughtful of you," she added, looking deeply into my face.

My guess, that I'd just met Omar O'Malley's cook, was confirmed when we reached the door leading to the rooms she shared with Mr Campbell. When we entered the living room, Mr Campbell was asleep on a patterned couch, snoring very loudly. I led Mrs Campbell to a chair, and helping her to sit down, glanced around.

The room was packed with everything and anything. Dark furniture filled every space. Nests of tables decorated the corners. Ornaments found their way on to every surface, and pictures and photographs covered every inch of the walls. My eyes continued to scan the room, and stopped at a photograph. It showed a picture of a couple. I assumed it was the Campbells in their younger days. Mrs Campbell wore a long gown. On her head was a large hat with a feather, which seemed to have been plucked from a cockatoo. She was blowing a kiss at the photographer, whoever that was. Mr Campbell looked awkward, his nose in the air, as if the feather on the hat had just tickled his nostrils.

A snort drew my eyes back to the couch. Mr Campbell was still fast asleep. His mouth was gaping. Another snort emanated from his throat, fit to blast a hole in the wall. All I could see were his tonsils. I really didn't like the guy. If I'd had a gun, I'd have cocked the trigger and fired.

I turned to the other pictures on the wall, and as I did so, another photograph caught my attention. I stared at it as I tried to make sense of it. What was *that* doing there? I'd seen a similar one tucked away in a drawer back home. It was a picture of Jim as a young man.

But that wasn't all.

As I left the room, I noticed a telephone in a corner. Now, there was nothing surprising about a telephone, but in a household that purported to have no telephone, that was bizarre.

The next day, Mrs Campbell was still under the weather, so I felt it was time to offer my philanthropic services, even if it did mean another sore ass. I ventured out alone, with the same tired old donkey, to do the shopping. I made my way down the hillside to the nearest market, conscious that by the time all this was over, I'd probably have recurring haemorrhoids.

The market was very active, and just as smelly as my transport. I fought off the usual attentions of the local kids, and when I saw a young boy trying to sell matches and beads to Europeans, I turned in the opposite direction, only to find myself in amongst the snake charmers. I did another about-turn, this time narrowly avoiding an angry-looking baboon.

I rode on into the thick of it. Market traders bickered and haggled, but seemed to keep everything under control. Deformed beggars held out their bony hands, whilst donkeys brayed and halal butchers slaughtered goats. I passed a flock of roosters, ranging freely about the market. They were strutting their stuff, their cock-a-doodle-doos shrilly slicing the air with the force of a rocket. It was at that point that a voice stopped me.

A man and a woman walked swiftly past, and as the man spoke, his voice loud, I realised he was a cockney Londoner. A hat covered his face. The woman, who seemed to be some kind of self-styled fashion guru, was dressed from head to toe in red. She wore a shawl over her head, but as she turned to the left, I caught a glimpse of her profile. I was certain I'd seen her before, but couldn't remember when, or, where. I wondered who they were. A cocker spaniel trotted at their side on a lead. I continued to stare as the pair melted into the crowd.

Two days later, matters took a turn for the worse. Omar O'Malley's land in the hills was so extensive, it required a jeep to get from A to B. It turned out that O'Malley *was* going to turn it into farmland, but the development of that was in its very early stages. Truth be told, I found that far more interesting than the film industry, but when I began to ask questions, O'Malley brushed them aside. He told me to get ready, for I'd just been granted the privilege of a grand tour round the property.

A toot of a horn soon identified my guide. It was a persistent tooting, and when I turned, I saw Mr Campbell in the driver's seat of the jeep. My heart fell into my stomach, and my right hand began to twitch.

Control, Bette, control. The twitching stopped.

"Come on!" shouted Campbell, his voice rasping from his throat. "Get in!"

The jeep was a right-hand drive. I stepped forward, disappointed that there were only two seats, and eased myself into the passenger side. Campbell turned the key in the ignition, but nothing happened.

I smiled and began to get out. "If it's too much trouble," I said, my foot hitting the ground. I got no further.

Campbell turned the key again, and coaxing the engine with a stream of profanities, he managed to get it started. He engaged the clutch, and the exhaust blasted. I sincerely hoped the brakes were working.

"So, how's things?" he muttered, as the jeep chugged forward.

"Things?" I repeated. He'd caught me off guard.

"Your article," he clarified.

"Fine," I lied.

My right hand started to twitch again, so I shifted position, and sat on it. We continued to drive in silence, until the road turned into a dust track. I felt the onset of panic, but calmed down again when the villa came back into sight.

"Let's have a wee break," said Campbell, as he brought the jeep to a halt. He switched off the engine, and leaned back. Then raising his left arm, he placed his hand across the back of my seat. I moved away. "Don't see a wedding ring," he said.

I didn't reply. The bastard was making fun of me. I stared at the windscreen, my mind racing. I was *not* in a good place: either the freak suspected me, or he fancied me. Well, he could keep his designs to himself, and think again, for not only was he a creep, he had the added affliction of poor oral hygiene.

He licked his lips. "Want to stop here?"

I didn't reply, just stared ahead.

Campbell laughed. "I quite like redheads, you know," he whispered through his gums.

"Really?"

"Feisty and interesting!"

"Sure." My right hand, which was still under my ass, was twitching again, and threatened to push me off the seat. *Control, Bette, control.* The twitching stopped.

"I'm still a virile man, you know."

"Virile?" I repeated, my tone disdainful. I turned to look at him.

"I love a cruel woman!" he gasped. "Go on. Talk dirty to me!"

I looked him in the eye. "Mud, dirt and bog!" I said tartly. As I spoke, my attention was drawn to the villa, where at a window, on the upper storey, I saw a figure. It was Mrs Campbell. So, he thought he'd make his wife jealous? For a moment I felt sorry for her, then I thought: *no way*! She could probably read him like a book, and in any case, if he was out annoying other women, at least that meant he wasn't chucking her down staircases.

It was time to give the broad something to smile at.

"Hey, Fuck Face! Guess what? I've an affliction. A twitch." I lifted my right hand from under my butt and held both hands out in front of me. "Wanna see the fuckers *really* work?" I yelled, as with an all-out effort, I punched him in the groin.

Campbell groaned. I felt no remorse, and examined my knuckles. They hurt like hell, but at least they were under control.

Make the most of it, Bette!

I drew back my hand and punched him in the eye. The onslaught was magnificent. Another groan. It was time to go. I clambered out my seat, left the jeep and ran.

The next day Stephen invited me down to the film studios to meet the cast and the production team in his latest film.

"So, what's the scoop? How are you getting on?" he asked, as we went in.

"I'm having a ball!" I lied.

"Just wondered how the article was progressing,

since I haven't actually seen you interview anyone."

Now that was something I hadn't anticipated. Stephen was watching me. "Yeah, just finding my feet!" I hastily replied.

"Well, come and have a look." The actors were showing off their artistic brilliance in front of cameras that were perched on top of dollies. Their operators bounced around, taking film and replacing spools. "It's the opening sequence," whispered Stephen. "I'm not in this bit."

"Scene one, take six!" shouted a voice behind me.

The sound of a clapperboard reverberated in the air, and made me jump to attention. I jerked my neck. "Fucking dodo!" I yelled. The pain was like a bullet through the heart.

Stephen smiled. "Not quite under control yet?" he said.

"Fuck no! Anyway, is the film in English?" I asked, trying to regain my composure.

"No," he said. "You'll have to rely on subtitles."

Great, I thought. "Do any of the actors actually speak English?"

"In a manner of speaking, but I'll make a list of their names for you."

"Thanks," I mumbled. I'd been hoping to avoid any actual interviews, but now realised that wasn't an option.

"Tell you what," continued Stephen, "when we're finished here for the day, we'll go and eat. How about Shepheard's?"

*

"What do you fancy?" asked Stephen, as the maître

d' led us to our table.

I picked up the wine menu. My eyes widened in anticipation, as I examined the huge selection. "What about champagne?" I suggested, deciding that now was not the time to succumb to a guilty conscience.

But Stephen wasn't making it easy. "If you like," he replied, ordering the most expensive bottle. It came in an ice bucket. We toasted one another, and then quite unexpectedly, Stephen raised his glass for another toast. "To Jim," he said. "To the father we had, but never really knew. May he rest in peace."

"To Jim," I said, raising my glass. I took a large gulp. The champagne was beautiful. "Do you think there's an afterlife?" I asked, putting my glass down.

"No idea," said Stephen, "but if there is, I can guarantee Jim's sitting here with us. He wouldn't miss the opportunity of a free bottle of booze."

"No, he would not."

"Anyway, I've got something for you."

"What?"

Stephen produced a parcel. "This."

"What is it?" I asked.

"Just a little welcome gift."

I opened the parcel. It was a camelhair coat. "It's beautiful," I exclaimed, the pangs of guilt returning.

"Not that you'll need it out here," he said, "but you'll need it in Scotland."

That was the truth. I felt myself flush and continued to feel uncomfortable. I wasn't used to gifts, and certainly not from people I was investigating.

"Are you ready to order?" said a voice.

I looked up. It was a waiter. So engrossed had I been in my gift and thoughts that I hadn't even looked at the food menu.

"Give us a couple of minutes," said Stephen.

I perused the menu and ordered spiced lentil soup and lamb kofta. Stephen chose the same. When we finished our meal, he went to settle the cheque, and I went ahead and made for the exit.

I skipped down the steps, giddy with champagne, and on to Kamal Pasha Street, where I stopped short, as a familiar figure appeared on the other side of the road. Captain Bentley Ford-Jenkins. I knew he'd seen me, because he turned abruptly, and walked in the opposite direction. Well, at least he was still in Cairo, which meant that in all probability, so was Joe.

I awoke abruptly the next morning. I'd spent the night in the villa, and was surprised to find the Doberman and mongrel lying at the bottom of my bed, fast asleep. They were supposed to be guard dogs, but had turned out to be a fundamental tactical error on the part of Omar O'Malley. I glanced at the clock. It was seven o'clock.

I got myself ready, and leaving the dogs sleeping, I made my way downstairs to the dining room for breakfast: only I never quite got there. As I passed the living room, I realised that something wasn't quite right. I'd only ever been in there a couple of times. It was an interesting room with Persian rugs and fancy furniture. I looked in, but the drapes were shut, so it was dark.

Strange, I thought.

Everyone was usually up at the crack of dawn. Well, nothing to do with me. I was about to continue on to the dining room, but was overcome by a sense of misgiving. Something still felt wrong. I turned back, and looked in again.

As I focused my eyes, I could see the outline of two large wooden bookcases, divided by a high marble fireplace, black in colour. The dark green walls looked grey in the sombre light. I ventured in, careful not to trip on the couch that was slightly askew of one of the bookcases. I felt my way round it, and as I did so, my right foot kicked something, and I stumbled. I regained my balance, and bent down. It felt like a shoe, but it certainly wasn't mine. I knew that because as I continued to examine it, I realised it was attached to someone's foot.

Just at that, a light went on. I turned and saw Mr Campbell. He'd switched on the red standard lamp in the corner. I turned my attention back to the floor, and stared in total disbelief. Lying in a crumpled heap was Omar O'Malley. He was dead. I tried to absorb the scene. My right hand twitched a couple of times, and then my head went dizzy. O'Malley's head had been whacked, his throat had been slashed and a knife protruded from his left side. I remembered Farida's comment about picking his brain: I'd no idea then, that that might mean picking it off the carpet.

As the truth sank in, I turned back to Campbell. His face was grim, but a brief sense of satisfaction comforted me, as I noticed his right eye, where he still sported a bruise from my attack in the jeep.

Satisfaction was soon replaced by another sense

of misgiving, as I realised there was every possibility Campbell was the killer. I opened my mouth to scream, but it was just then that Mrs Campbell appeared. She was the one who screamed, giving me ample time to leave the room, run up to the telephone, and call the cops.

19

Central Police Office, Glasgow

DI MacLeod

"Well, well, well!" muttered Detective Inspector MacLeod. "Would you credit it?" It was all happening now: two very interesting incidents.

The first had occurred that morning. Clara MacNab had got into a fight with a drunken male outside the Clelland Bar in the Gorbals. He'd managed to stab her, and now MacNab was lying on a mortuary slab at the police office. The male had been lifted, and was in one of the cells, pending his appearance at the custody court the following afternoon.

That was a straightforward murder.

MacNab had stolen drink from the accused the previous day, and had now suffered the consequences.

The second incident was not so cut and dried. In fact, if anything, the situation was getting worse.

MacLeod was clutching a telegram. An Egyptian

police officer had contacted him to say that Bette Milligan was staying at an address where a murder had been committed. It also stated that someone had been assaulted, but no complaint was being made.

Funny the way crime and death seemed to follow the girl.

First her father, who *fell* down the close stairs.

Fell? MacLeod wanted to laugh. Unfortunately, the inheritance theory would be hard to prove. Everyone knew about the clause in the trust. Furthermore, it had become common knowledge that the meagre way Jim Kipper had spent money, meant that any further spending would have made little difference to his savings, assuming, of course, that seven years hence, he'd be dead. Not an impossibility, given his history of alcohol abuse. MacLeod smiled. Jim Kipper was very aptly named, for he had, indeed, drunk like a fish.

But now he had the start of a case: a case that might well uncover actual evidence of wrong-doings.

The owner of a villa in Egypt, who happened to be a friend of Bette Milligan's brother, had just been murdered in his own home. MacLeod tapped the desk with the telegram. *Gets better,* he thought. Omar O'Malley was half-Egyptian and half-Irish, but it was the Irish bit that interested him.

"MacTaggart!" he called. "MacTaggart! My office!"

There was a knock on the door and Jessie came in. "Sir?"

"Sit down, MacTaggart, and listen." MacLeod

waited until Jessie was seated in front of his desk. "This, MacTaggart," he said, waving the telegram in the air, "explains it all."

"What does it say?" asked Jessie.

MacLeod thumped it down on the desk. "Read it!" He watched Jessie retrieve the piece of paper and absorb the contents. "Omar O'Malley is half-Irish," continued MacLeod, "and affiliated with one of the Irish-American gangs in New York, and murdered by another Irish-American gang, also New York. Here is a perfect example of mobsters falling out with mobsters. Vendettas! Call it what you will! Only in this case they used the services of one Bette Milligan, who happens to be affiliated with the disgruntled mob who had a score to settle!"

Jessie raised her eyes from the paper. "Are you sure?" she asked, a frown inscribed across her forehead.

"Of course, I'm sure! Milligan has just carried out the duties she was trained to do whilst a youngster in New York. And in this case, the particular mobsters she's associated with have an affiliation with the IRA, who in their turn, have been cavorting on and off with the Nazis since 1937!"

"But it doesn't say that, sir," said Jessie. "It just says that Omar O'Malley was found murdered, and that a resident from Scotland happens to be one of the witnesses. The Egyptian police are simply asking for information on her."

MacLeod got to his feet. "And I'll give them information! You mark my words! I'll give them information!" MacLeod's mind was in overdrive, his eyes almost popping out their sockets. Suddenly conscious that Jessie was still sitting in front of him, he barked, "Dismissed!"

Jessie complied.

MacLeod didn't care what anyone else thought.

As far as he was concerned, things were looking highly suspicious. The Procurator Fiscal had decided the incident with Milligan's father was an accident, but if Milligan did have Nazi connections, or mob connections, she could quite easily have given her father that fateful shove. The post mortem had revealed he'd drunk an abundance of alcohol. Easy target.

Then there was the fact Milligan probably knew the police weren't satisfied with the Fiscal's verdict, because she'd upped and left the country in a hurry, and landed back in Egypt, where not only had she murdered an elderly man, she'd assaulted another.

Once a criminal, always a criminal, and Bette Milligan certainly had more to her than met the eye. There had to be something wrong with her. He didn't buy Jessie's explanation that it was Tourette's. That was something made up by the medical profession. They were always making things up. Always found a medical reason for bad behaviour. As far as he was concerned, she was evil, and if anything, the swearing and twitching probably had something to do with her trying to invoke the power of the devil, which duly brought him back to Mrs Ellen Fairbairn.

He wondered if the woman ever held séances: the ones that supposedly produced stuff. If she did, he'd need to get MacTaggart to attend one of them. Good chance the woman was using a piece of cheesecloth to manufacture her own ghosts. If they could catch her with that, then they could prove she was a fraud.

He had to do something. The Chief Constable was looking for results.

MacLeod's mind was in a state of flux. This was something he didn't like. "Bloody woman!" he muttered, as his mind returned to Bette Milligan. Hanging would be too good for her. If she were in France, it would be the guillotine. Here he'd accept summary justice, followed by a good old-fashioned kick up the arse! But back to Ellen Fairbairn. If all else failed, there was, of course, the Witchcraft Act. "MacTaggart! Back in my office!"

Jessie

"Sir?"

"Sit down," said MacLeod.

This doesn't sound good, thought Jessie, seating herself back down in front of MacLeod's desk. She'd barely had time to breathe before this second summons.

"We still have the problem of Ellen Fairbairn."

This really didn't sound good. "The problem?" Jessie shifted position and smoothed down her skirt.

"Top-secret information. Operation MPRS."

Jessie was finding it hard to keep up with MacLeod's theories, which were spinning back and forth like a disorientated yoyo.

"What's going on, sir?"

"Ever heard of the Witchcraft Act?"

"Witchcraft Act?" repeated Jessie, leaning forward. "Did you say, *Witchcraft Act*?"

"Indeed, I did! The Witchcraft Act of 1735."

Jessie sat back. "1935?"

"No, *1735*," affirmed MacLeod, slamming his fist down on to the desk. A pencil that had been balancing on a pile of paperwork began to roll towards Jessie. She held out her hand and caught it.

"We're talking about the eighteenth century?"

"Indeed, we are."

"Isn't that when they burned witches?"

"I believe they did."

Jessie's eyes widened. "Surely you don't want to *burn* Mrs Fairbairn, sir."

"Not exactly. Anyway, the maximum penalty isn't burning, it's one year's imprisonment, which is ideal. We only want to put her away temporarily."

Jessie was finding it difficult to take her boss seriously.

"You mean, put her away for a spell?" she suggested, a wry smile across her face.

MacLeod didn't appear to hear her. His concentration seemed fixed on what he had to say next.

"The Chief Constable is *very* worried, and so is his contact in MPRS."

"What exactly *is* this MPRS?"

"Military Psychical Research Section. It's all to do with national security."

Jessie smiled. "So, the Chief Constable is liaising with a department that investigates ghosts?"

MacLeod's face flushed. "Don't be impertinent,

MacTaggart."

"Sorry, sir, I didn't mean to be rude."

"Never mind what you did and didn't mean, MacTaggart! It's what the Chief Constable means that's important. And what he means is that in order to prevent Ellen Fairbairn from spying for the Nazis, we have to find a way to get her off the streets."

"But sir, why are you so certain?"

MacLeod sat back in his chair. "Do you *know* what's going on in Germany?"

I'll treat that as a rhetorical question, thought Jessie. She remained silent.

MacLeod, however, was in full flow.

"Hitler is advancing through Europe, and *we* must do all we can to stop him landing in Britain."

Jessie felt her hand go to her throat. "So, what you're saying is, you want me to do something to incriminate Mrs Fairbairn, so she'll be locked up for a year. That way she can't pass on secrets to Nazi spies?"

"In a nutshell: yes!"

Jessie narrowed her eyes. "But what if she's *not* passing on secrets? What if she's really receiving information from the Spirit World?"

"Spirit World? Don't tell me you've fallen into her trap?"

Jessie paused. She knew now wasn't a good time to discuss whether or not there was such a world out there, but she still had to reason with him.

"Just supposing, sir."

"Sorry, MacTaggart. Can't indulge in fantasy. This is far too important. And as far as I'm concerned, either she's conjuring up spirits, or, she's pretending. Either way, she's getting done!"

20

The Villa, Muqattam Hills

Bette

The Egyptian police had been and gone, and it was established that the rich and prominent tycoon, Omar O'Malley, was well and truly defunct. Things weren't looking good. It seemed that the scope of my investigation was steadily expanding. On top of that, there was something else that had occurred to me. No one seemed to know where Farida was.

I went into the kitchen and made myself a cup of coffee. I was getting annoyed again. Where the hell was Bentley? Once again, he was incommunicado. I didn't even know if he knew that O'Malley was dead. Then, quite out the blue, my question was answered.

"One of your colleagues from *Amber St Claire*," announced Mrs Campbell, later that day, and in came Bentley.

"Well," he said, "another one bites the dust."

I stared at him. "What's going on? And where have you been?"

"Rumours are abounding," he said.

"Rumours?"

"The locals. They believe that once upon a time, Omar O'Malley found a tomb, and now he's just played into the hands of the vengeful pharaohs."

"That's convenient," I said, "especially for the killer."

"You might be right there," he agreed.

But something didn't sit right. I began to think of my conversation with Farida. According to her, Omar O'Malley *had* been involved in archaeological digs. Then there was Jim's reference to the Dead Army, so, I supposed I couldn't totally discount the involvement of a couple of irate pharaohs, no matter how illogical that sounded.

I swallowed hard. "I heard O'Malley got involved in archaeological digs in Iran. Not sure about Egypt."

"Interesting."

"So, what do we do now? Now our chief suspect is dead?"

"He might be dead, but there's a lot going on we don't know about, *and* there are two individuals, in particular, out there far more deadly: Adolph Hitler and his henchman, Heinrich Himmler.

"So, how's it all connected?"

"Let's just say, there's a lot to examine." He paused. "And remember one thing: if you don't fit into the Nazi criteria for a Master Race, well, that's you basically buggered."

He was right. Some of the more intrepid magazine

reporters had come back from Nazi Germany with frightening information. Stuff that people wouldn't believe. But stuff that meant if you happened to have red hair and an affliction, you were basically on Hitler's hit list: and there was no way my hair was going blond, whatever the emergency.

"Look at Hitler," continued Bentley. "He hates the Jews and he hates the communists. Spied his way up the ladder, until he finally brought down the Weimar Republic. And still, he's not happy. Austria's gone. Czechoslovakia's gone, and if we're not careful, his next step could well be Suez."

This was worrying. All the more so, because I'd just remembered that O'Malley had intimated the same thing.

"So, you really think the Nazis could push the British out?" I asked.

"If they want to."

"Giving power to the Nazis? Is that what the Egyptians want?"

"They certainly don't like the British."

"But the Nazis?"

Bentley shrugged. "Who knows?"

"And what about Farouk? You can't just displace a king."

"Can't you? When you've been pushed to the edge and left with nothing, I think you have the potential to do anything at all."

"Are you talking about the Egyptians, or the German people?"

"Come to think of it, probably, both. The treaties at the end of the last war weren't particularly helpful for Germany in the long run."

"But surely the German people can see it's all wrong?"

"Can they? They've lived in an angry country for a long time now, and suddenly a political mouthpiece pops up and tells them he'll save them. What would you do in their shoes?"

Keep a very low profile!

"Hitler has an education programme in progress, and it's geared towards the youth. They're being indoctrinated from school-age. He calls it political education."

"You mean, brainwashing?"

"And it's all been going on right under our noses."

"Can't anyone read between the lines?"

"What's there to read? It's blatant, but they're hooked. Hitler is like a drug. He mesmerises them. They hang on to his every word, and he's promised them national salvation."

"So, he's turning them all into robots?"

"He's creating young men who can easily be turned into soldiers. He's creating an army right under our noses. He wants what isn't his. He believes that if he doesn't fight, Germany is doomed to extinction. He wants war."

"But why does he want to steal other people's land?"

"It's for his Master Race. The Aryans. He needs to find new territories for its expansion."

"And the Dead Army?" I ventured slowly. "Where does *it* fit into all this?"

Bentley seemed surprised. "You know about it?"

"Well, yeah!" I lied.

"So, you'll get no surprises at the memorial service then?"

"Memorial service?"

"You've no idea what the Dead Army is, have you?" laughed Bentley. "Well, there's going to be a memorial service for Omar O'Malley, the day after tomorrow, here at the villa. You'll find out what the Dead Army is then, and I think it should prove very interesting."

21

The Villa, Muqattam Hills

Bette

The day of the service arrived, and I still didn't know what the Dead Army was. Not only that, Farida hadn't appeared, and I couldn't get hold of Stephen.

Mrs Campbell spent the best part of the morning in the kitchen, clucking like a hen, as she prepared a buffet. The table and chairs had been temporarily removed from the dining room, and replaced with benches set in rows. Something that looked like a shrine had been erected at the front, and the room now resembled the interior of a very spooky church.

There were two doors leading into the dining room. Bentley and I entered by the back. I followed him tentatively to the rear row, and sat stiffly, my feet planted firmly on the ground. When the rest of the congregation arrived through the other door, I noticed there were no women, only men, who assembled with the rigidity of constipated warriors.

The room was filled to capacity with a really strange bunch, all Nazis, of course, wearing military uniform, decorated with brass swastikas. Even Campbell was in uniform, attempting to keep up with his version of a goose-step and Nazi salute.

So much for the dig in Iran! I thought.

My mind went back to Farida. Then it went to Stephen. I was disappointed. Hell! I was mad! It was starting to become clear that the two of them had to be together. Not only that. They had to know exactly what was going on, and rather than get caught by whoever had murdered Omar O'Malley, had escaped. In fact, they were probably half way to Berlin by now.

Damn it!

"Concentrate!" whispered Bentley. "Watch what's going on."

He nodded his head towards the front of the room where one of the Nazis had started to address the congregation. He spoke in German. I had no idea what he was saying, but he had a loud, penetrating voice. I glanced at Bentley, but he wouldn't look my way. The speaker continued to shout, his tone prolonging the agony of tedium.

"Members of the Thule Group," Bentley finally whispered. "They're part of Hitler's National Socialist German Worker's Party: the occult side. Although by the looks of things there's a few members of the Vril Society scattered amongst them."

"Frill Society?"

"Vril! VRIL," he spelled.

"What?' I hissed.

"Keep your voice down! Tell you what, let's get out of here. Follow me." He patted my arm, and we slunk out of the room. "It was the Vril Society that started it," he said when we were out of earshot. "They're fixated with electricity. How it works and all that."

"Electricity?"

"These guys are trying to create energies using electricity to create a link between them and the afterlife," continued Bentley.

"Really?" I doubted the link, but could well believe electricity was involved. The way these guys were walking, they looked as if they'd been struck by lightning.

"They're very dangerous people, Bette. They think Hitler's been given special spiritual enlightenment, and who's he to dispute it?"

"Who, indeed?" I replied, cynically.

"Hitler's got people reading crystal balls, and dowsing all over Germany. He's even got a castle in the hills, Wewelsburg, which Himmler uses to practise what he calls magic and witchcraft. But it gets worse."

"How worse?"

"The *Lebensborn Programme*. He's introduced baby farms all over Europe to produce Aryan-type babies. They're being primed to become a future worldwide Nazi army. A living national army, that is."

"Fuck's sake!"

"But it doesn't end there. Hitler isn't satisfied with a worldwide living army, he's wanting to create another army: a formidable army of Nazi spirits."

"So *that's* the Dead Army!" I gasped, as things began to fall into place.

"You better believe it! He wants to create a link between his living army here, and an army on the other side. He thinks if he does that, he'll conquer the universe, and rule forever."

"So, how's he going to find this Dead Army?"

"He's already started. The Nazis have been purloining Aryan-type children for a long time now, taking them from other countries to train them up to be good soldiers."

"For his national army?"

"For both his armies. Human resources are always limited, even with baby farms, so Hitler thinks he'll increase the strength of existing manpower, by killing a percentage of them."

"Well, that doesn't make a lot of sense."

"He thinks he can find ways to control them once they're dead. Turn them into an army. A bit like the Hitler Youth, only far more powerful."

"Holy fuck!"

"And he's instructed that bastard Himmler to devise ways to connect with these children once they return to the afterlife."

"What ages are these kids?"

Bentley shrugged. "Anything from baby to toddler."

"He's killing babies?"

"You got it in one."

This really didn't make sense.

"What's he going to arm them with? Pacifiers?"

"He thinks he'll be able to start them young."

"When they're dead?"

"He believes their consciousness will be amenable to Nazi manipulation when they're on the other side."

"Spooky baby farms," I said, beginning to understand. "Mould them into the Nazi way of thinking."

"Yeah."

I shivered again as I remembered something else O'Malley had said: *You do know that a country's most valuable resource is its children?*

"It *is* all garbage, though, isn't it?" I stuttered.

"I don't know," replied Bentley, after a moment's thought. "Doesn't stop them trying, though. Himmler's a maniac who believes in magic. He's obsessed with manipulating energy."

"So, what you're saying is, supposing there is an afterlife, and Hitler and Himmler obviously believe there is, then they're going to try and do the same with the dead kids, as they're doing now with the living ones?"

"Yup. And a word of advice: don't discount the afterlife."

I pursed my lips, unable to share Bentley's conviction. "Really?" I mumbled.

"The Nazis are trying to develop ways to control the minds of the living and the dead. The Occult Bureau in Wewelsburg is being used for this. Unfortunately, there's another one here in Cairo. Only, we don't know where."

"So, how can electricity create contact between us here, and them over there? That is, if there *is* anyone over there?"

"How does a telephone work?"

"They're not going to try and phone them?"

"Who knows? Telepathy? Radio waves? All I can tell you is that magic and irrational ideas are all part of the Nazi way of thinking: and that's where *we* come in.

"We?"

"MPRS."

Now we were talking! Bentley had finally got down to brass tacks. "So, what exactly *is* MPRS?"

"We're part of army intelligence."

"And where do *you* fit in?"

"I coordinate the medical side of things." He paused. "Amongst other things, that is."

"A quack?"

Bentley frowned. "I could have put it better."

"So, if I cut myself, you'd know how to stick a plaster on?"

"I'd hope you'd know how to do that, yourself," he grinned.

"And what about the *other things*?"

"That," he said, his face now serious, "is slightly more complicated."

I shook my head. What the hell was going on? Why was a medical doctor involved with an organisation that appeared to be investigating an army of dead kids? "At least tell me what MPRS stands for. No! wait! I'll tell you! Medical Psychotics and the Really Stupid!"

Bentley rubbed his chin.

"Yeah, well. You could be right. I'm actually

psychic, although others might call me psychotic; and as for you, you're *definitely* stupid! So, there you go, we make a great team."

"Very funny! What *does* MPRS stand for?" I repeated.

"Military Psychical Research Section. We're here to investigate the paranormal, and that includes any kind of threat to national security."

So, Joe really was investigating ghosts. I opened my mouth to probe further, but Bentley pushed me back towards the dining room.

"We need to get back in there, before any of those bastards miss us."

We returned just as the congregation was being marched through the other door, into another room, where Mrs Campbell had laid out the buffet. The minutes were ticking away, and as beer fuelled the men, they became noisier. I looked around and wasn't surprised to find that Bentley had disappeared.

Since I had no idea what anyone was saying, I decided it was time for a gin and tonic. I poured my drink, and picking out a canapé, bit into it. Its contents oozed out its sides.

"Now, let's not get a reputation for being greedy," said a voice in my ear. It was Bentley.

"Where have you been?"

"Searching the villa," he said. "Couldn't have found a better opportunity. Everyone's drunk. Campbell's pie-eyed, and even Mrs Campbell's half way through a bottle of whisky."

"Did you find anything?"

"I'm not happy with one of the rooms upstairs," he replied. "It's very small, appears innocuous, but my senses tell me that something is going on in there." He paused for a moment, and looked across at the drunken guests. "Come on," he whispered. "I'll show you, and don't knock over the statue. It's rather large."

He was right about the statue. It sat next to the door, and looked like an Egyptian god. I couldn't decide if it was from an excavation, or from one of the local markets.

The room was small. In fact, it was more like a box room, and was furnished with a brown wooden table, two matching chairs and a rug.

"Well, what do you think they use this room for?" I asked.

"No idea," replied Bentley. "I just sense that it's not good."

I sat down on one of the chairs, and Bentley sat on the other. I looked across at him, and placed my hands steadily on the table. "So, if you're psychic, what do you know about ghosts and things?"

"The correct term is medium, but to answer your question, quite a lot."

I shivered. The very idea that one or two nosey ghosts might be watching us, made my right hand twitch. I started to fidget. "And is that why Joe uses you? I mean, can you read minds and the future and all that?"

"Something like that," he replied.

"Fuck it! If you can read minds, then why don't you know what those Nazi dodos downstairs are thinking about?"

"I'm good, but not that good."

"Whadda, ya mean?"

"These guys have been trained to close their consciousness, so the enemy can't get in."

This was getting weirder by the minute. "They think of everything, don't they?"

"They do that."

I was about to ask another question, but my fidgeting hands had just hit a knob on the side of the table, and for the first time, I noticed a drawer. I opened it and felt inside. It appeared to be empty, until my hand hit a book. I pulled it out. It was a copy of *Baedeker's Guidebook*. I examined the red cover, then flicked through the pages. As I did so, a piece of paper fell out.

"Egyptian parchment paper," whispered Bentley.

I caught it before it landed on the floor. At the top was a small design. I studied it closely. "An Egyptian eye? What does that mean?"

"The Eye of Horus," replied Bentley, the tone of his voice rising as he spoke. It didn't take a genius to see he was excited. "It's for protection."

He stretched his hand out towards me, but I didn't bite. The parchment paper remained firmly in my grip: my controlled right-handed grip, I might add.

"Protection?" I repeated. "What the fuck do *they* need protection from?"

Bentley lowered his hand and shrugged. It was obvious he was feigning disinterest. "They might be evil, but that doesn't stop them being superstitious."

By then I'd stopped listening. I couldn't forget

Bentley's first reaction. As bored as he might seem now, I knew he wasn't. The parchment paper meant something to him. I tucked it into my shirt pocket, but not before I'd noticed part of a map, surrounded by lines of numbers and letters. So, what was this? They looked like geographical coordinates. And maybe, just maybe, they had something to do with the location of Hitler's Occult Bureau out here in Cairo.

22

Shepheard's Hotel, Cairo

Bentley

Bentley was back in his room at Shepheard's with one humdinger of a headache. The American had just backed him into a corner. He'd nearly fallen off his seat when she'd produced the Egyptian parchment paper with the Eye of Horus. It had reminded him of the astrological chart on the wall in the dream.

But it wasn't just that.

Joe had briefed him, the week before, about the Occult Bureau in Cairo, and had told him that a piece of parchment paper, giving the coordinates, was missing, and that was why MPRS didn't know the location.

Bentley had thought that getting the paper off Bette would be easy enough, but he hadn't anticipated her next move. When she'd stuffed the paper into her pocket, he'd almost grappled with her, but that wouldn't have been a sensible thing to do. So, he'd been forced to reach a compromise: they would visit the locus together.

But before that, he had other things to do. He tried to concentrate, but the incessant noise outside the French doors made contemplation virtually impossible. He got up and closed them to afford himself peace and quiet. He then lay back on the bed, until he was finally overcome by a feeling of Africa...

German East Africa, 1914

Bentley was on the veranda, under the eaves of the bungalow, which looked out on to the garden full of rose bushes. Behind the roses, was a copse, comprising green foliage and plants.

Bentley turned his head. Baron Heinrich von Kosch was seated at a table, amidst sheets of Egyptian parchment paper. Now, that in itself was of great interest, so when he observed that the top sheet contained a chart with the signs of the zodiac, his attention was captured.

Bentley watched von Kosch flick through the papers. Some showed maps, some had designs of buildings, whilst others had images of guns and cannons. But always at the top was a picture of an Egyptian eye: the Eye of Horus.

Bentley opened his mouth to speak, but stopped himself. The young woman from his earlier dream had just appeared, and was now pouring coffee into a cup on the table. He remembered her name. Marisol. She turned to Bentley for a moment, her discerning eyes fixed on him, before retreating to a seat in the corner.

Von Kosch looked up. "We have a problem," he said. "There's going to be an attack on our port at Tanga."

Bentley scratched his chin, and for the first time, realised he had a beard. That in itself was confusing, but not as perplexing as the information that was slowly infiltrating his mind: the British, it seemed, were preparing to capture German East Africa.

"And the British Army is in the process of rallying Indian divisions from Bombay to fortify their defences in British East Africa," added von Kosch.

Information continued to enter Bentley's mind, and he was made aware that the Indian divisions were from the Bangalore Brigade, which had very little experience in fighting matters. "But the Indian divisions have no experience at all," said Bentley.

"Spot on, Jim!" cried von Kosch.

Bentley hesitated. Jim? At last! Now he knew his name here. Suddenly the word 'Moshi' came into his head. "What's happening at Moshi?" he asked, conscious that this was also part of German East Africa.

"We're pretty heavily fortified there, and if more men are needed in Tanga to fight off the British, there's the Moshi to Tanga rail link."

"Only, it's very slow."

Von Kosch leaned forward, and laughed with confidence. "But remember," he said, "the Bangalore Brigade have to find their way here using useless British maps!"

Bentley's eyes flickered open. He wanted to return to the dream, but the link was slowly dissipating. He tried to remember what had been discussed to make a clear distinction between what was German territory and what was British.

He could remember that there was to be an attack by the British on the Port of Tanga, which was part of German East Africa. Then there was the man, Jim. He was somehow involved, too. Bentley *had* to return to the dream to get more information. He shut his eyes tight, but no. When he opened them again, he was back in his room at Shepheard's.

23

The Pyramids of Giza, Cairo

Bette

Turned out I was right. The coordinates did lead to the other Occult Bureau: a forgotten tomb in the desert. So, it was on that note, Bentley and I made arrangements to pay a visit to Giza.

The first thing Bentley did, was deposit me in the garden café at the Mena House Hotel, with a pot of tea. He told me to sit and admire the Pyramids. When he returned, he had two donkeys, and was leading them with ropes attached to their bridles.

"Transport," he said.

"Haemorrhoids," I responded.

I mounted one of the donkeys, and hauled myself into its saddle, before following Bentley along the road leading to the Giza Plateau.

The heat was intense, and the combined effect of sun and flies was making my skin itchy. We continued past the Pyramids for about an hour. Then the ground grew rockier. Sand intermingled with stones. Stones became rocks, and finally, Bentley stopped at a boulder.

"Where are we?" I asked, as I drew level with him.

"We've arrived," he said, dismounting. He began to examine the boulder. "This has been moved. Give me your rope."

"Here," I said, dismounting. I watched him loop the ropes from both donkeys around the boulder, ready to pull. "Well, whoever moved it first must have had a fucking great tractor," I said, as a great stone gate gradually came into view. It was half open.

"Come on," said Bentley.

I followed him through the gap, and we were met by a flight of stone steps, descending into a downward sloping passage.

"Hurry up," he pressed.

"What about the donkeys?"

Bentley rolled his eyes. "They're tied to a ruddy great boulder, Bette. They're not going anywhere. They'll be there when we get back."

If we get back, I thought.

Bentley took a torch from his belt to illuminate the corridor ahead. "The passageway's getting wider here," he said, as we moved forward.

Eventually, we arrived at a brown wooden door. Bentley pushed it open. "Well, this door certainly wasn't built by the Egyptians," he said, as we entered a chamber. He flashed his torch around. The room was empty.

"There's nothing here," I said.

Bentley began to feel the walls. After a moment, there was a click, and the entire interior became electrically illuminated.

"And before you ask," said Bentley. "No, the Egyptians did *not* invent the electric light bulb!"

I ignored him and let my eyes scan the chamber. All the walls were covered in hieroglyphics.

Bentley made his way over to the far end, and ran his hand across some of the inscribed hieroglyphics. "Ekhtaton," he said. He turned to me. "Ekhtaton," he repeated.

I made a face. "Yeah! Ekhtaton. Who the fuck's Ekhtaton when he's at home?"

"Monotheism," replied Bentley. "We're looking at the worship of the Aton. One god. So, Ekhtaton, not Ekhtamon. That would be the worship of more than one god."

"Fucking illuminating!" I muttered. "Yeah! Light bulb moment!"

Bentley narrowed his eyes. "Follow me," he grunted. "Waste of time teaching you anything."

"Yup," I said, giving his retreating figure the finger. I followed him back into the wide corridor, where we soon arrived at a second wooden door. This one was bigger than the first.

I grimaced, as we heaved it open. "Where's a donkey when you need it?" I muttered, as we entered a second chamber.

Bentley flicked another switch, and the light went on. I blinked, and stepped back as a mass of gold struck my vision. I looked down. I'd almost walked into a gold chest.

"Beautiful," whispered Bentley.

I looked around and whistled. The entire chamber was filled with gold.

"Someone's been very careless, though," said Bentley.

He was right. A pile of gold daggers, decorated with precious stones, lay strewn about the ground. Next to them was a gold table, on top of which, was a small gold figure. I went over to touch it.

"Osiris," said Bentley. "God of fertility."

"Fuck that!" I said, withdrawing my hand. I glared at the figure's painted eyes. "Pervert!" I muttered, before turning my attention back to the room.

Bentley had made his way over to the gold chest near the entrance. "There's something wrong here," he said. "These things are all from the eighteenth dynasty, but they're in the wrong place."

"Whadda, ya mean?"

"This tomb is a necropolis from the Old Empire. The designs on the treasures imply they're from the New Empire, so either they've been taken from a tomb in Luxor, or, they've been stolen from a museum."

"What about the chest?"

"That as well." He paused to think. "Here, help me lift the lid."

The lid was heavy. When we got it open, I stepped back. "You got to be kidding me!" I gasped. Inside were sheets of Egyptian parchment paper with drawings of guns, cannons and rockets. Bentley began to sift through the papers. He picked out a few, and handed me the top one. On it was a drawing of a strange looking contraption. It was like something out a science fiction movie.

"Vergeltungwaffen-1," said Bentley, grimly. "A Nazi revenge weapon." He began to study the design. "They work by remote control."

"So, no one has to go near them?"

"Only the poor bastards that get splattered."

My eyes widened. "How d'you know all this?"

Bentley didn't answer. Instead, he handed me another sheet. "Rockets the size of the Empire State Building," he said. He passed me another. "Flying bombs. And this," he paused to study the sheet in his hand, "this is the sound cannon. It uses the natural energy of sound. According to this design it has a rigid steel combustion chamber. Methane and oxygen are ignited inside it under high pressure. A series of powerful explosions at rapid intervals create shock waves, which destroy the enemy."

I shook my head. Where was all of this going? What were the Nazis planning? By the looks of the designs, if the Nazis got them into working order, they really would take over the world: that is, if there was a world left to take over.

"Have they built any of these yet?" I asked.

Bentley picked out another sheet. "If this is anything to go by," he said, "they're just at the planning stage." He handed me the drawing.

"It's a factory," I said. "They're going to build weapons under the desert here in Egypt, aren't they?"

Bentley's expression answered my question. He handed me another drawing. "This is the sun cannon.

You see that huge mirror on the truck? It rotates and collects the sun's rays, which are sent back towards the sky to blind the enemy."

"Mental!" I cried.

"A travesty," corrected Bentley, picking out another drawing, which he passed over to me.

"The villa?" I whispered. I looked up at Bentley.

"Take a look at the land," he said.

Suddenly it all made sense. Crops, water irrigation and farmland. No wonder that fucker O'Malley didn't want to talk about it. "Enough to feed an army," I said.

"Looks like it," agreed Bentley.

But something else didn't make sense. "So, if that's them got the humans sorted out, what about the Dead Army? What are their plans for that? I mean, correct me if I'm wrong, but the last time I heard, ghosts don't use guns."

"That's what I'm afraid of," said Bentley. "The Nazis work with make-believe. But no one really knows the ramifications, or how much of it might actually work, so it could affect a hell of a lot of innocent people."

I walked over to the daggers, and stopped at Osiris. "And what the fuck are you looking at? Fertility, my ass! I bet you don't even have a weenie!" I grabbed hold of the figure to prove my point. It didn't move. I pulled again at it. Nothing. The third time, I yanked it. This time the figure moved forward in my hand, like a lever, and the sound of sliding stone filled the chamber.

"There's your answer," said Bentley.

I turned. The far wall had gone, and we were now looking into another room.

"What the hell is this?"

"Ekhtaton's burial chamber," said Bentley, "but not as it should be."

We stepped inside. Ekhtaton was lying in his sarcophagus, as if someone had attacked him with a tin opener. There was little left to salvage. He'd been stripped bare of his jewels, and after years of mummification, his shrivelled skin was beginning to rot.

"You'd think he'd been dredged up from a lake," I said.

Bentley turned to face me. "This is serious," he said. "Really serious."

"Thanks," I replied. "I feel better already!"

"We need to get out of here." He paused. "Whilst we can."

I wasn't going to argue. My morale had done a dive, and my thoughts were all over the place. But more importantly, I didn't want to die. I followed Bentley towards the exit: but first things first. I stopped at Osiris and put him back in the upright position. As the wall slid back into place, we scarpered.

24

Shepheard's Hotel, Cairo

Bentley

Bentley hadn't been told that his new partner had Tourette's syndrome, until after he'd met her. The only saving grace was that Bentley had once treated a young soldier who'd had Tourette's, but had grown out of it in his early twenties. Time yet for Bette.

At the start, Bentley hadn't known what to think. Joe had refused to discuss it, claiming that Bette was well in control and deserved a chance. But medical opinion was divided. Bentley had, therefore, been forced to draw his own conclusions.

The twitching and fidgeting: yes. As for the swearing, he wasn't so sure. He rather thought *that* was just Bette. Not all sufferers swore, and if they did, *Coprolalia* was the correct medical term.

Well, maybe she *did* deserve a chance, but why the bloody hell did it have to be with him?

Bentley rubbed the back of his neck. He'd got used to the twitching, but he'd certainly *not* be giving her a gun. Even then, an agent without a firearm? That was madness. For a moment, he wondered if Joe was drifting into senility. He shuddered at the thought of it. Still, no point in getting the deadhead killed. As much as Bette got under his skin, that would probably not go down as one of his best achievements. He'd managed to keep his cool, so far, but if he heard her say: '*whadda, ya mean*?' one more time, he just might knock her block off.

It was with that in mind that he began to review matters. After they'd cleared off out the tomb, Bette had said she was returning to the villa, so he'd gone back to Shepheard's.

That had been the previous day.

Now he was in the Dining Hall at Shepheard's, examining the décor. It was designed in the Renaissance Style, and was classier than the Grill Room, but less formal than the grandest of the three restaurants. He turned his attention to the food on his plate, but he'd lost his appetite.

Matters were becoming tiresome, and he was steadily reaching the conclusion that things could only get worse. He'd been involved in top-secret work for more years than he cared to remember, and he was tired. All he wanted now, was to bow out, and reclaim his former identity as a civilian. Unfortunately, the threat of war was making this increasingly unlikely.

A mirror occupied a large part of the opposite wall. He looked across at his reflection, and studied his face. He was beginning to look like an outlaw from a western movie. He still had his good looks, but the bags under his eyes were starting to become as floppy as a cow's udders. If he didn't do something radical about his sleep pattern, he'd soon be able to either pack or milk them.

He shoved his plate to the side, and getting up, returned to his room, where he helped himself to a whisky and soda, before reclining back on the bed. He held the glass to his mouth, and felt the fluid trickle slowly down the back of his throat. The pleasantness of its flow made him want to gurgle like a baby, until his limbs relaxed, and his eyes glazed over, and he felt himself drifting gently back...

German East Africa, 1914

Bentley was in Africa again, and just as he tried to determine what was happening, von Kosch appeared.

"By God! They've arrived!" squawked von Kosch. "The damned British have arrived!" They're on the coast of Tanga!"

Bentley blinked, as information began to enter his mind. "What about German reinforcements?" he asked.

"From Moshi, you mean?"

"Yes. The rail link."

"We've warned Colonel von Lettow, who's in charge of the men in Moshi. They're on their way now, but the journey is slow."

"What about our defences in Tanga? I take it they can't be particularly good?"

"Useless! Bloody useless!" snapped von Kosch. *"The civilians have gone, and the police have had to join with the only troops actually left in Tanga."*

"So, a mess?" said Bentley.

"It's diabolical! And we have another problem. The British are likely to launch an attack, tonight. We need to get to Tanga before it gets dark!"

Von Kosch left the room, returning a moment later with Marisol, followed by a German soldier. Bentley watched as Marisol was led away, but not before he'd noticed that her hands were bound behind her back.

"What's going on?" he asked.

"The girl is a spy," said von Kosch. *"She has been passing information on to the British."* He paused. *"She is being taken for interrogation. Then she will be shot."* He paused for a moment. *"And you are the one who will shoot her."*

Bentley felt the blood drain from his face. What was happening? He tried to force open his lids. For a second, or two, he managed, but they shut again almost immediately, and he was precipitated into a galaxy of blackness. He forced his eyes open again, expecting to find himself back at Shepheard's, but he wasn't. He was still in the dream...

Bentley found himself in a clearing in the jungle, following the girl, Marisol. Her hands were still bound, and his eyes were fixed on her back. He remembered von Kosch's instruction, and his stomach churned. His nerves were on fire, and his feet dragged beneath him. It would take a miracle to save this girl.

Bentley placed his hand in his pocket, and felt the bulk of a revolver. His heart sank further. How far was he to go? Surely the entity controlling his actions wouldn't make him kill this girl? Even if only in a dream?

"Are we going to Tanga?" asked Marisol, as she continued to walk.

Bentley's hand left his pocket. "Yes," he replied.

Bentley wanted to wake up from this nightmare, but if he did that, he would be unable to help, and that was something his heart wanted him to do.

Marisol stopped walking. "My feet are hurting," she said.

Bentley looked down, and noticed, for the first time, that she wasn't wearing shoes. Her feet were cut and bleeding. "Not far to go," he whispered.

Soon the foliage began to thin out, and dirty sand became visible between the branches of scraggy-looking trees. They had arrived at a beach.

Bentley paused, but Marisol continued forward. Bentley took a step towards her, and grabbed her arm. He pulled her behind a tree. "Stay back!"

His words were sharp, and this surprised him. But that wasn't all. A sensation had flown up his arm, just as his hand had touched the girl's flesh. It had been like a bolt of lightning.

Marisol didn't appear to notice. She leaned against the tree. "What's happening?" she asked.

What indeed was happening?

The beach was empty, and as Bentley cast his eyes to the left, he observed a ship lurking a distance from the coastline. "*I don't know,*" *he said.*

But even as he spoke, a voice inside his head was telling him that the ship ahead was HMS Fox. This was the British vessel, sent to attack.

"*Where are the German soldiers?*" *asked Marisol.*

"*I don't know,*" *replied Bentley.*

It seemed that the troops from Moshi had not yet arrived. Bentley remembered that von Kosch had said the civilians had left. But where were the German soldiers who had remained in Tanga? A sound to his right drew his attention to another part of the beach, where a group of men were walking across the sand. They looked like British soldiers, and were making their way towards the sea, where a small landing craft awaited them.

"*Are they British?*" *asked Marisol, her eyes following Bentley's gaze. She was still leaning against the tree, her hands tied behind her back.*

"*It would appear so.*"

"*What are they doing?*"

It was then that Bentley noticed a pile of rifles lying on the beach, next to the water. He continued to watch as the soldiers walked past them, and clambered on to the landing craft.

"*Has there been a battle?*" *asked Marisol.*

"*I don't know,*" *replied Bentley.* "*But I think the British have surrendered their arms and are leaving.*"

"*Why?*"

"*An amnesty?*"

"*But why?*" *Marisol left the tree, and walked nearer to the beach, her back now facing Bentley.*

"*Maybe it's just Africa,*" *said Bentley, his eyes fixed*

on Marisol's back. Such a delicate, elegant back. "Things might be different out here. Could be no one wants to fight."

"Except von Kosch," whispered Marisol, her back still to Bentley.

Bentley shook his head. This was crazy. The British were leaving and there was no sign of any Germans. How crazy was that? But there again, maybe not crazy enough. After all, this whole dream was nothing but crazy.

Marisol began to speak, but Bentley was no longer listening. He shut his eyes. Just how far was he to go? His hand went into his pocket, and he took out the revolver. Opening his eyes, he pointed it at the small of Marisol's back. He shut his eyes again.

"Turn round!" he growled. "Turn round."

"I have," whispered Marisol. Bentley opened his eyes. She was staring at the weapon in his hand. "Did von Kosch tell you to shoot me?" she asked, calmly. Bentley didn't reply. "Are you going to shoot me?"

The truth was, Bentley really didn't know.

He glanced across at the landing craft. It was still there. He felt his hand tighten round the grip of the revolver, until his grasp unexpectedly loosened. He lowered the weapon, and returning it to his pocket, felt at the inside of his jacket, and produced a knife. "Turn the other way!" he commanded.

"I don't understand. If you want to kill me, shoot me. You don't need a knife!"

"Turn round!"

Marisol obeyed him. "Just make it quick," she whispered, her head dropping.

Bentley stepped forward, and grabbing her wrists, cut the rope binding her hands together.

"Go!" he cried, shaking her arms, but not releasing his hold. Another flow of electricity rushed up his body, as he pulled her round to face him. Marisol didn't move. "Just go!" he cried. He let go of her. "Go with the British. It's your only chance of survival!"

Bentley's eyes sprang open. The dream had come to an abrupt halt, and he was back in his room at Shepheard's.

What the hell was going on? First, an amnesty between the Germans and the British? Well, that order certainly hadn't come from Baron Heinrich von Kosch.

But that wasn't all.

There were other things that disturbed him.

He remembered the emotion, rushing through his body when he'd touched the girl. What was this? Was it love? Or, was it lust? He couldn't be sure. If it was love, did that mean that the man, Jim, had been in love with the girl, Marisol?

Bentley recalled the anger, fear and sense of helplessness that had overcome Jim. He wondered if he had acted wisely, for it was becoming clear that Jim's feelings may well have backed him into an inescapable corner.

The truth was, Jim and the girl had inadvertently made a secret pact. They'd drawn up their own private amnesty, which was all well and good, but how on earth could that be explained to Heinrich von Kosch?

Bentley was in no doubt that von Kosch would consult his charts, and expect to find a tortured victim: a bludgeoned torso, battered, bruised and resembling little more than a pot of well-boiled stew.

25

The Villa, Muqattam Hills

Bette

That was my stint in the desert over and done with, or, so I thought. I'd returned to the villa and gone straight to bed, exhausted, but unable to sleep. Far too much was going on in my head.

First off, where was Stephen?

Secondly, where was Farida?

Thirdly, wherever Farida was, I could only assume that she was now the legitimate owner of the villa, and as such, had to be the inheritor of a vast fortune.

But why run away if they were innocent? It could only mean one thing: the bastards *were* both Nazis, and were biding their time till the Nazis took over the Canal Zone. Then Mr and Mrs High and Mighty could return and assume positions of authority.

But was that really true?

Hell! I just didn't know.

I wanted to stop thinking.

I wanted to cry.

To top it all, my brain was fit to burst.

Dawn was fast approaching, and I'd still not managed to conk out. My head continued to reel, but as I tried to work out who was in cahoots with who, I heard loud footsteps pass my door.

I didn't move. I listened hard, until the sound disappeared. Only then did I jump out of bed. I opened the door, and stepped into the hall. It was then I made a decision: time to revisit the small room with the two chairs and table.

I tiptoed along the corridor, and slunk into a small recess behind the stone statue, well out of view, but not before I'd noticed that the door was shut, and a gleam of light shone beneath it. What's more, I could hear voices.

"They're going to start constructing the factory," said a man. His voice denoted he was a Londoner. It had to be the man from the market.

"Good," said another. I knew that voice. It was definitely Mr Campbell.

"Which means it's starting again," said a woman. That was Mrs Campbell. Her voice was tired. "Haven't they got enough factories all over the place?"

"Never enough," said the Londoner.

"And who's coordinating all this, Peter?" said Mr Campbell.

Peter? The Londoner was called Peter.

"One of the Brits," replied Peter.

"Who?" said Campbell, his tone sharp.

"Can't name him," said Peter, "not yet, anyway."

"A double agent?"

"Yes."

"Who is he?" snapped Campbell.

"You'll find out in due course."

"We've to live on trust!" exclaimed Campbell, excitedly.

"Then trust me," said Peter.

"And what about Farida?" intervened Mrs Campbell, her voice low.

"Aye, what about her?" said Campbell, harshly. He paused for a moment. "What's wrong with you woman?" he spat. "Going *saft in the heid*?"

"Going?" repeated Mrs Campbell.

"Brain-deid whore!"

There was a gasp of breath. "What's the matter, Willie? Not pushed me down the stairs often enough?"

"Ach, get to fuck!"

"No, Willie! I'll get to my bed! I've been up all night, and that's the only place I'll get to!"

I held my breath. Farida? Was I about to learn the whereabouts of Farida? Maybe then I'd learn where Stephen was.

I waited expectantly. There was silence, then the sound of footsteps, followed by someone flinging open the door. I cowered further into the recess as someone stormed out and slammed the door. The sweat was pouring off me, and just as I tried to decide what was happening, the door was flung open again.

"Fucking whore!" spat Campbell's voice. "Fucking two-faced bastarding snitch! You *know* where she is!"

She? I swallowed hard. Did he mean Farida? Now that was a turn of events. Did it mean *they* didn't know where she was, either?

"Leave it, Willie," came Peter's calm voice.

What the hell was going on?

"Leave it, my arse!" returned Campbell. The sound of running footsteps was followed by the resonance of a scuffle.

"Bastard!" cried Mrs Campbell's tormented voice. I cringed behind the statue. I'd never heard her swear before. It had to be bad.

"Bitch!" shouted Campbell. There was another scuffle, followed by the sound of someone being dragged across the floor in the direction of the statue. Shit! What if they saw me? I needn't have worried. Campbell was too intent on trying to destroy his wife to pay attention to anything else. "Where is she?" he demanded, "where's Farida?"

"My foot!" cried Mrs Campbell.

"I said, where *is* she, bitch?" shrieked Campbell, his voice erupting from his mouth.

"I don't know," whimpered Mrs Campbell. There was a loud thump, followed by the slamming of a door. I assumed Mrs Campbell had been pushed back into the room. A muffled whimper was followed by a loud cry through the door. "You'll kill me, Willie! You'll kill me!"

My right hand began to twitch badly. It was in overdrive. I held my breath. *Control, Bette, control.* The twitching finally stopped, and I stepped forward a couple of inches, still out of view, and leaned against the statue. As I did so, the door flew open, and I saw Willie drag his wife out. I gasped and stared at the look of astonishment crossing her face, as she looked up into her husband's eyes. He'd produced a hand gun, and throwing her to the ground he levelled it at her face. His right hand was on the trigger.

As for me, I froze.

"Please, Willie, please," begged Mrs Campbell.

"On your face!" shouted Campbell. Mrs Campbell didn't move. "Did you hear me?" he screamed.

"She hears you!" said Peter, appearing at the door. I studied him from my corner. Definitely the man from the market, only he wasn't wearing a hat. He was bald. I remembered the woman who'd been with him. The one dressed in red. I wondered where she was.

"Stop giving her the third degree!" said Peter.

Campbell didn't move, and for a split second I thought he really would shoot his wife, but a moment later, he drew back, lowered the gun and pulled her to her feet. He stared into her face, and raising the gun, thumped her on the cheek with the grip. She let out a cry, and Campbell grabbed her arm and tossed her back into the room, her slumped body missing Peter by inches.

"That'll do," said Peter, his voice steady.

"That will *not* do!" said Campbell, storming away in the opposite direction.

I listened hard. In the distance a door opened, and then slammed shut. I waited patiently, until convinced Campbell wouldn't return.

I felt like shit. I had to do something. I should have

intervened, but what good would that have done? I'd have got caught, and the situation would have worsened. I crept forward. The door to the room remained half open. I knew it was risky, but I had to look inside. I stepped out of the shadows, and glanced in. Peter was leaning over Mrs Campbell, who was seated on one of the chairs at the table, her head in her hands.

"You're not crying, Myra?" he said.

Myra? Funny. I hadn't known her name until then.

"Crying?" she repeated, raising her head. There was a nasty gash across her right cheek, which crossed into the one healing on her right eye. "You don't see anything wrong with a split eye?"

Peter shrugged. "I don't get any vicarious satisfaction from your husband's violence, but I'm not taking part in your tiffs," he said, sauntering over to the other chair, and sitting down.

"No," said Mrs Campbell, "no one ever does. So, don't you trouble yourself about me, Peter Bellingham. It seems I don't deserve anyone's help."

"Listen," said Peter. "You know me for what I am, and I don't try to hide it. I was born in a brothel, which means I come from nothing. I've no idea who my father is, although looking at me, he was probably from somewhere in China. As for my mother, I don't even remember her name. She was some poor sod who earned a living as a prostitute, and was addicted to drugs. But I got out of it. I got out of it, and met my wife."

"I don't want involved anymore,' whispered Mrs Campbell through gritted teeth.

"Too late," said Peter Bellingham. "It only takes one to back out, and the whole plan splinters into bits. So, let's be a little more astute. In other words, wise up and shut up! You still have a part to play."

"I don't want to know!" cried Mrs Campbell, placing her hands over her ears. "I don't want to know!"

Peter Bellingham stared across at her. "But you already do, darling," he said. "You already do."

"Stop it!" she cried. "You know I don't keep well!"

"Vulnerability and ignorance don't count as excuses, my dear," he said. "You can deny any suggestion of your involvement. It really doesn't matter. The truth is: you *are* involved, and have been from the start. What's done is done. And please don't trouble to rhyme off all your health problems. I'm really not interested." He got up, and walking towards the door, slammed it shut.

I stepped back into the shadows again, and as I did so a howl emerged through the closed door. Mrs Campbell began to cry with such intensity, I thought she would choke.

I moved back into the recess, and leaned against the wall. The situation wasn't good. Mrs Campbell had clearly taken an active part in what was happening, and now regretting it, was threatening to throw a spanner in the works.

What was more, it was becoming clear that Hitler's national army and his Dead Army were to play an integral part in the entire affair. Factories and ghosts. Simple to say, but I was convinced there was more to it than met the eye.

Something stank.

Yeah, something stank, and smelled as rancid as a shit-filled puddle next to a garbage tip.

I rubbed my eyes. I was exhausted, but it was time to get up. I went back to my room and started to dress. I eventually gave in, toppling back into bed, my head as mushy as a plateful of runny scrambled eggs.

Myra Campbell

Myra stared at her strained image in the mirror. The face looking back was cut and bruised. Hardly recognisable. But as much as her injuries hurt, it was the indifference that pierced her heart. It was that which deeply pained her, and caused a torrent of passion and despondency to form in her mind.

Life had never been kind to Myra. As a child, she'd been used and abused by most of the adults around her. Uncle Tam in particular. Uncle Tam was her mother's brother. On her eighth birthday, he'd identified her as suitable fodder. From thereon in, he'd admire her blond curls and girly smile. He'd embrace and cuddle her, as an uncle might, but always with a difference: a hard erection.

Not that she'd known what it was at the time, except a voice in her head had told her it wasn't right, especially when Uncle Tam had said it was their own special little secret.

And so, it had continued and progressed.

By the time Myra was ten, she was the only girl and the oldest of seven. Not only that, there was another one on the way. Her family lived in a single-end tenement in the east end of Glasgow, so when Uncle Tam offered to take her in, her parents were glad to get rid of her.

"Gie the lassie a bit of space," they'd all agreed, pleased that Uncle Tam was always there to oblige.

"Aye," Uncle Tam had said. "Canny beat peace and quiet."

When Myra's father had suggested he take a couple of the boys, Uncle Tam had been quick to decline. "Canny cope wi boys. Too tricky," he'd affirmed.

But no one was trickier than Uncle Tam. He lived alone in his own single-end. His bed was in the kitchen behind a curtain, and he had his own tin bath. Imagine! A bath of your own, there to use, any time you wanted.

And the friends! All the little girls in their torn, ragged clothes. They would appear for food: and who could blame them? Hungry and abandoned, they too sought the confines of warmth and peace.

Then it changed.

Uncle Tam now insisted he wash her. "Hey lassie," he'd say. "Behind yer lugs." But in truth, it wasn't behind her ears he was interested in. His hands would roam, then stroke her between her legs. "Hey lassie, I sore forgot. Yer lugs are on yer heid and no doon there."

Myra had laughed at first. It was a game. A daily game: until his fingers ventured further. Now that hurt. And that was *not* right. "Please stop, Uncle Tam!" she'd plead. "Yer hurting me!"

But Uncle Tam wouldn't stop. "Now lass," he'd

say. "This is one of the pleasures of womanhood. Something every woman desires!"

But Myra wasn't a woman. Nor did she desire it.

When the other little girls were invited to bathe, the younger ones screamed, but the older ones remained silent, and succumbed to the humiliation, in the knowledge that although it was Uncle Tam's hand that abused them, it was also the hand that fed them.

So, life continued, until Myra was eleven and she finally said: "No."

Uncle Tam had progressed from the bath to the bed. "No," said Myra, as his hand had slid up her thigh. He'd said nothing in reply, but had stared hard into her eyes. Then he'd unzipped his trousers, and raped her.

As numb as she'd been, that was something she would never forget. When he'd finished, he'd struck her on her face, and kicked her from the bed on to the floor, where he'd left her, indifferent to her pain.

When one of the older girls had turned up later that evening for food, the girl had succumbed in silence, well used to such requirements. When Uncle Tam had praised her, he'd stroked her face and given her half a crown.

"That my darling, Myra, is how to behave," he'd said, when the girl had left. "That is how you earn your keep."

"And if I tell ma maw?"

"Yer maw doesny care. She'll call you a dirty wee whore, and throw you out on the street!"

"I wish I was on the street!" Myra had cried.

"Like yer maw wis?" laughed Uncle Tam.

"Ma maw?"

"How d'ye think she had you, you stupid wee bitch? Do you think she *wanted* you?"

And that was the problem. Nobody wanted her.

When the older girl came the next day for her half crown, Myra was made to watch.

"This is how you earn yer pennies, ma darling. It's easy. Just dae as yer telt, and ye can have anything in the world."

So, Myra had stayed. She'd succumbed to Uncle Tam, in the knowledge that he, at least, put food on the table.

Then came the day of comparisons.

"Ye ken, Myra, yer gonnae have to up the ante."

"What d'ye mean?" she'd said, "I've no got an aunty."

Uncle Tam had looked at her in disdain. "Yer no earning yer keep, lassie. No like the other wee lassies."

Myra had swallowed hard. It was true about the lassies. Four of them would come round every day, do the business, and collect their half crown.

"Ye see, hen, it's all about showing appreciation." He'd paused. "Or, at the very least, pretending to show appreciation."

Myra had looked at him in ignorance. It wasn't until later she'd understood he was grooming them. Preparing them for the use of others, and all for a nice fat fee.

But something in Myra's head had told her that it wasn't worth it. If she was to pretend, she might as well do that in another way. She'd had enough. She'd learned to accept humiliation. She'd learned to listen and obey, and never question. She'd been pushed around and manipulated. She'd been indoctrinated, her head filled with toxic facts, and the more this had happened, the more she'd sought praise, which, of course, had never materialised.

"Pretend, Myra, pretend."

These were the last words she'd heard Uncle Tam say. "Aye", she'd replied. "I'll pretend! I'm going to be an actress! A great actress! And the world will love me!"

But her decision to join the theatre wasn't a great success. She'd hoped that the music hall would provide happiness, and lay the foundations for a glittering career.

But none of that had actually happened.

26

Shepheard's Hotel, Cairo

Bette

I'd let a week go by, and things were still no further forward. It had become something of a waiting game. But what was of most concern, was the fact I didn't know how much longer I could stand being under the same roof as the Campbells.

As for Bentley, that was something entirely different. I'd formed the impression he was trying to avoid me. Well, he might want to chuck me out like a piece of trash, but since we were supposed to be working together, we really did have to meet up on occasion.

It was time to pay him a visit at Shepheard's.

When I arrived, I began to climb the outside steps leading into the lobby. As I did so, I heard a vehicle pulling in. I turned, and clocked a red Cadillac coming to a stop. The rear passenger door opened, and a svelte figure in a red dress stepped out on to the pavement. It was the dame from the market. She had to be Peter Bellingham's wife.

I carried on through the Grand Entrance Hall, and sat down on a wicker chair behind a statue. The dame entered the building. She walked across the Hall with extroverted elegance.

I continued to observe her, and wasn't surprised when she flouted convention, and entered the Long Bar, which was attached to the main restaurant. I got up, and tracing her steps, stopped at the door.

I glanced in.

The room was filled with very noisy men, some of them in British army uniform. They seemed to be burbling on about nothing. The setting was the ultimate in luxury, although the heavy mahogany furnishings gave the room a mannish appeal. Huge bevelled mirrors adorned the walls, and I used them to scan the room.

I soon clocked the broad.

She was sitting at a table on her own, her back to me. She raised her left hand, displaying crimson nails and a gold wedding band. With slick unobtrusiveness, she beckoned over the barman. He'd been slicing limes with an air of swanky ease, and understood at once that this lone female, who really shouldn't have been there, needed attention.

I decided to leave her to it. I had other business to attend to. I needed to find Bentley.

I made enquiries at reception, and learned that Bentley was in his room. Taking the stairs, I reached the fourth floor. A wide corridor led me past rows of watercolours, depicting various local scenes. These were divided by doors that led into the individual rooms. I breezed past them, only stopping when I reached room number 490.

I rapped on the door. It was opened almost immediately by Bentley, who stood there, clearly surprised to see me. He rubbed his eyes, then let me in.

"Thought it was room service," he said.

The room reeked of booze, and whatever he'd been up to, Bentley was definitely the worse for wear. His eyes were puffy, and he looked as if he'd just consumed a bottle of whisky. Either that, or his internal organs were playing up.

He sat down on the bed, and I plonked myself next to him.

"Everything all right?" I asked.

"Actually, no," he replied. "I'm tired, I've had a lot to drink, and I want to be left alone."

"But I've only just got here."

"Please, Bette. Please."

The guy looked ill. In fact, he looked as if he was about to conk out. I actually felt sorry for him.

"Well, stay in touch," I murmured, getting up to leave.

"Yeah," dragged his voice.

I pulled the door behind me, and leaving it slightly ajar, peered in. God, he was bad. Was he ill? Had he caught something?

I continued to watch, as he lay back on the bed.

What if he died?

Fuck that, Bette!

When, eventually, audible snorts filled the air, I knew he was asleep. He continued to snore with the intensity of a fired-up engine. There was nothing more I could do. It was time to go. I pulled the door quietly shut, and as I did so, it suddenly occurred to me, that I hadn't had a chance to mention anything about the incident involving the Campbells and Peter Bellingham.

Bentley

Bentley was jittery. He was beginning to resent the persistent intrusion of the American. It made him feel weak and vulnerable, and threw him off his game.

As for the dreams, each one was sapping more and more energy from him, and he still wasn't sure what they meant.

He shut his eyes. He needed sleep. No dreams. Just deep, uninterrupted, blissful sleep. So, when the sounds of Africa began to permeate the room, he forced his eyes open and got up. He grabbed his gun, and shoving it into his holster, made his way to the Long Bar.

A table had been set aside in the corner to accommodate the needs of the professional card players: and there were plenty. Bentley would have loved to join them, but his head was sore.

Instead, he sat at the bar, and ordered a Turkish coffee. When it was served, he swivelled round to get a better view of the room. A woman was seated in the far corner, her back to him. He wondered what she was doing there, but it didn't really matter. She was exquisite. He admired the blonde coiffure, piled high on her head. It contrasted well with her red dress that was rather like a piece of lingerie, and was very sexy.

The woman was eating black olives, and washing them down with a glass of white wine. As she turned her head, Bentley caught the profile of a fair complexion with cheeks that had the natural blush of a peach.

Just as she lit a cigarette, someone coughed in Bentley's left ear. He turned. It was Joe, and he was carrying a briefcase. "She's well out of your league, mate," said Joe, sitting down next to Bentley.

Bentley grinned. "I wonder if her underdaks are red?"

"Definitely out of your league." Joe turned to the barman. "Gin and lime, if you would, my good man."

"Cheers," said Bentley, when Joe's drink arrived.

"Don't know how you can drink that stuff," said Joe, pointing to the Turkish coffee. "There must be enough caffeine in there to kill a horse."

"Helps keep me awake," replied Bentley.

"Ah, the dreams," said Joe, understanding. "Must get a bit annoying at times. Still, have you come up with anything interesting yet?"

"One or two things."

"And the reason for the dreams?" said Joe, taking a sip of his drink. "Have you worked that one out yet?"

"Not really," sighed Bentley. "Except there's a man called Jim involved."

Joe put his drink down. "Anything significant

about him?"

"He's involved with something in Africa. German East Africa."

"Ah," said Joe. "Are we looking at the war?"

"Yes. He's working with the Germans."

"And I take it, he's British?" said Joe, smiling.

Bentley paused to reflect. "You know something, Joe," he said slowly. "It's just occurred to me. Jim is from Scotland."

"How bizarre," said Joe. "And very interesting."

"There's also another person. Baron Heinrich von Kosch."

"A German," commented Joe.

"And a woman called Marisol."

Joe raised a brow. "So, there's a woman involved?" he said, retrieving his glass, and taking a large sip of gin.

"What about you," said Bentley. "Anything to tell me?"

"Actually, yes." Joe took another gulp. "We've come up with new information: the International Hospital for Sick Children."

"Go on," said Bentley.

"It's in the eastern part of the desert. It runs in tandem with Wewelsburg Castle."

"A hospital that practises magic?"

"Alleged magic," said Joe.

"Alleged, or not, it still doesn't sound good," said Bentley.

"You're right there. Heinrich Himmler coordinates the activities of the hospital. It was built in 1935, within striking distance of the Suez Canal, but sufficiently isolated to supposedly confine infectious diseases to one spot. It's managed by a man called Peter Bellingham."

"Never heard of him," said Bentley.

"His wife is called Deborah Bellingham. She's a paediatrician. I'm afraid we don't have any pictures of them, but they are definitely ones to watch."

"So, what's actually going on there?"

"It's being used as a centre for recruitment purposes."

"Recruitment of what?"

"That's what we're trying to find out. All we know is that sick children are getting sent there from all over the world. They're supposed to be getting treatment, but we have our doubts."

"Human resources for the Nazis?" suggested Bentley.

Joe opened his briefcase and withdrew a file. "This is all the information we have," he said, sliding it across to Bentley.

"In that case," said Bentley, taking the file, "I'll update you with what I have. We found the tomb."

"Fill me in then," said Joe excitedly.

"I will. Only, buy me a beer first."

27

The Villa, Muqattam Hills

Bette

Something had happened, but for the life of me, I couldn't think what. All I knew, was it had something to do with the room with the table and chairs.

What the hell was it?

The incident with the gun had scared the shit out of me, but I'd stayed remarkably calm: that was until now. My right hand twitched. *Fuck it!* And it didn't help that Bentley remained incommunicado.

I had to do something.

I finally decided to make a Victoria sponge.

I mixed the flour and butter together with a vengeance. What was going on? I shivered. I'd witnessed an incident that might well have turned into another murder. What the hell would have happened if Peter Bellingham hadn't intervened?

My attention went back to the cake. I'd beaten

the mixture into a lumpy pulp. Great! I couldn't even make a Victoria sponge. Whatever! I started to pour the ingredients into a baking tin. When my right hand twitched, some of the mixture landed on my foot.

"Fucking dodo!" I yelled. "Fucking dodo!" I scraped the mess off with my other foot, and put the rest of the mixture in the oven. Then I stopped short.

Something had just triggered something.

Something to do with a foot.

Come, on Bette, think!

Then things became really freaky.

An image flashed before my eyes. Mr Campbell was dragging Mrs Campbell by the hair into the small room.

Holy fuck!

It wasn't enough I'd already seen the incident for real, it was now being repeated. Then another flash. Campbell was still dragging her, only this time, one of her shoes flew off, and rolled down a large, gaping hole.

The memory returned.

So traumatised had I been by the gun, I hadn't paid attention to the fact that one of Mrs Campbell's shoes had come off. It had then rolled across the floor for a bit, and fallen!

I knew it had rolled, because one minute I'd seen it, the next I hadn't.

I knew it had fallen, because I'd heard the sound of something hitting a hard surface, once twice, and then I'd lost count.

I'd been so scared, that my mind had totally dismissed the incident with the shoe falling. I'd totally disregarded the sound. The shoe had rolled across the floor, fallen, and then bounced downwards. It had bounced down steps, so that could only mean one thing: the room had to communicate with an underground passageway, and that was what Bentley had sensed.

I left the kitchen, retrieved my torch, and scurrying to the small room, threw open the door and looked in.

Think, Bette, think.

Where would a falling shoe go?

I looked down. To the left of the threshold, was the rug. I hadn't paid much attention to it before. Now, I kicked it aside, and hey fucking presto, there was a trapdoor! I didn't hesitate. I drew it up, and a flight of concrete steps appeared. Well, it was now, or never.

Now, was the decision, even if it should have been, never.

My foot touched the first step, and I descended slowly, switching on my torch, and carefully shutting the trapdoor above me. I continued down a couple more steps, then stopped, and looked around to get my bearings. There wasn't much to see, so I continued to descend. When I was almost at the bottom, I noticed a passageway, and decided that it had to pass through the hills. But if it passed through the hills, where the hell did it lead to?

I got to the bottom, and as predicted, there was Mrs Campbell's black leather shoe. I didn't touch it, but continued on. Red brick walls now ran on either side of the passageway. I must have walked five hundred yards or so, when I stopped. To my right was a metal door.

Well, Bette. You've come this far. Go for it.

I reached out, and opening the door slowly, was surprised to find myself in a brightly lit forecourt, full of ambulances. I blinked, and tried to understand what was going on. The smell of diesel was overpowering. I blinked again, and tried to focus. What the hell were ambulances doing under the villa?

I wandered over to the nearest vehicle, and stopped at the rear doors. I turned one of the handles. The door swung open, and I looked in. There was nothing inside.

I climbed in, and shut the door quietly behind me.

A solid panel separated the front from the back, but a small skylight, above me, let in enough light to see. I looked around. Nothing. No sign of any medical equipment. I was still trying to process this, when I heard the sound of a key being inserted into an ignition, followed by the roar of an engine, and the ambulance began to chug forward.

I held my breath, only to become part of a sudden commotion. The rear doors were flung open, and Bentley, his eyes ablaze, jumped in, feet first.

"Grab my legs!" he hissed, through his teeth.

"What?"

"Grab my legs, or I'll roll out!" He was out of breath. The driver changed gear. "Help me in, or we're going to lose the doors!"

I pulled him in, and sat on his legs. Then I grabbed one of the doors, and pulled it shut. Bentley rolled forward, and grabbing the other door, slammed it shut.

"Whadda, ya know," I gasped, looking at my hands. Not a twitch. I laughed at the irony. I was probably about to die, but at least I was cured.

I looked across at Bentley, who was leaning back against the panel, trying to catch his breath.

"Do you know where we're going?" I asked.

"Unfortunately, yes, I do," he replied. "The International Hospital for Sick Children."

I'd never heard of the place, but it didn't sound good. "So why are we going there?"

"*You* shouldn't be going anywhere."

"Whadda, ya mean?"

"We're dealing with dangerous stuff here."

"Stuff?"

"Things *you* shouldn't be involved with."

"Well, stuff you!" I gasped. "Joe got me here, so, here I'll stay!" I paused. "And I'll be having a word with him when I see him next."

"*If* you see him!"

"Whadda, ya mean?"

Bentley's eyes narrowed. "*If* you survive," he clarified.

"Listen, Fuck Face. Joe sent me on an assignment, and I'm here to work with you, so you can like it, or lump it!"

Bentley looked grim. "Then I guess I'll have to lump it."

"Yeah!" I agreed. "Lump it!"

Bentley shut his eyes, his head still against the panel.

"You can shut your eyes, but I'm still here!" I taunted.

Silence.

"I'm not going anywhere."

The ambulance continued to bump across the ground, and I counted the minutes. We remained silent, neither one of us wanting to speak to the other. After about an hour, the vehicle drew to a halt, and Bentley opened his eyes. He looked up at the skylight, and leaping to his feet, produced a screwdriver and began to unscrew the glass.

"You normally carry a screwdriver?" I asked.

He ignored me and carried on with what he was doing. He removed the glass and placed it on the floor. Then with a jump, he heaved himself through the gap, and disappeared out of sight.

I stared, my body tense. What was he doing? What was the driver doing? Hell! What was *I* doing?

Suddenly the vehicle lunged forward.

Holy fuck!

I jumped up to the skylight, and popping my head out, was in time to see the distant form of a body lying on the sand. It didn't look like Bentley, and I was about to jump back down, when I caught a glimpse of a cluster of buildings. One was very tall, and I was in no doubt that this had to be the International Hospital for Sick Children.

I jumped back into the ambulance, and it was then, I remembered the Victoria sponge.

28

International Hospital for Sick Children

Bette

It didn't take a genius to determine the likely fate of my cake. It would be carbon by now. As I pondered over this, the ambulance took a sharp bend, and I tumbled down from the skylight. It took another bend, and then accelerated.

My bowels began to grumble, and my right hand twitched.

No. Definitely *not* cured, and the likelihood of death, was not helping.

By the time the vehicle screeched to a halt, my nerves were shattered. I was about to hammer on the partition wall, when the ambulance started up again, this time crawling like an ant, before finally stopping.

After a moment, Bentley opened the rear doors.

"What the hell's going on?" I cried.

"Quiet!" he whispered.

I jumped out the vehicle, and looked around. We were in some kind of compound, surrounded by fencing. Most of the ground was well-compressed sand. The rest was grass.

Grass in the middle of desert? That was just as bad as grass in the Muqattam Hills. I shivered, as I thought of the connection.

We were parked at the rear of the tall building I'd seen in the distance: the hospital. A couple of hundred yards away was a small bungalow, and beyond that, another building that looked like some kind of warehouse.

"Listen," said Bentley. "I have to get back to the Canal Zone, so I need you to cover for me."

I narrowed my eyes. "What's going on in the Canal Zone?"

"I need to tell Joe's contacts what's going on, and *you* need to get into the hospital, whilst I'm gone."

"Can't we both go back?"

"No." His tone was firm. "I need you to act as a distraction."

"What?"

"You'll have noticed there's a casualty back there?"

"You mean the dead guy? The dead guy you dumped on the sand?"

"Yeah. The dead guy. And very soon they'll know he's dead."

"They?"

"A man called Peter Bellingham, and his wife, Dr Deborah Bellingham. They're Nazis, and they run the hospital here."

That didn't sound good, but it was the distraction bit that worried me most. "So, whadda ya want me to do?"

"I want you to introduce yourself to them, and tell them you're writing an article on the work being done at the hospital: and by that, I mean the treatment of sick children."

Unbelievable!

I glared at him. The whole thing was verging on a case of disturbing déjà vu.

"How many fucking articles am I supposed to write?"

"As many as it takes," he replied. "Remember, we're talking about national defence, here."

"Fine," I responded, wondering if a career change was in order: that was, if I got out of this mess, and *had* some kind of career.

"And I suggest you try the bungalow first. Time's moving on, so I guess the staff will have finished up for the day."

"Staff?"

"Yeah. Dr Bellingham has a team of scientists. Their quarters are in the hospital, but the Bellinghams stay in the bungalow."

I turned to look at the bungalow. "Do you think Dr Bellingham locks her staff in the hospital at night?" I asked dryly.

No reply.

When I turned back, Bentley had already done an about-turn. Then he was off in the ambulance before I could blink.

Great!

A lamb to the slaughter.

I made my way towards the bungalow. When I reached the door, I stopped.

Oh boy!

How would I bluff my way out of this one?

I was about to knock on the door, when a man opened it. I stared at him, my mouth agape. He was tall and well built, with blue eyes and very pale skin.

Human, not an alien from another planet, I thought.

I continued to stare, and he stared back. Five seconds of silence passed. "Hello," I finally quacked, my voice breaking. "Bette Milligan from the magazine, *Amber St Claire*. I'm afraid I didn't make an appointment, but I'd very much like to meet Dr Bellingham and discuss her work at the hospital."

The man narrowed his eyes. "Your driver was in a bit of a hurry, skidding away like that."

"Not the most patient man," I replied, hoping he'd only heard the ambulance and not actually seen it.

"Clearly."

I took a deep breath. "And you are?"

"Dr Andrew Witherspoon," he replied, with a stare that was as fixed as the eyes on the stuffed head of a dead moose.

Well, this one was definitely *not* locked up at night. So, maybe I was wrong. Maybe he *was* an alien. And if he was, my guess was he was from very deep outer space.

My thoughts were suddenly interrupted.

"Miss Milligan," said a loud voice. I knew, at once,

who it was, and jumped to attention as the familiar bald head, and hawk-eyed features of Peter Bellingham came into view. His voice pierced my eardrums with the sharpness of thorns. "Please, come in," he said, modifying his tone with an obsequious smile.

"Thank you," I replied.

The entrance led directly into the living room, which had a stone floor. A green three-piece suite occupied a corner, and a coffee table dominated the centre. My eyes travelled to the far end, and rested on the back of a woman. She sat on a chair, next to a display cabinet full of ornamental wares. She was small and elegant, and her red blouse served to identify her.

She turned to look at me, and beckoned me over. I took a couple of strides, and the first thing I noticed was the lips. Blood red lips. She was holding a drink, so I could see that her nails were painted as crimson as her mouth. I took another couple of strides, and stopped at a chair opposite her. I sat down. She smiled, and her teeth sparkled like pearls, their whiteness accentuated by the bright red lipstick. It all looked extremely civilised.

"Chin-chin," she said, raising the glass.

What the hell was going on?

Play along, Bette, play along!

"Please join me in an aperitif," she continued. "Mine's a cocktail. My husband will prepare one for you. It's called a Ginny-Hooker. Very sharp flavour. Just the right amount of lime, a dod of syrup and a great big dollop of gin."

I was thirsty, but knew I had to keep my wits about me. "Maybe later," I replied, wondering why her drink was named after a prostitute called Virginia.

"Are you sure?" she persisted.

"Well, maybe a ginger ale," I conceded.

"Deborah," said Peter Bellingham, as he began to pour out my drink, "let me introduce you to Miss Milligan. She's a reporter with the magazine, *Amber St Claire*. Sorry, I didn't catch your first name?" he pondered, as he handed me my drink.

"Bette," I said. "Bette Milligan."

"She wishes to write an article on the hospital and our work out here."

"How lovely," purred Deborah Bellingham.

Lovely? Not the word I'd have used. "Yeah. If you don't mind, that is."

Her eyes remained fixed on my face. "Not at all," she said, sipping her Ginny-Hooker. "At the moment, I'm looking at how infection impacts on the nervous system."

Yeah! Finding ways to create infection, I bet, not cure it!

Dr Bellingham laid down her drink. "I'll show you round the hospital if that helps."

"Sure," I said, my tone buoyant, but my heart beating nineteen to the dozen.

The main entrance to the hospital led into a wide reception area. We turned left towards a lift. Its doors opened, and as we stepped in, I noticed a series of buttons. Dr Bellingham pressed the top one, which was for the eleventh floor.

"Tall building," I said, wondering if I'd ever leave it, alive.

"Yes. We'll start at the top. That's where my laboratory is. Shall we begin?"

An image of Frankenstein and his monster popped into my head. "OK." I said slowly.

The lift zoomed up at the speed of light. When it stopped, my stomach was still at the bottom. The doors opened, and I followed Dr Bellingham out.

The walls were white, and we were enveloped by an overriding smell of disinfectant. She paused at a door. "This is my laboratory," she said.

I looked in, and clocked about a dozen scientists, all wearing white overalls.

Must be doing overtime, I thought.

"We won't go in," she said. "That would disturb my staff."

Yeah! Let's not disturb the staff!

"How about we meet some of the patients?"

I followed her back into the lift. We stopped on the third floor, where I was met by a room full of screaming babies. A nurse was running back and forth, trying to pacify them.

The second floor wasn't any better. A group of kids were throwing biscuits at one another. It was like a chimpanzee's tea party, and I felt like joining them.

Dr Bellingham shrugged. "Part of the course," she said. She looked at her watch. "It's getting late now. Do you have transport?"

"Not tonight. He's coming back tomorrow. I kind of assumed you'd put me up for the night?"

Her eyes were fixed on my face. She smiled. "Then I think we should carry on with the tour tomorrow morning, before your transport returns. The bungalow has a spare room. You can use that."

"Thanks," I murmured.

"Breakfast is in the dining room at eight thirty. We'll resume the tour tomorrow morning at ten o'clock sharp."

She took me to my room, and left me there. I sat in silence, and looked around. I could see nothing of interest, except two boxes that seemed to have been abandoned on top of a wardrobe.

I dragged one down. It was full of toys. I shoved my hand into the pile, and pulled out a doll with flexible limbs.

"Hi," I said to it. It smelled musty. I examined its face. The eyebrows were squint, and I wondered if it was the prototype of something showcasing *before* and *after*; and if it was, whether this was the *before*, or the *after*.

The fact it had copper-coloured wire hair standing on end, didn't help. Maybe the Bellinghams were experimenting with voodoo? Either that, or the doll had passed through a dynamic force, and was now being used to conduct electricity.

"Hey doll," I said, my eyes fixed on the contraption's face. "Let's give you a name. How about Ginny-Hooker? Yeah! Ginny-Hooker! Why not? If it's good enough for a drink, then it's good enough for you."

I jumped into bed, Ginny-Hooker reclining on my pillow, but as I began to drift off, I found myself faced with another dilemma: I just couldn't remember if Bentley had actually said he *would* be coming back.

29

Central Police Office, Glasgow

DI MacLeod

"MacTaggart! In my office now!"

MacLeod scratched his head as he studied the report on his desk. It was from a certain Captain Shawar, who was stationed at police HQ in Cairo. It had arrived at lunch time, amidst a pile of other paperwork. MacLeod had highlighted the parts he felt were important to his own case, and as he reviewed them, he realised the investigation was continuing to yield yet more unpleasant results.

People were dropping like flies. Murder was becoming epidemic, and as for the Milligan girl, she was driving him mad.

"You know sir," said Jessie, appearing at the door. "They've actually come up with quite a few sensible points."

"Who?"

"The Spiritualists," she replied, entering the office.

This was *not* what MacLeod wanted to hear. "Like what?" he grunted, nodding in the direction of the empty chair on the other side of his desk.

"Like trying to get on with one another," said Jessie, sitting down. "Not that that always happens, of course, but the important thing is, it's more a way of life: to try and make the world go round as smoothly as possible."

"Only that's not exactly what's happening here, is it MacTaggart?"

"We have choice, sir, so, if we choose to make a mess of it, then we're going to make a mess of it, and suffer the consequences."

"Well, some of us are making a bigger mess of it than others."

Jessie smiled. "I take it you're referring to Bette Milligan?"

"You know, MacTaggart, I think we might be dealing with a *double* murder here."

Jessie leaned forward. "You think Bette killed *two* people?"

"I think she killed her father *and* someone in Egypt."

"Someone else?" Jessie's face appeared blank.

MacLeod looked down at the report. "Omar O'Malley."

Jessie sat back. "Quite a unique name," she said.

"And quite unique circumstances," said MacLeod, his eyes not leaving the report. After a moment, he looked up. "Tell me, MacTaggart. Does that woman Fairbairn ever do séances?"

Jessie paused. "Well, sir, I wasn't going to say until I'd been, but I've actually been invited to one."

"And why didn't you want to tell me?" MacLeod was annoyed that she was keeping him out of the picture. In fact, he was more than annoyed. Jessie MacTaggart was doing that just a little bit too often, and he didn't like it.

He'd brought her in to work with the CID on the assumption that, as a woman, she'd gain the trust of the female criminals, and pass on all information given, like a dutiful informant. But that wasn't happening.

"In case you wouldn't let me go, sir."

She was right, but he wasn't going to tell her that. Besides which, circumstances had changed, and he couldn't see a better way of getting her into enemy territory.

"Well, as far as I'm concerned," he said, "you have carte blanche. Only remember, I want updates."

"Yes, sir."

"Do you have a date for it?"

"Not yet, sir."

MacLeod leaned forward. "Well, just you make sure you tell me when you know," he hissed, between clenched teeth.

Jessie smiled. "I take it you're still after that piece of cheesecloth, sir?"

MacLeod's face flushed. "That and anything else that might incriminate her."

"So where exactly do you want me to look, sir?"

MacLeod felt the flush spread down his neck. "Anywhere you can, and by anywhere, I mean anywhere."

"An intimate search?"

"If necessary. That and anything else that proves Ellen Fairbairn is a fraud."

"That might be difficult, if I don't have the grounds to do an intimate search, and I'd need a doctor."

"Find the grounds," ordered MacLeod.

"Would there be anything else, sir?" asked Jessie.

"No. You're dismissed!"

Jessie got up and left the room.

MacLeod stared after her. Was it just MacTaggart, or, was it women in general? Why couldn't they follow a logical train of thought? It was simple. It was so clear. Why couldn't she see they were dealing with a *double* murder?

He shook his head.

Unfortunately, it wasn't just that. Other matters were compounding the situation. Firstly, MacTaggart, his investigating officer in the Fairbairn case, was maybe getting a bit too close to the daft folk she was investigating, but not in a good way. He'd have to keep an eye on that girl.

Secondly, the report in front of him stated that the daughter of the murder victim in Egypt had disappeared. He glanced again at the report. Farida O'Malley. No one knew where she was, and the Egyptian police were afraid she might have been murdered, and her body dumped.

Thirdly, according to witnesses, his prime suspect, Bette Milligan, had just vanished into thin air.

MacLeod then had a sudden thought.

He felt the flush return to his face. What if this

wasn't simply a *double* murder? What if it was a *triple* murder: Jim Kipper, Omar O'Malley *and* Farida O'Malley?

He pursed his lips together. No one seemed able to grasp the facts, especially when it came to Bette Milligan. For a start, MacLeod still couldn't get it round his head why a drunken father would suddenly accept the added responsibility of a thirteen-year-old daughter, who was shoplifter, to boot. Unless, of course, it was for a more sinister reason.

MacLeod shifted a pile of paperwork, and retrieved an old copy of *The New York Herald Tribune* from the bottom of it. His younger brother had started taking trips to New York, on business, and always brought back piles of newspapers, which MacLeod had, recently, decided to read. The one now in his hands, had yielded results.

MacLeod flicked through the pages, until he found what he was looking for: an article he'd read earlier, reporting on a rally that had taken place in Madison Square Garden, New York. Twenty thousand supporters of Nazism in New York. Not an insignificant number.

He'd already carried out a bit more research, and discovered that back in 1936, a Nazi camp had been created: Camp Siegfried.

And where was Camp Siegfried?

Long Island, New York.

And the connection?

Bette Milligan had come over from the State of New York.

And which part?

Long Island!

As far as MacLeod was concerned, the Nazis, the IRA and some of the Irish-American mobsters were all in cahoots. The ones that weren't, were being bumped off. Simple as that. MacLeod was pleased with himself, but not with his counterparts in Egypt. They certainly hadn't got their act together. All the police had ended up doing was locking the stable door well after the horse had bolted.

30

International Hospital for Sick Children

Bette

"My wife's running late," said Peter Bellingham, entering the dining room at nine o'clock the next morning. "A few complications with an amputation. But she should still manage the final tour before lunch."

Amputation?

"Look forward to it," I lied, wondering what had gone wrong. Had she chopped off the wrong foot?

"She will, of course, have to clean up and prepare herself," he added.

"I understand," I said, not understanding at all.

It was clear that Peter Bellingham didn't like me, but I didn't care. As far as I was concerned, the feeling was mutual. That, however, didn't resolve the next problem. In a couple of hours, I'd be left alone with his wife, the butcher. It didn't bear thinking about.

I glanced round the room. A photograph of the Bellinghams sat on the sideboard.

"Quite a beauty, isn't she?" said Bellingham. I turned to face him. He stared into my eyes for a moment, saying nothing, then he spoke. "Just stay where you are. I've things to do. My wife will get you here. She'll hopefully not be too long."

"Yeah. The amputation."

Bellingham narrowed his eyes. "You can listen to the wireless if you get bored," he said, his eyes fixed on me again. "It's around now we get an hour of classical music. Great compositions, but it's important to pay attention to the theme underlying each piece." He paused, and his lips curled back into a half-smile. "There's nothing better than a symphony in the key of F major," he finished, stomping out the room.

I didn't bother with the wireless. As far as I was concerned, F major could have been D minor.

I poured myself a cup of coffee.

Where the hell was Bentley?

And where were reinforcements?

It was then I remembered the other building: the one that looked like a warehouse. It was time to explore.

I slipped out the bungalow. The door leading into the other building was made of steel, and had a large metal handle. To the right, was a roller shutter, which was shut. I turned the door handle. The door was heavy, but it wasn't locked. I shoved it with my shoulder and went in.

It was cool inside. There were no windows, and the only illumination came from the sunlight that streamed in through the door. I blinked hard as I adjusted my focus.

I was inside some kind of store area. I looked around. Rows of shelves adorned the interior, each one packed tightly with containers that looked like urns.

Holy fuck!

I was in a funeral parlour.

As I tried to work out what was what, a powerful smell of diesel drew my attention to something else.

At the far end was another large steel door. I walked over to it, and pushed it open. There was nothing but darkness on the other side. I felt at the nearest wall, and finding a switch, flicked on the light.

I whistled loudly, as I observed another fleet of ambulances, parked closely to a couple of battered-looking motorcycles. I looked to my right, and there was the roller shutter I'd seen from the outside.

The smell of diesel was overpowering.

I approached the vehicle nearest the shutter: it was a right-hand drive. Opening the driver's door, I saw that someone had left a key in the ignition. I hopped in, and made to examine the glove compartment, but never got the chance. The sound of a rolling shutter, and a transfusion of light, stopped me in my tracks.

"Get out of there," shouted a voice. "Whatever you're doing, stop it, and get out of there!"

I looked up. It was the alien from outer space. As Dr Andrew Witherspoon came nearer, I could see he was carrying a gun, and it was pointed in my direction.

My right hand twitched, but just the once.

Control, Bette, control.

I began to exit the vehicle, slowly. My right foot hit the ground, my hands remaining as steady as a rock.

No explanation.

And then it occurred to me: if it was good enough for an ice-cream vendor, it was good enough for him. No point in having an affliction if you couldn't take advantage of it. I jerked my body, rolled my eyes and began to drool.

Witherspoon looked surprised. He took a step back and tripped. I grabbed the opportunity, and leaping forward, kicked the gun out of his hand. As it crashed to the ground, I jumped back into the ambulance.

"Huh!" I yelled. "Take that Doctor Doolittle!"

I slammed the door shut, just as the passenger door opened, and a woman jumped in, pulling the door behind her. She was dressed in a nurse's uniform. I recognised her at once. It was the dame from the train, and going by her expression, she clearly knew who I was.

"Drive!" she cried.

I turned the key, and released the handbrake. The vehicle jumped backwards, then stalled.

"Fucking dodo!" I yelled.

It had been left in gear. I slammed it into neutral, turned the key, changed back to first and felt my hand go for the indicator.

"Never mind the bloody indicator!" screamed the

broad.

My hand went back to the gear stick. I hit the gas and the vehicle lunged forward. We screeched out the warehouse just as I hit fourth. I glanced at the fuel gauge. Full.

"Special Agent Jacqueline Brown," said the dame. "MPRS. I won't shake your hand. I can see it's otherwise engaged. Let's just show these bastards what we're made of!"

The vehicle continued forward, and the perimeter fence got closer.

"Holy fuck!" I cried as we crashed through it.

I glanced in the wing mirror. Witherspoon had grabbed one of the motorcycles, and was now in close pursuit.

"Who the hell taught you to drive?" demanded Jacqueline.

"Taught myself!" I shouted over the roar of the engine.

"That explains it."

"Well, if you want to take over?"

"Just drive!" she retorted.

So, I did.

We continued forward, but then the tyres began to skid.

"Fuck it!" I yelled.

"Cadence braking!" she cried.

"Cadence what?"

"Deliberation, not speed! Pump on the brake pedal, or we'll end up in orbit!"

I began to pump on the pedal. "Like that?" I gasped.

"And pause, don't bounce!"

I shifted gear, and made a turn. When a gun was fired, I realised that Dr Witherspoon, who had just shot passed, was now turning back, and firing at us.

"Check the glove compartment!" I cried.

"Don't worry," said Jacqueline. "I've already found it!" I glanced in her direction. She had a gun in her hand. "Just as well," she continued. "That bastard out there stole mine!"

I turned my attention back to the windscreen, just in time to see a large vulture swoop down and land on the bonnet.

"Fuck's sake!"

"Just keep going!" yelled Jacqueline.

The vulture stared at me through the windscreen as I drove, its glare piercing the glass, but when there was more gunfire, it took off.

"Fucking hell!"

A series of bullets followed, which were emitted in rapid succession.

"Get that foot down!" screamed Jacqueline, as she leaned out the passenger window, and fired back.

I shoved my foot down again on the gas. The sun was blinding, but when the glare disappeared for a moment, or two, I realised I was about to drive into a large rock.

"Fuck!"

I swerved to the left, and felt the tyres lose their grip again.

"No point in suggesting you get a swear box, is there?" said Jaqueline, pulling her head back into the vehicle.

"Fuck no!" I gasped, as the ambulance continued to skid across the surface.

I tried to brake, but to no avail. Jacqueline stuck her head back out the window, and continued to fire as we skidded. I wondered if I'd ever stop, my biggest fear being that the ambulance would flip over, trap us both inside, and then ignite.

Another gunshot filled the air, and then another one, followed by silence. I turned to the passenger seat, and noticed that Jacqueline was leaning out the window, her body limp.

"No!" I cried. "Not now!" I leaned over, and grabbing her, managed to pull her back into the seat. "Not you, too!"

She'd been shot in the head, but what was more, she'd dropped the gun out of the window.

I had no idea what to do.

I was about to give up, when there was another loud bang, followed by an explosion. I thought at first it was one of my tyres, but as the ambulance gradually came to a halt, a flash of light in the wing mirror soon made me aware of the facts. Witherspoon had just driven into the rock I'd narrowly missed, and his motorcycle had ignited. It lit up quickly. Flames struck the sky like a blast of pyrotechnical brilliance.

"Well done, Bette," I whispered. "One very damaged vehicle, and *two* very dead bodies."

I then remembered the gun. I had to find the gun.

I reversed the ambulance, and began to search. Luck was on my side, and I found the weapon within minutes. It glistened in the sunlight, next to a lizard.

The creature's tail was hanging over the barrel.

I jumped out the vehicle to retrieve it. As I bent down, the lizard opened an eye, stared at me for a second, then made off. I slipped the gun into my pocket, and returned to the vehicle, where I found a stash of bullets at the back of the glove compartment.

I sat in silence. I was tired, thirsty and in a state of shock. What now? I had no idea what to do next, but eventually decided my first port of call should be Shepheard's. There was no way I was going back to the villa.

Couldn't tell you how I found my way back, although a series of flashing images, and whooshing sounds in my head may have helped. I booked a room, deciding that MPRS could foot the bill. And as I sat on a wicker chair in the Entrance Hall, I reviewed the situation.

There was still one more thing to do.

I went outside, and sitting at one of the tables on the veranda, ordered a large gin and tonic. No Ginny-Hookers here. I swallowed it in a gulp, my head quickly feeling its effect, but I didn't care. I was working myself up to the task ahead.

Get the job done, Bette, said a voice in my head. *And take a good look at yourself.*

Take a look at myself?

That wasn't very difficult. I'd already done that. That's how I knew I had one more thing to do. Things were *not* looking good. For a start, I was in possession of a stolen vehicle *and* a dead body. I was also in possession of a gun, *without* a licence.

And to crown it all: I was about to drive with a belly full of alcohol! Not wise! But I had no choice.

Act now, Bette, said the voice.

Yeah, I had to act now.

It wouldn't be long before people started to take an interest in the ambulance, parked outside the hotel, with a woman apparently sleeping under a blanket. I knew I had to convey both vehicle and body to Military HQ in the Canal Zone, but I had to be discreet.

A couple of minutes later, I was ready for action. Ready, because it had just occurred to me that since my moment of drama with the good Dr Witherspoon, my hands hadn't twitched once.

31

The Villa, Muqattam Hills

Myra Campbell

Myra Campbell had always made the wrong choices in life. Not that her choice to leave Uncle Tam had been wrong, but her next move had proved to be a total disaster.

The funny thing was, she always knew she was about to make a mistake, but simply couldn't stop herself. She met Jim Kipper in 1913. He was a number of years older than herself, a married man, who regularly frequented the music hall. He lived with his wife and son, and was a reporter with one of the local newspapers.

But Jim had a weakness: women.

He and Myra soon became lovers.

To begin with, Myra had tried to rationalise Jim's marriage. He'd told her that his wife was punishing him by refusing him his conjugal rights, and that was why he only had one son. This served to satisfy Myra. She never thought to wonder *why* the woman might be punishing him, or, if indeed, she was. So, as far as Myra was concerned, it sealed the bond tying together their own relationship.

But then, in 1914, war broke out.

Jim was now a war correspondent, and spent most of the war years abroad, so was unable to satisfy Myra's needs. It pained her, but she waited, until, quite out of the blue, she learned that in 1916 Jim's wife had given birth to a daughter.

So, Jim had lied.

He *had* returned to Scotland, on at least one occasion, but had never once contacted her.

Myra had suffered the pain of abandonment yet again. She'd been dumped and forgotten.

But six months after the birth of the girl, Mrs Kipper had died, which meant that Jim, who had returned to Scotland for the funeral, had just become a free man.

Maybe, just maybe?

Myra waited with patience for the day Jim would visit and ask for her hand in marriage, but it didn't happen.

So, Myra had been forced to get on with her life.

She continued to perform in the music hall. She sang and danced, and did anything that was required of her. One day, she was approached by a sly-looking individual. She knew his name was Willie Campbell, for she'd seen him sniffing around the streets, over the years. He was a snitch, and Jim Kipper had used him a couple of times to get information on the criminal underworld.

Willie had fingers in every pie, and more importantly, he knew of the relationship that had existed between Myra and Jim.

"You want him back?" Willie had said, after the death of Mrs Kipper.

"More than anything," she'd replied.

"Then you have to become part of the New Movement."

New Movement? This was not what Myra had expected, but if it meant a new way of life and a happy future, what had she to lose? So, Myra, who had been in the depths of despair, could now think of nothing more wonderful. She didn't care what it was about. The only thing that concerned her was that life was about to get better: or, so she thought.

She happily signed on the dotted line.

Myra was at once reunited with Jim, who, strangely, appeared more distant than before. Undeterred, she would go with him and Willie to underground meetings. When the New Movement became the Dead Army, she did not question it. When she was told that the successful future of all humankind depended upon a hidden astrological formula, she didn't care.

As far as she was concerned, she had cornered the love of her life, and very soon, Jim would seduce her again.

But that didn't happen.

When Jim returned to Africa later that year, he went without her. He left his children with a distant relative on the side of his deceased wife: and it was *that* that pierced her heart.

Myra was heartbroken.

It would have been so easy to slip into the role of Mother. A ready-made family. Children who would need her, and a husband to love her. But that was something Jim had clearly never envisaged, so, life had continued to go round in ever decreasing circles.

Willie had been too old to join the regular army, but as war raged, Myra learned that he was secretly flying in and out of Africa, where he liaised, not only with the founder of the Dead Army, one Baron Heinrich von Kosch, but also with Jim Kipper.

This also broke her heart.

Would Jim ever return to her?

Myra had been misunderstood and misguided by every man she'd met. She should have realised that her experiences had presented her with a vast knowledge, and from that knowledge, she could have calculated options, and then made constructive choices.

But had she learned anything?

No.

She had allowed her confidence to erode over the years, and when she eventually agreed to marry Willie Campbell, at his insistence, in order to protect his criminal activities, she felt herself slowly descending into a pit: a pit filled with belittling lies, toxic spillage and rancid excrement.

Myra was now ashamed of herself.

She'd mismanaged every aspect of her life, and had become nothing more than a misfit.

She turned her head, and caught a glimpse of

herself in a small mirror on the wall opposite her. She glared at the dark circles under her eyes. They were as dark as the blemishes making up her own damaged soul. She sighed, for she knew it was she, herself, who had allowed the bad things to happen.

She'd allowed herself to be drawn into matters through her own inactive participation and unquestioning acceptance of facts. She'd allowed herself to be manipulated and controlled by all the men around her.

Her mind went back to the facts.

By the end of 1918, things had started to change. The war was reaching its conclusion, and Germany was on the losing side. Heinrich von Kosch had escaped to Egypt, where he'd got his hands on a villa in the Muqattam Hills. Jim also resided there. And then something dreadful had happened, and Jim was forced to return to Scotland.

But this was a different Jim. This was a broken man, who would never be the same again.

However, it didn't end there. Before leaving Egypt, Jim had sired yet another child, and that was when the problems had really started.

32

Shepheard's Hotel, Cairo

Bentley

"You have to be kidding me!" Bentley sat back in his chair, a large glass of water in his hand. He began to laugh. "You mean she blew the bastard up?"

"Motorbike hit a rock and burst into flames!" exclaimed Joe.

"And where is she now?"

"Here," said Joe.

Bentley was confused. "*Here*? What do you mean: *here*?"

"I mean *here*," repeated Joe. "She booked into a room on the first floor, and refuses to come out."

Good, thought Bentley. That meant she wouldn't come knocking at his door. If she did, he'd ignore her. "And how do you know all this?"

"I have my spies." Joe paused. "And fortunately for you, I also have a clean-up team."

Bentley felt bad as he remembered the ambulance driver. "I had no choice. It was him, or us."

"Doesn't matter to me. Hopefully, by the time they realise the man's missing, it'll be too late for them to do anything."

"You mean, we should have the upper hand by then?"

"Yes." Joe paused. "Unfortunately, we lost an agent."

"Surely not down to Bette?"

"No. But she was a good agent. I mentioned her to you a while back."

"Yeah. I seem to remember you saying someone was compiling a report."

"She was posing as a nurse at the children's hospital, gathering information. She got a lot of good stuff on that pair, but never quite managed to put the report together. Too bad."

"Yes," agreed Bentley. "Too bad." He paused. "So, who killed her?"

"It happened during the chase. That Nazi bastard, Dr Andrew Witherspoon, got her in the head, just before he drove into the rock."

"Anything left of Witherspoon?"

"Nothing," said Joe. "Nothing except charred remains. Even the gun he used on our agent was annihilated."

"The murder weapon," mused Bentley. "Still, I don't suppose it matters now. Can't try a dead man."

"Indeed," said Joe. "You can't try one, but how about we try and speak to one."

Bentley studied the glass in his hand, and took a

gulp, resisting the temptation to swallow the water in one go. He lowered the glass and let it rest on his lap.

"Give me a moment," he said.

As Bentley shut his eyes, Joe waddled over to the window. "Ready?" said Joe, after a moment.

But Bentley was far from ready. He opened his eyes and watched as Joe began to pace.

If only it was as easy as that, he thought.

But life wasn't easy. Never had been. In fact, it was downright bloody difficult.

On completion of his medical degree, he'd taken the Hippocratic Oath, but hadn't realised just how complicated circumstances would prove to be. How difficult it would be to preserve life.

Bentley continued to watch Joe pace. He wished the daft bastard would stop.

"Everything all right?" shouted Joe from the window.

"If you'd sit down and give me bloody peace," replied Bentley, bluntly.

Joe took a couple of steps forward, and drew up a chair. He took out a notepad and began to doodle. "Not there yet?" he asked in a matter-of-fact tone.

"Nope!" replied Bentley, as his mind delved into his subconscious, like an antenna searching out the thoughts and voice of the spirit, Jim.

Finally! A connection!

Feeble at first, but growing steadily stronger. Clearer and clearer, and to the point.

Remember the Oath? said Jim's voice.

Bentley swallowed hard. "Indeed, I do, Jim," he whispered. "Indeed, I do."

"Is he there?" interrupted Joe's voice.

But Bentley was no longer connected to the physical world. It was time to commune through thought. A tear dropped slowly down his left check, as he remembered the Oath.

I will follow that system of regimen which, according to my ability and judgement, I consider for the benefit of my patients, and abstain from whatever is deleterious and mischievous.

I will give no deadly medicine to any one if asked, nor suggest any such counsel, and in like manner I will not give to a woman a pessary to produce abortion.

With purity and with holiness I will pass my life and practise my Art.

I will not cut persons labouring under the stone, but will leave this to be done by men who are practitioners of this work.

Into whatever houses I enter I will go into them for the benefit of the sick.

I will abstain from every voluntary act of mischief and corruption.

"Mischief and corruption," sighed Bentley, opening his eyes. He stared for a moment at Joe's confused expression, before shutting his eyes again, as he prepared to enter yet another dream.

33

Shepheard's Hotel, Cairo

Bette

It wasn't so much the fact that there had been an unexpected turn of events, but rather the fact I'd come to a sudden halt, that made me realise there were still things to do.

I'd disposed of the body and the vehicle at the Canal Zone, signed in at Shepheard's, hidden the gun in a drawer, and strangely enough, had had a good night's sleep.

That was until the early hours, when the crazy dreams had started to bombard my brain.

Crazy dreams about going back to Ekhtaton's tomb. Crazy dreams telling me the truth lay there. Crazy dreams, real at the time, and gobbledegook on waking up.

Only when I did finally wake up, the message was still there. *Go back*, said a voice in my head. *Go back*.

The words were clear and concise.

No mistaking.

I was going off my rocker.

Or, was I?

I waited a half hour for reality to settle in, only to find that reality had already well and truly settled in. Problem was, I didn't like it, and I certainly didn't relish the prospect of going back, but I knew that unless I did, the voice wouldn't disappear.

I remembered the piece of parchment paper with the Egyptian eye, and wondered where the hell it was. That dodo, Bentley, had finally prised it from my possession. Well, not strictly true. He'd asked for it, and me, like the dumb shit I can be, I'd given it to him, thinking that was me finished with Egyptian tombs. Problem was, I wasn't finished, and he'd fucked off with it.

So, where was he?

Maybe he'd returned to the tomb?

Somehow, I didn't think so.

Well, I hope you've gone back to the goddam hospital, and discovered I'm not there!

And then another thought.

What if he had gone back, and someone had shot him?

Goddam it! My mind was going mad. I shut my eyes and lay back.

And then, a miracle.

Colours merged in front of my closed eyes. Purple, black and splurges of green. What the hell? Then sparkles, shooting out like tiny stars, followed by a fireworks display; and finally, words began to form into sentences in front of my closed eyes.

Goddam it!

I tried to read the words, but they didn't make sense. I crinkled my brow, afraid to open my eyes. I tried to zoom in, but it was like a foreign language. Letters from the alphabet, put together like words, only they didn't form words, at least, none I knew.

What the hell are you trying to say?

You? Who the fuck was I talking to? I zoomed in again.

Now there were numbers. One number jumped to the next with speed, as if calculating an important equation.

Equation?

The whole thing was a puzzling equation.

What are you trying to say?

When the image of a map suddenly appeared, it clicked. The letters and numbers made sense. I'd seen them before. They were the coordinates leading to Ekhtaton's tomb.

34

Ekhtaton's Tomb

Bette

By the time I arrived at the tomb, I knew it was too late to turn back. I paused for a while, wondering if the Pharaoh still lay exposed in his shroud, like an exhumed body.

Well, I'd soon find out.

The boulder at the front had been moved, enough to give me access. I swallowed hard. Somehow, that seemed far too convenient. But it didn't matter. I was probably just being paranoid.

I switched on my torch, and went in.

When I reached Osiris, he was in the upright position, and the wall was in place.

"Pervert!" I mumbled, grabbing hold of the fucker's head, and yanking it forward. The wall slid back.

I was in.

I shone my torch around the walls. Macabre shapes began to form, until the beam of light finally rested on the sarcophagus. I made my way over towards it.

Ekhtaton's smiling skull stared ahead, and I noticed for the first time a small, thin crack across the forehead.

"Hey pal!" I laughed loudly. "Frontal lobotomy?"

I snorted, then stopped abruptly, as a voice hissed in my left ear.

Shut your pie hole! You just might be next!

I stared at the skull. "Did you *say* something?"

Of course it hadn't, but that just made things worse. From a medical perspective, things were bad. I might have got over the twitching, but now I was hearing voices.

Control, Bette, control.

What fucking control?

Deep breaths, Bette. Deep breaths.

One, two, three.

I pointed my torch to the far end of the chamber, and was surprised to see a large wooden door, decorated with panels. Like the other doors, it was totally out of character with the rest of the place.

"Hello! You weren't there before!"

I moved towards it, and my fingers began to explore the panels. Someone certainly liked wooden doors. My hand went to a part of the wall, which was to the right of the door, and as it did so, it hit something.

"Goddam it!"

I stopped short, as another wall jumped out,

sliding over the door with eager vengeance.

I jumped with fright, and dropped my torch. It was as if the door no longer existed. I stood in silence. A gap of twenty seconds told me that the commotion had passed unnoticed. I bent low, retrieved the torch, and shone the light on to the new wall.

Hell! I'd just lost a door. How could anyone lose a door?

I examined the wall, where the door had been. It was covered in hieroglyphics. I looked closely, and realised it lay very slightly back from the rest of the wall.

As I pondered over this, one of my fingers hit a groove, and rested on something that felt like a lever.

"Eat your heart out, Osiris!" I hissed, as I took hold of the lever and pulled.

The wall began to slide away.

"Anyone else want to yank my chain?" I yelled, stepping back.

Beware the might of the Nazis, cackled another voice in my ear.

"And beware the might of my skinny white ass!" I responded, as the door returned.

I was back on track.

But my bravado was short lived.

I'd just noticed a cast-iron handle.

I paused as a sense of misgiving took hold of me. I'd no idea what lurked behind that door, but was pretty damned sure I was about to find out.

I turned the handle, and with single-minded determination, opened the door an inch.

The hairs on the back of my neck rose, as a third

voice, this time in my head, clearly indicated I was about to leap into something out of the Dark Ages.

35

Shepheard's Hotel, Cairo

Bentley

Bentley continued to dream. He was now in a library. He recognised the room, and if his senses were correct, he had to be in the villa in the Muqattam Hills...

Villa, Muqattam Hills, 1918

"There's a lady to see you," said a small Egyptian manservant.

"And who might that be?" asked Bentley, his voice controlled by the man, Jim.

"She says her name is Marisol."

A rush of emotion surged through Bentley's body. "Send her in."

"May I sit down?" asked Marisol, as she entered the room.

"Aye, sit down," said the voice within Bentley. He regarded her for a moment. Her hair was as black as ever, and she was so, so beautiful.

"I never thanked you," she said, making her way to a chair in the far corner. She sat down.

"Thanked me for what?"

"For saving my life."

Bentley examined her face. He recalled the dream where he had almost killed her. "You're a very brave woman in coming here."

"How so?"

"My orders were to kill you, and von Kosch believes you are dead."

"Despite his charts?" she said, a wry smile crossing her features.

"You can't stay here," said Bentley, his tone abrupt. "Von Kosch will find you and kill you."

Marisol narrowed her eyes. "Why does he hate me so much?"

"He says you are a spy."

"And you," she said, getting to her feet. "Do you think I'm a spy?"

Bentley didn't reply, but watched as she walked slowly towards him. He could sense the effect her presence had on the man, Jim.

"Well, are you?" he said, his voice breaking.

Marisol continued towards him. Bentley felt Jim perspire. She stopped by the side of his chair. A bolt of lightning shot through Bentley's body, when without warning, she knelt at his feet, and placed a hand on his arm.

She leaned towards his face. "I am no more a spy

than you are a British patriot," she whispered in his ear.

Bentley turned his head away, but sensed a power that strengthened, as she turned his face towards her. She looked into his eyes with the intensity of a huntress.

What now? thought Bentley.

Gently, she caressed his face, and he felt his lips relax as she covered his mouth with her own. He got to his feet, taking her with him. His arms encircled her waist, and the sensuous rapture that ensued was totally unexpected.

36

Ekhtaton's Tomb

Bette

The curse of the Pharaohs, I thought, as I continued to push the door open. Things weren't looking good. I was as trapped as a maimed prawn, caught in the claws of a boiling lobster. Simple qualms were fast turning into nagging doubts. I was in a quandary.

Did I continue to open the door, or, did I shut it?

I paused for a moment, my reaction surprisingly philosophical. Maybe it wasn't that bad. I'd sauntered into the hub of things, and dodged the odd bullet, so perhaps, despite all obstacles, things were destined to fall safely into place. I certainly hoped so.

My right hand was still on the doorknob. I gripped it tight. My knuckles went white. I pushed the door further, vowing that if I ever did get out of this mess, I'd never be so fucking stupid again.

37

Shepheard's Hotel, Cairo

Bentley

Bentley stirred from the dream, only to return to it a moment later, and found that time had moved on...

Cairo, 1919

Bentley advanced through the city towards Al Azhar University, which was situated in the medieval quarter of Cairo. As he walked, his mind slowly assimilated new information.

Marisol had conceived a child, and was into her ninth month of pregnancy; the man, Jim, was the father. Unbeknown to von Kosch, Jim had rented private rooms for his pregnant lover, which overlooked the old University.

So, it seemed that von Kosch's charts had not revealed the truth.

Bentley continued forward, past ramshackle buildings, until arriving at Marisol's residence, he climbed three flights of stairs, and knocked on her door. There was no reply, so he turned the handle, and went in.

Marisol was asleep at an open window that looked out on to the courtyard of the Mosque, which was attached to the University. She reposed in a large armchair, facing the window, the back of her head peeping out over the top.

Bentley smiled. He could sense that Jim was changing. No longer controlled by indiscriminate, self-centred needs, Bentley could feel that new aspirations now fought with the old.

Jim wanted a new way of life.

For the first time, he was prepared to accept a new responsibility. He wanted to share his life with this woman and their unborn child. He felt calm, as a sense of warmth enveloped his heart, something he'd never experienced before. It altered his mood. He felt happy. A lifetime of indifference was being slowly replaced by a feeling of love.

"Marisol," he whispered. "Wake up." She didn't respond.

He knew he should let her sleep, but there was so much to discuss. There was marriage, and their new life together. Jim wanted away from the evils of the Dead Army. He wanted to hide from von Kosch. He wanted to be alone with his love, when she brought their child into the world.

And then someone coughed.

Bentley turned. Standing behind him, was Baron

Heinrich von Kosch.

"I did warn you," said von Kosch.

"No!" cried Bentley, as wild panic engulfed him.

"You were instructed to kill her. But no. Instead of killing her, you fuck her."

Bentley swallowed hard. "What have you done?" he whispered, as the truth began to strike him with the force of a slow-moving sword. He turned back to the chair at the window, and ran forward.

It was the pool of blood at Marisol's feet that struck him first. Why hadn't he noticed it before? There was so much blood. He touched Marisol's arm, but her static body simply proved she was dead. She had been shot in the heart, and as he glared at the point of impact, he slowly realised that the child, Jim's child, was no longer in her womb: someone had sliced the flesh, and dragged the infant from its dead mother's bleeding body.

The expression on Marisol's face registered shock, and showed that the transition from life to death had been quick and unexpected. Beads of sweat were still ranged across the top of her mouth, and shone like lacquer against her dark skin, whilst her dull, glazed eyes stared up at the ceiling.

Bentley's eyes moved to Marisol's neck. He stared at the chain and gold locket with its embedded diamond and emerald. Also attached, was a cartouche pendant.

As Bentley studied the necklace, more memories possessed his mind. Jim had given her that cartouche pendant, and it bore Marisol's name in hieroglyphics.

Then one more final memory.

The last time Jim and Marisol had been together, Marisol had taken a lock of hair from her head, kissed it gently and placed it inside the locket. She had then stroked her large belly and said: "For you, my love, should I die in childbirth."

The memory proved too much. Bentley fell to his knees, and wept inconsolably.

38

The Villa, Muqattam Hills

Myra

Myra sat in her room. She stared at herself in the bedroom mirror. Her eyes, bruised and angry, filled with tears.

"Stupid, stupid, stupid!" she gasped aloud. She rarely drank, but today was an exception. The glass in her right hand was half-filled with neat whisky. In her left, were twelve sleeping pills.

"Evil man, von Kosch," she said to her reflection.

As pain seared up her arms, she took a gulp of the drink, but the pain continued, and steadily moved to her stomach. Von Kosch *was* an evil man. And as Myra remembered what he'd done all those years ago, she wanted to die.

Von Kosch had believed that Marisol, the mother of Jim's third child, was a spy, so he'd shot her in the heart. As much as Myra had resented the relationship between Jim and the woman, she still shuddered at the very thought of what von Kosch had done next.

Convinced his charts were telling him to keep the child, von Kosch had removed the baby girl from her dead mother's womb, and hidden her.

Myra shivered at the memory of it all, recalling how it hadn't stopped there.

"Just couldn't stop yourself, Heinrich." Myra's lips trembled, as she spoke the words. The pain in her stomach intensified, as she remembered what had happened then.

Von Kosch had discovered a tomb, which was ideal for his purposes. But plans for the Dead Army hadn't yet had a chance to come together. When he'd murdered Marisol, he'd disposed of her body; but neighbours, noticing the absence of the heavily pregnant woman, had summoned the police, who had begun to sniff around.

So, things had been put on hold.

Myra smiled at her reflection. "You didn't count on that, did you, you bastard?" she said. "Never occurred to you that other people might care. Always went by your own standards."

And that was the truth. Myra recalled how von Kosch had shut the tomb and sent Willie and Jim back to Scotland to join her.

"Didn't care what you did to Jim, either. Took his other children and sent them away."

Myra remembered the day von Kosch had told Jim that Stephen and Bette were going to America.

"But they're my children!" Jim had pleaded, tears

streaming down his face.

"And you are a drunk!" von Kosch had replied.

"And my third child?" Jim had gasped.

"Farida is coming with me to Ireland."

"Damn your charts!" Jim had hissed.

"And you, sir, are in no fit condition to look after yourself, far less a family. You are going to a mental hospital. Arrangements have already been made."

And that had been that.

Then a number of years later, and quite out of the blue, she and Willie had been summoned to Egypt, where Von Kosch had been waiting for them, only this time in the guise of Omar O'Malley.

But he'd been alone.

"Where is Farida?" Myra had asked.

"The girl is in Dublin at boarding school," von Kosch had replied. She will be called upon when ready."

"Ready?" This was what Myra had feared. "Ready for what?"

"Ready for duty," von Kosch had replied.

The subject had never been raised again.

Then, quite unexpectedly, in 1929 Jim had made contact with her. He'd been discharged from the mental hospital, and for some reason his daughter, Elizabeth Kipper, aged thirteen, had left America and was now living with him in Glasgow.

"My darling Jim," Myra had written in her first secret letter to him, *"I'm so happy you are out of that dreadful place."* She had then poured her heart out to him in every one of her letters. Jim would reply faithfully, and had even sent photographs of

Elizabeth. Myra didn't know if contact had ever been resumed with Stephen, for Jim had never mentioned him, and she had no idea what he looked like.

Then just as suddenly as the letters had begun, they stopped with an abruptness that pierced her heart: and that was when things had started to spiral out of control.

They'd begun the day the journalist arrived. On their first meeting, Myra had assumed that Bette Milligan, the sister of Stephen Milligan, simply resembled the girl, Elizabeth Kipper, until she finally realised, they had to be the same person.

Having identified Bette, it had then been well within her capability to identify Stephen, and it was at that point she realised that Stephen had unwittingly been dating his half-sister, Farida.

"But it got worse, didn't it, von Kosch," whispered Myra. "You and your ties with Nazi Germany. You and your instructions from the Fuhrer. It all backfired!"

As indeed it had.

Adolph Hitler had discovered that Farida, who spent time in the same household as von Kosch, who of course was now O'Malley, was not, in fact, O'Malley's daughter. What was more, it had been revealed that she was not genetically correct. Her grandfather had come from the Dominican Republic, and as such, she was considered by the Nazis to be racially inferior.

"You took the orders from your damned Fuhrer," hissed Myra. "You were ready to carry them out, and have her arrested. Only the girl got wise to you, didn't she? She escaped. Where to, I don't know. But she got away! She got away from you, you bastard!"

Myra sighed, and began to think of the limited options now open to her. She drew on all her mental resources, and prayed for inspiration.

Life was unfair.

But Myra had learned that a long time ago. Her downfall had been her belief that hope would deliver fortune, and that by adulating the men around her, she would get what she wanted. She'd thought Jim could provide, and then she'd thought that Willie could provide. In truth, no one could provide, and she'd been a fool to seek the unattainable.

But now there *was* a way out.

Myra had chosen the ultimate sacrifice, and the process itself would open the way for retribution. Von Kosch was dead, but Willie had to go. It was time to get rid of one more cause of evil, and it was consoling to believe that she might be the one to do it.

Myra looked at the pills in her hand. She got to her feet and made her way to the top of the stairs. She hesitated for only a second, before gulping them down. She felt rapture as the pills and whisky slid down her throat.

The process was simplicity in itself.

Myra stood still with the serenity of a priestess, and waited for the medicine to work. Very soon, the empty glass slipped from her fingers, and her mind began to float like a butterfly...

39

Ekhtaton's tomb

Bette

I'd remained rooted to the spot for what seemed like an eternity, but now I strode into the room on the other side of the door, and stopped short.

My eyes skirted the walls, next to which, were stone columns that reached up, and stopped at a high ceiling. Hieroglyphics adorned the beige stone: images and writing that formed illegible strokes, some of them like the ones that had popped into my head. There were even one, or two, Egyptian eyes: the eyes of Horus, if I remembered correctly.

Some of the carved and sculpted stone was covered in matte paint, on top of which, were inscriptions and symbols.

I assumed this was a biographical account of Ekhtaton's life.

The chamber was long and narrow, and as my

eyes ventured to the front, I observed rows of shelves containing urns, very similar to the ones I'd seen in the warehouse.

It didn't take a genius to guess what was inside them.

40

Shepheard's Hotel, Cairo

Bentley

Bentley had found his room at Shepheard's oppressive. Deciding that a change of scenery might help, he'd gone along to the Long Bar, where he now sat alone. It was past lunchtime, and although the bar didn't normally cater for customers until half past seven, the barman, a debonair-looking individual, had opened it for him.

Bentley had been sitting in the same position for nearly an hour. He wasn't at his best. The barman had served him a whisky, half an hour before. He'd then hovered for a moment, but noting that the hardy-looking Australian was uncommunicative, had departed.

Now the barman had returned. "Suffering Bastard?" he said.

Bentley turned to face him. The man looked

American, but sounded Egyptian. He was wearing a white jacket, and sported a black bowtie.

You could say, thought Bentley.

"Suffering Bastard?" repeated the barman.

Bentley nodded his head, in the knowledge that the man wasn't actually referring to him, but to an aptly named cocktail drink.

He watched the man prepare the drink. Gin, Angostura bitters and bourbon, all mixed together. Then he added ice, dry ginger ale and sweetened lime juice, before decorating the concoction with a slice of lemon and a sprig of fresh mint. He passed the beverage across the counter towards Bentley, and smiled. "On the house," he said, before departing.

Bentley stared at his drink, before taking a gulp. He returned the glass to the counter, and turned in his seat to scan the room.

His eyes crossed the mosaic floor, and rested on one of the huge bevelled mirrors, directly across from him.

"Well, Jim, my man," he muttered truculently, looking at his own face in the mirror, "'whoever you are, and wherever you are, I do believe it's time for a showdown! Time to tell me what the hell's going on."

Nothing happened.

Bentley scrutinised his face. It looked tortured, but why did that surprise him?

Still nothing happened.

He swung back to his drink, and finishing the contents, placed the glass on the counter with a thud.

"Enough!" he shouted. He spun round again, and glared at his angry image. He was about to speak, but was surprised to see the faint outline of a form beginning to develop behind him. "Ah, you *are* there," he said.

Yes, came a voice. The temperature in the room had dropped. Bentley continued to stare, squinting his eyes, as slowly, slowly, the apparition continued to emerge.

"And where are we now?" asked Bentley. "The present? The past? Maybe even the future?" Bentley glared into the mirror, and watched as the form rose above him, until it seemed to dominate the room. A face was beginning to take shape, a sad face, with a white beard that stared back in grim silence.

"Who exactly are you?" asked Bentley.

My name is Jim Kipper, said Jim, his voice vibrating inside Bentley's head.

Bentley wanted to laugh. He recognised the energy from his dreams, but of all the ghosts, in all the bars, in all of Cairo, he had to find one named after a fish.

"Kipper?" Bentley repeated. "As in a fish?"

Unfortunately, *so*, confirmed the entity.

"Well, at least I know you reached old age," smiled Bentley, as he examined the white beard. "So, what is it you want of me, Jim Kipper?"

The Dead Army.

"Ah," sighed Bentley, understanding. "We're talking about the work of the Nazis, and we know that *that* has something to do with you."

Had, corrected Jim.

Bentley smiled again. "If it were only as easy as that."

Lessons learned.

"And the consequences?"

I am thinking of the consequences.

"Tell me what you know about the Dead Army," said Bentley.

You already know, said Jim.

"Humour me and remind me", returned Bentley.

We're talking about Himmler's desire to create an army of dead children. He believes that since the soul of the child has not yet been influenced by human experiences, it cannot know the difference between right and wrong. He desires to manipulate the soul to the Nazi way of thinking.

"But he has to be wrong!" cried Bentley.

This is a lesson in greed, said Jim. *Human greed and its consequences on a very large scale.*

"Another world war?" ventured Bentley.

Some of the spirits that have incarnated into these murdered children are older than time as humans know it. They are strong and fit for what is to come.

"And the others?"

That remains to be seen.

"You don't know?" gasped Bentley. "What about the probable consequences!"

There are always probabilities and possibilities in human life. One thing leads to another, but the important thing is, choice. Choice will affect the progress of each of our spiritual paths, and that includes yours, too, Bentley.

"Some bloody choice!"

That's why you, Bentley, you have the choice to stop them, and in the process, save yourself.

41

Ekhtaton's Tomb

Bette

Once more, I remained rooted to the spot, only this time, I was on the wrong side of the door, and my nerves were getting the better of me. What the hell had Joe got me into?

I glanced around, and clocked a couple of other doors, one to the left and one to the right. I carried my gaze down the length of the chamber, and my attention became fixed on a pair of red velvet drapes. They were drawn shut, and were as wide as a double doorway, creating the illusion of elegance and resplendence.

Move, Bette! said a voice in my ear.

"Fuck off!" I hissed.

I was traumatised. I was hearing voices, and my legs wouldn't budge. I looked down at them. They were shaking.

"Fuck's sake, Bette! Get a grip!" I growled.

And just as I was about to raise a toe, I tumbled forward, and landed on my knees.

"Fucking hell!"

Someone had just pushed me. I turned abruptly. There was no one there. That did it. The only thing that was worse than invisible voices and unknown dangers, was being pushed over by something that wasn't really there.

I jumped to my feet, and ran to the drapes. I gulped, and remembering the push, slowly parted them. On the other side was a large annexe. A Gothic gloom shrouded the entire atmosphere. My eyes raced down an aisle, along a red carpet to the front. A metal gate and fence sectioned off the front area. Next to these, were pillars, which stretched up to create arches that melted down from another high ceiling.

I glanced from left to right.

I had no idea what was behind the metal barrier, but in front of it, was an altar, on top of which, was a black cloth which hung to the ground.

On it were the letters: "SS".

Well, that sure as fuck didn't stand for 'Sunday Service'. And just as I was trying to work out what Hitler's SS forces were up to, a malevolent vibration began to fill the air. It was the sound of footsteps ascending stone steps, which had to be situated behind the metal barrier.

The sound was coming from a crypt.

42

Police HQ, Cairo

Willie Campbell

Willie Campbell thumped the table with all the aggression he could muster. "The bitch!" he growled. He'd been arrested and incarcerated in a cell, which was no better than a hovel. He'd then been interviewed by a couple of Egyptian police officers, and charged with the murder of his wife, Myra Campbell.

It was when he'd been left alone to digest the facts, that the truth of the matter had finally sunk in. He'd been framed!

He was in no doubt that Myra had thrown herself down the stairs. She'd done that to get at him, and the stupid cow had killed herself in the process.

And then another thought.

What if she'd meant to kill herself?

He'd known about Myra's early adultery with Jim

Kipper, and had derived great pleasure in taunting her, by placing a photograph of the idiot on a wall in their sitting room.

Then there was the other photograph, which Jim had taken, showing Myra blowing a kiss at him. Willie had insisted the pictures adorn the room, for they were all reminders of her infidelity.

But now he'd never forgive her.

The bitch had got what she wanted.

She'd created her own web of lies, and ruined and betrayed him in the process.

Vindictiveness.

That was what this was all about.

Instead of being thankful that he'd taken her off the street, grovelling and whimpering, she'd turned on him. The woman was as inconsiderate as she was unfaithful.

He thumped his hand down again.

Why hadn't she accepted that he owned her? Every bone in her body belonged to him, and the stupid bitch had broken half of them. He owned the flesh covering the bones. He owned the organs within the flesh. He owned the blood that should have been pumping through the veins and arteries.

But the stupid bitch had stopped them working.

He wondered if she had a soul, and if it lived on. If so, where was it now? He'd heard stories of ghosts and phantoms returning to haunt their tormentors. But he wasn't a tormentor. He'd been her saviour, only the stupid bitch hadn't seen that.

But now there were other things to consider.

He felt a shiver run through his body. The future

wasn't looking good for him. The police had told him that he would be kept in custody, pending trial, and they were in no doubt he would eventually face the gallows at the legal system's earliest convenience.

43

Central Police Office, Glasgow

DI MacLeod

Detective Inspector MacLeod's thoughts were all over the place. His mood alternated between hope and despair. What was it with this girl? She was a walking crime wave! What was more, his concerns were not helped by the telegram he'd just received from Captain Shawar.

Bette Milligan, aka Elizabeth Kipper, had been sighted at Shepheard's Hotel, after being on the rampage. Three more people were dead, and an ambulance and a motorbike had been badly damaged.

In fact, *damaged* was an understatement.

The motorbike and rider had been blown to smithereens, and the ambulance had been crashed, and left within the vicinity of the Canal Zone, after Miss Milligan had dumped the body of a dead woman at the back entrance of British Military HQ.

To top it all, there had been another death at the villa in the Muqattam Hills, only in view of his history of domestic violence, a man called William Campbell had been arrested.

But MacLeod had his doubts.

Further information revealed that Miss Milligan had been staying at the villa some time earlier, and the circumstances concerning the death, were almost identical to those relating to Jim Kipper's death. Both were definitely linked, and he was of the opinion that Miss Milligan was responsible.

Then Captain Shawar, who'd been keeping a close watch on Miss Milligan, had somehow slipped up. He'd been on the point of bringing her in for questioning, when he'd discovered that her recent sojourn at Shepheard's had come to an abrupt end, and now she seemed to have vanished from the surface of the earth, yet again.

MacLeod was awaiting further updates that would hopefully clarify a few more points. The girl was still at large, and the sooner they found her, the better.

44

Spiritualist Church, Glasgow

Jessie

Jessie knocked on the door, and it was opened, immediately, by a lanky man, who'd clearly been expecting her. "I'm here for the séance," she said.

"Come in," he replied.

Jessie was led up a flight of stairs, through a couple of rooms, and into a third, which she assumed was the séance parlour. She'd been surprised that action was taking place in mid-afternoon, until she observed the long black curtains, which were shut. The only illumination came from a small lamp in the corner, next to which, was a gramophone. Both sat on top of a table. Next to the table was a wooden chair.

Jessie's eyes scanned the room. There was nothing fancy there. Fifteen chairs had been set out in three rows, all of them facing a strange-looking box-like contraption, which was open at the front. The box itself was black, and inside it, was a chair. Behind the chair, was a door, but it was the unlit red bulb, attached to the top of the structure, that really captured Jessie's attention.

"The cabinet," said the lanky man. "We're doing the cabinet today."

"I see," said Jessie.

"I think you'll find it interesting."

Jessie wasn't sure what she would find, but knew she would soon find out. "How long do these things normally take?" she asked.

"However long it must," replied the lanky man.

"And will we be joined by anyone else?"

"Another five."

Jessie sat down in the front row, and waited. When the others arrived, three men and two women, they sat in the row behind her.

"This is the cabinet," said the lanky man, pointing to the contraption. "Mrs Fairbairn will be sitting on the chair."

The portal leading to strange and wonderful things, thought Jessie.

The lanky man made his way over to the gramophone and lamp, and very soon, music filled the room.

"Energy," said the lanky man. He sat down on the wooden chair, and taking out a notepad, opened it at a clean page.

Although the room was cool, Jessie was tired. She was about to nod off, when someone opened another door. Jessie hadn't noticed it. It was to the left of the cabinet, behind a curtain.

"We're looking for a female volunteer," said a plump woman, who'd emerged from the doorway.

Out of the frying pan and into the fire, thought Jessie, as she raised a hand.

"It's very important that Mrs Fairbairn is properly searched before she does anything," said the woman. "Stops the rumours of fraud."

Interesting, thought Jessie, getting to her feet.

The woman led Jessie back through the door, and into another room, where a bed was situated in the corner. Mrs Fairbairn was there, standing next to a window. She was dressed in a long black robe.

"Hello Jessie," said Mrs Fairbairn.

"Hello," replied Jessie.

"Are you ready, Ellen?" said the woman.

"Aye, on you go." As Mrs Fairbairn spoke, she lifted her arms in the air, allowing the plump woman to remove the robe.

Bloody hell! thought Jessie. *She's starkers!*

Mrs Fairbairn made her way to the bed, and lay down.

"What's happening?" asked Jessie.

"I'm about to carry out an intimate search," said the woman.

"You need a doctor for that," said Jessie.

"I *am* a doctor," affirmed the woman.

"Of people?" asked Jessie, before she could stop herself.

"I'm a gynaecologist, so I'm well used to what should and shouldn't be up a woman's vagina."

Jessie swallowed hard. "And how do I know you're

telling the truth?"

"Because when I've searched her, you're going to search her too, under close supervision, of course."

Twenty minutes later, they were back in the parlour, where the rest of the group had already made a very thorough examination of the room.

Well, thought Jessie, *DI MacLeod can certainly throw his theory of cheesecloth out the window.*

Mrs Fairbairn, who was back in her black robe, was seated in the chair in the cabinet.

"And now we need two male volunteers," said the gynaecologist, a long rope in her hands. Two men from the group got up. "Mrs Fairbairn must be tied up, so she can't move."

The men secured Mrs Fairbairn's wrists at the front, then returned to their seats.

"Now the lights," said the gynaecologist, switching on the red bulb above Mrs Fairbairn's head. As she did so, the lanky man switched off the lamp on the table next to him, so that the only light remaining came from the red bulb, which lit up Mrs Fairbairn's face with its dim red glow.

"She's going into trance," said the gynaecologist, who'd seated herself next to Jessie. "Watch."

"Who *are* all these people?" whispered Jessie.

"They've come up from London: The Society for Psychical Research."

"So, they're carrying out a scientific evaluation of what's going on?"

"Very much so."

Jessie smiled, as she imagined the expression on

DI MacLeod's face when she told him that. *Apoplectic*, was the word that sprang to mind.

"It's all very interesting you know," continued the gynaecologist. "Our two worlds are closely entwined."

"And by that," said Jessie, "you mean them and us?"

"You make it sound too divided, and it isn't that at all," responded the gynaecologist. "You see, we're spirit too. We just happen to be residing in a human body at the moment."

"That's what I don't get," said Jessie.

"We're here, as spirits, to learn," said the gynaecologist. "Human experiences will shape our knowledge, but the only way to get that experience is to live as a human."

For a moment, Jessie felt sad. She was thinking of Charlie. *What was your lesson, Charlie? And how did leaving me help you evolve?*

The gynaecologist looked into Jessie's eyes, and smiled. "Ellen has told me about Charlie," she said. "And for your information, his human body *did* die for a reason."

"Charlie?" whispered Jessie.

"He's doing important work, Jessie, and that's why he wants you here."

Jessie was about to probe further, but the lanky man silenced her. "Ssh!" he said. "The medium is about to start."

Jessie turned her attention back to the front, and began to watch closely. Mrs Fairbairn had closed her eyes. No one spoke. Then just as Jessie thought nothing would happen, Mrs Fairbairn leaned forward, and her eyes popped open.

But these weren't Mrs Fairbairn's eyes.

These eyes belonged to someone else.

"Charlie?" whispered Jessie.

"Transfiguration," said the gynaecologist, her voice low. "A mask."

"I know" said Jessie, still unsure if it was true.

"Very exciting."

What's going on, Charlie, thought Jessie.

Then without warning, Mrs Fairbairn began to laugh, but the sound of laughter appeared to come from somewhere in the cabinet, not from her mouth. Jessie sat bolt upright. What was going on? Was this a trick? Was it a distraction? Only that didn't explain the mask. It didn't explain how Mrs Fairbairn had somehow managed to place a mask of Charlie's face on her own face. The laughing stopped, and Jessie heard a voice.

"Jessie," it said. "It's me. It's Charlie."

Jessie was confused. The mouth on the spirit mask remained still, and the voice appeared to come from Mrs Fairbairn's left shoulder.

"This is independent direct voice," said the gynaecologist, her voice low, "and a wonderful example of physical mediumship!"

"Physical mediumship?" repeated Jessie.

"Well, the trance bit is mental, although the transfiguration is physical, so it's actually both."

Jessie wanted to ask more, but couldn't think of one single question. None of it made sense.

"You see, the Spirit World can create a larynx,"

continued the gynaecologist, "and each visiting spirit can speak through it. Everyone in the room can hear it. That's why it's physical."

"Larynx?" whispered Jessie.

"Voice box," clarified the gynaecologist. "It's made of ectoplasm."

But Jessie had stopped listening. How could this happen? Her eyes moved from the mask to Mrs Fairbairn's shoulder. It was definitely a voice, but not just *any* voice. It was Charlie's voice.

Jessie scratched her head. The last time, Charlie's voice had come from the middle of the room. She began to feel impatient. It was just so like Charlie to change things on a whim, without telling her first. She wished he would make up his mind.

"Charlie?" she whispered. "Charlie? Is that really you?"

The sound of a crackle emerged from Mrs Fairbairn's shoulder. "Yes, Jessie, it's me!" said Charlie's voice.

"Why are you talking out of a shoulder, and not a mouth?

"You haven't changed, Jessie. Always the practical woman! Truth is, I'm training students here. Teaching them the art of communication from the spirit side. I'm afraid we haven't quite got to the correct positioning of the voice box yet."

"So, I need to talk to the shoulder?" smiled Jessie.

"You can talk to anything you like! Just talk!"

"And why are you laughing?"

"I'm laughing because I'm so happy to see you here!"

"You're really here?"

"I'm really here."

"And I can talk to you?"

"Isn't that what you're doing?" The voice laughed again. "You daft thing! Of course we're talking!"

Jessie's eyes swelled with tears. "Oh, Charlie!"

"Now, come on lassie! Don't get all mushy on me. You know I can't stand these things."

"Nor can I. Well, not usually. But at the moment, I don't even know what to say, Charlie!"

"Doesn't matter. I've got plenty to say! And the first thing is that you've got a lot of work ahead of you."

Jessie sighed. "Some things never change."

"I don't mean police work." The voice paused. "Well, that's not strictly true. I do mean in a police sense, but at the same time, not just in a police sense."

"Sense? Charlie! You're not making sense!"

"That's because nothing in the world is making sense just now. The world is in a terrible mess. This has to stop, and you, Jessie, have to play a very important part."

"Me? How?"

"First you need to learn to blend your energy with mine. Do that, and then we can talk any time you need to."

"I don't understand."

"Remember how we used to lie in the grass together, looking up at the sky?"

Jessie felt herself blush. "Charlie! Please! We're in company!"

"Well, I want you to do that again. I want you to lie back in the grass, and study the sky. Look hard, until you see the tiny white sparkling balls of energy. When you see them, you'll know you're beginning to attune with my energy."

"But why do I need to do this, Charlie?"

"We're not allowed to interfere, Jessie, but we can suggest. However, in order to suggest, you have to hear us, and in order to hear us, you have to listen."

Jessie didn't know what to say. Charlie had stopped speaking, and the room was silent. She felt that her heart was breaking.

"I miss you so much, Charlie!" she sighed.

You have to listen, communed Charlie's voice, this time in her head.

"I will, Charlie! I will!" A tear began to fall down her cheek. "I love you so much, Charlie," she whispered.

The mask across Mrs Fairbairn's face began to fade, but something else was happening. A trickle of mist had started to drip from her nose, and was collecting on the floor.

"Ectoplasm!" exclaimed the gynaecologist, excitedly. "It's ectoplasm!"

Suddenly the door burst open, and the light went on. "This is a police raid," cried a familiar voice. "No one move! You're all under arrest!"

45

Ekhtaton's Tomb

Bette

"Hilarious!" I muttered, under my breath.

Of course, it wasn't. I'd just slammed shut the crimson drapes, in the knowledge that what I'd walked into, was tantamount to a horror movie.

German SS officers were filling the annexe, three of them seated behind the altar, like a panel of judges, whilst the rest assembled within the chamber. Each was carrying an urn, and they were chanting something in unison, which, of course, I didn't understand.

Then I remembered Bentley's reference to electricity.

Well, at least the soles of my shoes were rubber, but I doubted even that would stop an excessive surge of electricity turning me into a Ginny-Hooker lookalike.

I took a deep breath, and slowly opened the drapes an inch, hoping the men would be too engrossed in their activities to notice me. I watched, in horror, as the officers stepped forward, one by one, placing their urns on the altar, crying out in loud voices, as if summoning the devil.

Each then turned, and got to his knees. I glanced at where they now faced, and observed, for the first time, a man sitting in the corner. It was Heinrich Himmler.

"Fucking dodo!" I muttered, under my breath.

A moment passed. I realised I was on the edge of a precipice. It would have been expedient to leave, but my feet refused to budge. It didn't matter, anyway. Before I could chart my next move, an unexpected blow to the back of my head knocked me to the ground, unconscious.

46

Police HQ, Cairo, Egypt

Captain Shawar

Captain Shawar sat in his office, reviewing the report he'd just received from Detective Inspector MacLeod, the police officer in Glasgow. It was in response to a report Shawar had submitted to him a short while before, but no matter how many times Shawar read it, things were simply not falling into place.

Earlier that day, Shawar had had a long discussion with the Government Director of Egyptian Antiquities, and the curator at the Egyptian Museum of Antiquities, about the theft of valuable exhibits from the Museum. It had been reported at the time, but it was now being suggested that the theft might have something to do with the murder of Omar O'Malley, who funnily enough, had been a director of the Museum.

The phone rang.

Shawar picked up the receiver. The caller was British, and was inviting him to attend a meeting that had been arranged by a Colonel Joe Bannerman. It was being held at Shepheard's Hotel.

Shawar confirmed he'd attend, and was advised a car was waiting outside. There was no indication as to what it was about, but Shawar had a strong feeling that the matters about to be discussed would have something to do with Omar O'Malley, and by the end, they might have clarified one or two core issues.

47

Shepheard's Hotel, Cairo

Stephen Milligan

"Colonel Bannerman," called Stephen Milligan, as he ran up the steps leading into the Entrance Hall at Shepheard's.

He'd dropped his pompous, anglified tone, and now spoke in a clear, Scottish voice. The sweat on his forehead gleamed like raindrops, but this didn't detract from his appearance. He was dressed in British military uniform, not a prop, but the real thing. And he looked very handsome.

But he didn't feel good.

The annoying lustre of the strong sun that day had given him a headache, and the pain refused to leave. For once, he'd have appreciated a cool day in Britain, with its lush pastures and blustery winds.

Joe Bannerman had been about to enter the private room to the left of the Entrance Hall. He stopped. He was also in British military uniform, only he looked more like an overweight teddy bear.

"Stephen?" he said, walking over to him. "What's the problem?"

"My sister," replied Captain Stephen Milligan. "Bette's disappeared, and I'm very worried."

"What do you mean, disappeared? She's booked in here at Shepheard's. I was told she'd retired to her room, following a session with a gin bottle."

"Well, not any more. I've been looking for her. I've been up to her room several times, and I've waited out here for her, but she's vanished."

Joe looked at him. "Vanished?" he muttered. "That's a bit of a nuisance. She definitely came back here. I've checked the register."

"Well now she's vanished," said Stephen.

"That's not good."

"Do you know who saw her last?"

"Not sure about that one," admitted Joe. "Last I heard, she was sulking, and wouldn't come out her room. But I thought that was good. It meant she wouldn't see us all in uniform."

"And about that," said Stephen. "Why aren't we having this meeting at Military HQ, out of the way, in the Canal Zone?"

"I'm afraid that doesn't suit everyone," responded Joe. "Shepheard's is seen as neutral territory, and that's very important in view of the political climate."

Stephen's face darkened. "You know, as well as I do, that I only agreed to Bette's involvement, on the condition she wouldn't be placed in any kind of danger."

"Have you checked the villa?"

"Of course, I have. There's no one there. No one, except the police. It's a crime scene. Everyone else is either dead, or in jail!"

"And the police haven't seen her?"

"For fuck's sake, Joe! There's no trace of her!"

Stephen sat down on a wicker chair, and put his head in his hands. The whole thing was turning into a nightmare.

Why had Joe allowed matters to go so far?

He supposed that to answer that question, he'd have to look well into the past, and examine how it had all begun.

It had started with his recollection of his father's inebriated ravings. At the time, Stephen had been a young teenager, and knew nothing about the occult: and certainly, had had no knowledge of the Dead Army. All he remembered was that in 1919, he and his three-year-old sister, had been shipped off to America, and put into foster care. But it wasn't until much later, that matters had started to fall into place.

Stephen had fought with the Americans at the end of the war, underage, of course, but having spent most of his life in Scotland, he'd never lost his accent, and that had been a source of amusement for his fellow grunts. He'd been nicknamed 'Scottie', which he hadn't liked, so after the war, he'd upped and left America, and joined the British Army.

In 1935, Colonel Joe Bannerman had traced and contacted him. Joe was British, and worked for a military organisation called MPRS: Military Psychical

Research Section. The first shock had been to find that the British Army actually investigated ghosts; then Joe had gone on to explain more: including rumours of the existence of the Dead Army, and its links to Stephen's family.

Joe explained how he'd managed to track down his father, Jim, who'd been committed to a mental hospital in Scotland, and how, in 1929, he'd got him discharged. Joe had then recruited Jim to MPRS. Joe already knew the identity of the actual founder of the Dead Army – Baron Heinrich von Kosch – and how he had created a new identity for himself – Omar O'Malley – and was living in Dublin.

Joe had already tracked down Bette in America; so, in 1935 he re-introduced Stephen to his sister. At the time of their meeting, Bette was working as a reporter with *Amber St Claire*. What Bette didn't know was that the magazine had been created by MPRS, as a cover for clandestine military operations, which meant that Joe had plans for Bette: whether she liked it, or not.

But that's when the investigation into the Dead Army took on a momentum of its own.

In 1937, MPRS discovered that Omar O'Malley, who'd moved away from Ireland, was heavily involved in Cairo's film industry. Stephen was ordered to take up acting, in order to infiltrate. 'Angel' had been one of Joe's little jokes, but it had backfired somewhat when Stephen's acting career had very unexpectedly taken off.

Stephen was, unfortunately, now in the limelight, something that would probably have to change when the investigation was complete, whenever that would be, because to compound issues, things had become even more complicated.

New information had come to light, so the focus had shifted slightly, and that was where Bette came in. She thought she was investigating him, and she certainly wasn't making a very good job of it. Still, that wasn't the important thing. The new angle was the one to focus on.

So, where the hell was she?

He was still deep in thought, when someone coughed in his left ear: Captain Bentley Ford-Jenkins, also in British military uniform.

"Afternoon," said the Australian, smiling.

"Good-afternoon," replied Stephen.

Bentley turned to Joe. "Am I late?" he asked.

"No," replied Joe. "But I'm afraid we have something of a situation here. We're going to have to fly you back into the International Hospital for Sick Children later tonight. Meantime, we have a meeting to attend, so shall we get started?"

48

International Hospital for Sick Children

Deborah Bellingham

"Do you anticipate an abdication?" called Peter Bellingham from the bathroom in the bungalow.

"You mean Farouk? Egypt's King?" asked Deborah from the bedroom. She yawned and sprayed herself with perfume. Talking to Peter could be laborious at times, especially during moments when she wanted to be silent and relax. Peter didn't reply, and Deborah took this to mean, yes. "He may well be forced to," she said. "I think he'll do whatever is asked of him to avoid any kind of trouble."

"You think so?"

"Trouble seems to follow the man."

"That's because people don't react well to him," continued Peter, like a prophet of doom.

Deborah raised her brows. "Well, it's up to him," she said. "Kings can abdicate for a hundred and one different reasons. You only have to look at the scandal caused by Edward and Mrs Simpson."

"How about a small libation, before retiring to bed," said Peter, entering the bedroom.

Deborah smiled. "I'll have a Ginny-Hooker," she said.

She turned to the mirror on her dressing table, and admired the angelic features that stared back, with demure detachment. Deborah was in her forties, but knew she looked good for her age. She stretched her arms leisurely above her head, and yawned again.

"Beautiful!" said Peter, as he left the room.

Deborah puckered her lips. People thought she was perfect, but she knew that her delightful face covered a sea of complexities and carefully orchestrated plans.

"Your Ginny-Hooker, Ma'am," said Peter, as he appeared at her side.

Deborah turned. She eyed her husband up and down, then took the glass from his hand. She sipped her drink, but it stuck in her throat. He hadn't got the flavour right.

Deborah shut her eyes. Should she say anything? She was tired, and really couldn't be bothered. She'd had enough on her plate, dealing with the charred remains of Dr Andrew Witherspoon, and the unexpected arrival and departure of the American.

At that precise moment, all she wanted was to be left alone within the sanctuary of her bedroom, and not to be in the presence of her annoying husband, Peter.

She swallowed till the mouthful was finally down, then taking a deep breath, she gave Peter a coy look, and wished he'd just go away. He aimed to please, but that evening, his ineptitude had just spoiled the end of what might otherwise have been an almost perfect day.

49

Shepheard's Hotel, Cairo

Joe Bannerman

Joe got to his feet. "On behalf of MPRS, I'd like to extend a very warm welcome to you, and thank you all for taking the time to attend this emergency meeting."

Joe was positioned at the head of a large oblong table, Stephen to his left, and Bentley to his right. In front of them was a large global map of the world. Delegates from different countries sat around the table.

Joe looked at them, but all he could see was a sea of bewildered faces. He'd been hoping that this meeting would enhance cooperation, but now, as he studied each expression, he was beginning to doubt it.

I should have gone to the bar first, he thought, catching both Stephen and Bentley's eyes, and understanding that they thought the same.

"Before we go any further," said Joe, "there are one or two things we really have to address." He'd been preparing this talk for a full day, and had managed to reduce the vast bulk of what he wanted to say into a fairly brief, but comprehensive summary. He wanted to talk about the paranormal, but couldn't quite find a way of expressing it.

"What the Colonel is trying to say," said Bentley, getting to his feet, "is that we have information that the Nazis are doing extensive research into mind control, but not as we know it. The parameters have, in fact, widened to such a degree, that we're now looking at the potential consequences of Hitler's belief in paranormal warfare: and that is a problem."

Bentley paused, and looked at Joe, who'd sat down again. Joe nodded his head for Bentley to continue.

"So, not only do we have to address Hitler's theories," said Bentley, "we have to understand the influence his actions could have on normal warfare in the event of another war."

Joe stood up again. "The decision to discuss this hasn't been an easy one," he resumed. "As you can see, we have representatives here from many different countries. Each of you has a wide spectrum of different political ideas. Not everyone agrees, but I've called you all here to seek a solution to a very difficult problem. We need to find a sensible strategy to help avert the inevitable, that being Nazi dominance." He paused. "Stephen, if you'd like to explain."

Stephen got to his feet, and pointed to the large globe of the world. He spun it halfway round. "This globe charts the progress of the Nazis," he said. "They're stealing land, and they're stealing national treasures. The Museum here in Cairo has lost a number of its artifacts. We believe they're being laundered by the Nazis, and used for nefarious purposes. If we allow this to continue, every country in the world will lose its national heritage and wealth."

"So, what has paranormal warfare got to do with this?" asked one of the delegates.

"I'll take it from here, Stephen," said Joe, getting up again, and turning to the delegate. "The enemy is talking about exploiting paranormal phenomena, which means it's up to the rest of us to take this as seriously as our acceptance of natural phenomena. It's also important to consider the possibility that should enemy paranormal forces exist, these forces might well harm us."

"The fellow's mad!" cried a voice in the room.

Joe couldn't make out the nationality, but it didn't matter, for very soon the room was filled with outrage, as delegates remonstrated with one another, offering critical and unhelpful remarks.

"Never mind ghosts!" challenged one of the delegates. "Let's deal with the living."

Joe examined him. He was a strange-looking man, with long arms that hung loosely, as if they'd been dislocated from their sockets.

"The entire threat affects the living," said Joe, when the noise in the room calmed down a bit. "No one knows the exact truth of the matter, but if successful, and in the hands of the wrong people, it could add a new dimension to warfare, and the problem isn't in its initial phase."

"No," said Bentley, who'd remained standing. "It's in advanced development."

"No margin of error," resumed Joe. "As disinclined as you are to believe in the possibility of it, you have to, and we have to work together. We have to do this in order to consider one very important thing: the overriding threat of Nazi domination.

"Where's your proof?" demanded a delegate.

"Crazy rubbish!" shouted another.

Delegates remonstrated with one another again, and the room became a hive of disorder.

Joe rolled his eyes. He had to convert opinions, before the meeting turned into a free-for-all. Everyone was missing the point. No one was prepared to work with an open mind, and all Joe wanted to do was wash out minds, and recycle each delegate, one by one.

It didn't help that MPRS needed to recruit more agents. They were dying like flies. It was a damned shame, especially Jacqueline Brown. She'd been one of the best, but that wouldn't have lasted for long. The post-mortem had revealed something quite unexpected: she'd been pregnant.

Joe hoped Bentley had had nothing to do with that. He hadn't had time to look into any updates concerning her private life, and didn't know with whom she'd been cavorting. That would have to be done at a later date.

Joe took a deep breath. This meeting was one of the hardest things he'd ever had to tackle, and almost as sensitive as the measures the Chief Constable had had to take to ensure that a certain medium kept her mouth shut, and stopped disclosing things about Operation MPRS.

That woman Fairbairn was too truthful for her own good. He knew that for a fact. He'd met her once when recruiting Bette for the magazine. He'd tried to get Fairbairn on board, as the psychic for the magazine's monthly horoscope. That could have led nicely to other things, but she'd flatly refused.

Next, he'd tried her niece: or, was it the daughter of a friend? Somebody MacNab. Volatile girl. She would have been good for the less orthodox activities of MPRS. But she'd refused, too. Pity.

Joe's mind went back to the matter at hand.

He had to impose order.

Of course, he'd anticipated conflicting ideologies: this *was* Egypt after all. And he'd expected opposing opinions, which was why he'd invited the Egyptian Police Captain along, so he could mediate, should needs arise.

Unfortunately, it had now become easy to infer from the expression on the man's face, that he was equally bemused.

No one was prepared to believe in ghosts.

"Gentlemen!" shouted Joe above the din. "Order! Please! Order!" The room became quieter. "I really would appreciate a bit of order."

"And does that include magic?" laughed one of the delegates.

The room broke into raucous laughter.

Joe shut his mouth. It was obvious no one was taking him seriously. He could really have done without the drama, and he certainly didn't want to do anything else that might initiate further ridicule and rancour.

He was about to speak again, when the door burst open, and a man in British uniform hurried towards him. The room became silent, as the man pressed a telegram into Joe's hands. Joe wiped his brow, as he read the contents.

When Joe finally spoke, his voice broke. He cleared his throat. "Gentlemen, we have a situation, here. If you don't want to believe in ghosts, at least believe this. Germany has just invaded Poland."

He paused for effect. "I have a telegram in my hand that states that this morning the Luftwaffe and Nazi land infantry invaded the Polish towns of Wielun and Mokra." Gasps filled the room. "As I speak, more Nazi troops are being marched in. Nazi Germany has now occupied Poland."

Joe paused again to read further, then began to read aloud.

"A German battleship has opened fire on the Polish military transit depot at Westerplatte." He raised his eyes from the telegram, and looked grimly into those of the delegates. "It's the start of a ticking time bomb. We're on the brink of war, and I cannot overemphasise the increasing potency of the Nazis, and the threat they pose."

He got no further.

"How can you criticise the possibility of a Nazi

occupation, when you yourselves occupy part of our country? Why shouldn't we let the Nazis in to get the British out?" It was the delegate with the long arms. The question annoyed Joe. It revealed that no one truly understood how dangerous the Nazis really were.

"Transferring control of the Canal Zone to the Nazis isn't an option," said Joe.

"And do you really think the Egyptian Army would assist the British, if there were an assault on Cairo by the Nazis?"

Joe turned towards another delegate, who'd remained silent throughout the meeting. He was wearing the uniform of an Egyptian army officer.

"We would simply ask," said Joe, "that the Egyptian Army understands what's really going on, and takes the existence of paranormal phenomena, seriously. We would ask it not to resist the British."

Joe kept his eyes fixed on the officer, who eventually spoke.

"I take it there are things you know," he said.

"In the eyes of the King of Egypt," said Joe, "you are an officer of his armed forces. In my eyes, you are also an officer of a clandestine section of the Egyptian Army, and you and your fellow adherents are preparing a military coup."

"You are well informed," said the officer. "What else do you know?"

"King Farouk is unaware of this cell. Indeed, the Egyptian Army doesn't know it exists, with the exception of the officers involved."

The officer blinked, and nodded his head. "We act

for the Egyptian people," he said.

"In that case," said Joe, "I really do expect you to cooperate." He paused. "For the time being anyway."

50

Central Police Office, Glasgow

Jessie

"What's going on?" cried Jessie, bursting into MacLeod's office.

"Funny," said MacLeod, swinging back in his chair. "I must be going deaf in my old age. I didn't hear you knock."

"That's because I *didn't* knock," retorted Jessie, marching forward, and plonking herself down on the chair that always seemed to be positioned in front of the Detective Inspector's desk.

"So, how can I help you, Constable MacTaggart?" asked MacLeod. "And by all means, take a seat," he added, sarcastically.

Jessie ignored his remark. She leaned across his desk, ready for battle. "I'm just back from Greenock Prison, where I visited Ellen Fairbairn!"

MacLeod stopped swinging backwards. He leaned

forward, and the chair clattered with him. "Who detailed you to go there?"

Jessie's expression was grim. "No one!" Her eyes darkened. "It was in my own free time, and it's as well I did. She's in the hospital there, and she's very, very ill."

MacLeod shrugged. "Happens to us all at some time in our lives."

"No sir, it doesn't. It doesn't happen to us all!" Jessie could feel herself shaking. "Why did you do it?"

"If you're talking about the raid, I ordered it to collect evidence to put a very dangerous woman behind bars!"

"Her nose was bleeding, and her cheeks were burned!"

"Probably used matches," said MacLeod.

"No! Not matches! Spontaneous burn marks, caused by ectoplasm firing back into her system!"

MacLeod examined Jessie's face. "Have you been drinking, MacTaggart?"

Jessie shook her head. "I saw it coming out her nose! And now you've injured her, but not only that, you've put her behind bars! Why?"

"Evidence, Constable, evidence!"

Jessie got to her feet. "Evidence, my arse!"

MacLeod raised a brow. "Watch your language, Constable."

Jessie refused to be daunted. "So, where the bloody hell is the *cheesecloth* then, the thing you keep going on about?"

"Clearly secreted somewhere."

"I searched her, sir. I searched her in the presence

of a gynaecologist. And just for the record, it was a *very* intimate search!"

MacLeod flushed. "What do you mean?" he demanded.

"A *very* intimate search," repeated Jessie, her words slow, "in a very private place."

She smiled grimly as MacLeod's right eye began to twitch. He scraped his chair back, and getting to his feet, leaned across the desk, until his face was inches from hers. She could smell his breath, and it wasn't very fresh. Sour milk sprang to mind.

Jessie moved back from the unpleasant odour.

"We can't let her go!" hissed MacLeod, through gritted teeth. The smell permeated further, passing quickly in Jessie's direction. She held her breath. "Something wrong, Constable MacTaggart?"

Jessie shook her head, and shut her eyes. After a moment, she opened them, exhaling slowly. Then a quick breath in. Fortunately, the smell had dissipated in another direction. It was safe to breathe.

"So, we're back to the spies, and the Witchcraft Act, are we, sir?"

"That woman disclosed classified information."

"She gave someone a reading."

"Then we have the correct legislation!" spat MacLeod. "She was clearly talking to the devil."

Jessie gasped. "Is that really what the Chief Constable is wanting to prove?"

"Report's already been sent to the Procurator Fiscal," said MacLeod, sitting down. He seemed pleased with himself.

"If you *have* to punish her, why not make it a

misdemeanour, and fine her twenty pounds, and let her go?"

"Not good enough."

Jessie paused, and narrowed her eyes. "Is it because you think she *is* talking to the dead?"

MacLeod's right eye twitched again. "There are things you don't understand, MacTaggart."

"No, and I'll never understand until you tell me!"

MacLeod took a deep breath. "Operation MPRS is a top-secret project. It relates to the identification of a Nazi spy in the ranks."

"The police ranks?"

"No. The army ranks."

Jessie paused to take in this new information. "So, who's the spy?"

"I don't know. But what I do know is that Mrs Fairbairn made reference to Operation MPRS. We don't know where she got this from. All I know is that the Chief Constable can't risk anything that might affect national security."

"So, what you're really saying is, you don't know if Mrs Fairbairn was passing on this information as a spy, or, if she really was talking to the dead!"

"Have you listened to the wireless, today?"

"Yes, sir. The Nazis have invaded Poland, and the world's in a bloody mess."

"So, you see the predicament we're in? Mrs Fairbairn is a danger to national security. We can't risk treason."

"You're not thinking of hanging her?"

"It's a hanging offence, but no, the courts won't go that far. We'd be looking at a year behind bars."

Jessie's mind began to work quickly. "So, by the time Mrs Fairbairn gets out, would I be correct in saying that Operation MPRS would be dealt with?"

"I believe so."

But somehow it still didn't make sense. "She's not a spy, sir. She's the real thing. I can vouch for that. She's given me evidence about Charlie."

"That's enough, MacTaggart. I'm not going down that path."

"Just talk to her."

"Can't take the risk."

"Risk? You're risking the life of a sick woman. How do you know she'll even survive a year behind bars?"

"That's one risk I *am* prepared to take."

Jessie stared at MacLeod in silence. The man was soulless. In fact, he was worse. He actively enjoyed the discomfort he generated for others.

"Really?" she finally managed.

"Anything else, Constable MacTaggart?"

Jessie shook her head. "No, sir."

"And don't expect to find your name on the list of prosecution witnesses," added MacLeod, when Jessie was almost at the door.

Jessie stopped in her tracks, engulfed in anger. She turned to face MacLeod. "No, but I'll make damned sure I'm on the list for the defence!"

51

International Hospital for Sick Children

Bette

I woke with a start, not a clue in hell where I was. All I knew was I was lying down, and my head was aching, as if someone had hit it with a polo stick. I couldn't move, and it took me a while to gather my thoughts and do the math.

Firstly, my solo performance as a secret agent hadn't gone well.

Understatement of the fucking year, Bette!

I'd tottered along, oblivious of the facts, and allowed myself to be backed into a corner, until finally I'd nosedived into a pile of crap.

So, here I was, confined to a bed in what looked like an isolation ward, inside the International Hospital for Sick Children, or, so I assumed from the noise of crying babies in the room next door.

Fuck! Even they were part of it!

I was still coming to, when a person, wearing a ski mask, entered the ward. He was carrying a pistol, which at that moment in time, was pointed in my direction. "Get up!" It was a man's voice, but not one I recognised. I moved a toe, and then a finger. My neck jerked, and pain shot through my body. "I said, get up!" screamed the voice.

"Fucking hell! Give me a moment! You try to knock my brains out, then expect me to get up and trip the light fantastic! What do you want? A fucking miracle?"

The man stepped forward. "Let's try a miracle," he said, slowly.

"Yeah! Fucking right." I raised my head and then my shoulders. I sat up, and slowly swung my legs round till my feet hit the ground. Pain shot up my spine, and I gnawed at my teeth. "See," I began, as I managed to stand. "A fucking miracle!"

The man clearly didn't care what it was. He had me on my feet, and that was all that mattered. He led me through a labyrinth of corridors, and up a flight of stairs. I stopped for a moment, and was about to ask if we could use the lift, when a hard object, presumably the pistol, was pushed against my head to encourage me to walk on.

My feet didn't want to comply. The miracle was becoming no more, but a dig in the head made me realise that loitering and malingering were not part of the course.

I began to climb the stairs, and counted the landings. Then I did the math. If the babies were on the third floor, we'd soon hit the eleventh.

Nine…ten…eleven.

I looked up, and clocked a set of ladders. We were at the top — and that was high. Problem was, whatever was up there couldn't take me up any further. So, either I was going to be left there to die, or worse still, I was going to be made to jump.

Whichever way, it wasn't good.

I climbed the rickety rungs, and found myself in a tiny room with a window. There was no doubt about it: I'd well and truly blown it.

52

Eastern Desert, Egypt

Bentley

The aircraft maintained a steady course, which was more than could be said for Bentley's racing pulse. He got to his feet, and began to pace.

What the hell was Bette up to?

She was driving him to distraction. Why did she always want to do her own thing? Why couldn't she follow orders like the rest of them?

He'd tried to warn Joe, but as usual, anything Joe didn't want to hear, he didn't hear. What the heck was the daft girl up to, and why was Joe so certain she was back at the International Hospital for Sick Children?

Bentley hadn't been happy about leaving Bette at the hospital, but she'd created that situation for herself. Someone had had to go for help before they were both annihilated. He had, however, been relieved to learn that she had escaped in an ambulance, albeit with the dead body of an MPRS agent.

Bentley still didn't know who the agent was, except that it was a woman. Bette had dumped her at British Military HQ in the Canal Zone, after crashing the ambulance. She'd then made off on foot, before anyone saw her: except Joe's spies, of course.

Bentley smiled, wryly. Spies? Great job they were doing! Couldn't even keep track of a twenty-three year old girl. Simply left her at Shepheard's, until she'd consumed so much booze, anyone could have taken her.

He sighed. Life was turning into a piece of shit. Nothing was certain. He felt at his parachute pack. At least that was there, well tied to his back.

The plane began to circle. They must be near the drop zone. Bentley began to fidget. He hated this part of any mission. As the sense of butterflies in his stomach intensified, he made his way to the exit.

The light went on, and he jumped.

The wind pressed against his cheeks, causing a concentrated flow of air to strike his teeth. It hurt. Faster and faster, he fell. He began to count, then released the parachute. He felt it tug at his body, and as he floated under it, his mind went back to his conversation with Jim Kipper.

You have the choice to stop them, and in the process, save yourself.

Bentley still wasn't quite sure what Jim had meant by this, but as he continued to drift, the cool air eased his way into introspective analysis.

He shivered.

What now?

He lowered his eyes as he approached the hospital compound. His concentration turned to the ground, just as his foot hit the sand. He fell forward, and his parachute tumbled down on top of his prostrate body. He wriggled from under it, and brushed himself down. He tried to get his bearings, but a karate chop to the back of his neck pushed him back on to his knees, and he fell unconscious.

53

Central Police Office, Glasgow

DI MacLeod

Detective Inspector MacLeod took a gulp of warm milk from the chipped mug in his left hand, and prepared to read an urgent telegram from Captain Shawar. It had arrived on his desk a few minutes before.

His eyes scanned the first line, and he realised it was reporting on a meeting that had taken place the previous evening in Cairo. All very interesting. No doubt a consolidation of the facts, which in all probability, would have a bearing on the Ellen Fairbairn enquiry.

He read the telegram in full. When he'd finished, he read it again, then again, each time, becoming increasingly bemused.

Paranormal warfare?

MacLeod read the telegram a fourth time. How on

earth could the British Army be taking this seriously? There was no mention of Ellen Fairbairn, but then he remembered that only certain individuals knew about her, and that was on a need-to-know basis. And he'd been reliably informed by the Chief Constable, who had been reliably informed by his military contact, Joe Bannerman, that very few people needed to know.

MacLeod shook his head and shivered. He'd been brought up as a good Christian Presbyterian, but everything this telegram suggested went against the grain. It wasn't right.

Things were happening in Cairo, things he hadn't known about, or expected. However, the facts before him were beginning to fill in a few blanks. Unfortunately, and much against his wishes, they also meant he had to change the direction of one part of his investigation.

He raised his head from the telegram, and smiled contritely at the mugshot of Bette Milligan, aka Elizabeth Kipper, that was hanging on his wall. He wanted to growl, and fought a sense of shame, for he was slowly realising that it was just quite possible his deductive reasoning had been somewhat off base.

54

International Hospital for Sick Children

Bette

Now, it would be fair to say that this was probably one of the many instances, Bentley wouldn't have been particularly happy with me. Not to say he'd any particular right, for although I'd been caught, so had he.

Five minutes before, the door had sprung open, and his sprawling body had whizzed towards me, missing me by inches. "Hey, Fuck Face!" I'd cried. "You nearly hit me!"

I'd expected an equally virulent retort, but from the moment he'd stopped rolling, and crash-landed, bolt upright, against the far wall, he hadn't budged.

Now I stared at him, unsure what to do next.

Bentley's face was like an empty shell. His eyes were shut, and his right cheek was lacerated, where someone must have hit him.

Was he unconscious?

I began to panic. "Hey! Wake up!"

Bentley didn't move, and nor did I. I was glued to the spot, engulfed in confusion. He looked far from right. "OK, just fucking die on me you thoughtless bastard!"

But die? What if he *wasn't* unconscious? What if he *was* dead? His face was sure as hell a funny colour. No. Surely the Bellinghams wouldn't leave me in a room with a dead body? Unless it was a warning.

I forced myself to my feet, and lunging forward, slapped Bentley hard on the left cheek, although I should maybe have made it the right: that sure as hell would have sent shivers up his spine.

"Hey! Wake up!"

Bentley opened his eyes, fleetingly, and I breathed a sigh of relief.

"Hell! Knew you wouldn't do the dirty on me!"

I stopped. He'd just shut his eyes again, and I realised he was phasing in and out of consciousness. But that wasn't all. Something very queer was beginning to happen. He was starting to groan.

"Goddam it! Don't do that!"

Still, he groaned, until totally unexpectedly, he opened his eyes wide, and the colour rushed back into his face. As his gaze met mine, he began to laugh.

"So, put me out my misery! What's the joke?" I gasped.

Bentley didn't reply. He stopped laughing, and just stared at me. I didn't like it. Brain damage? No. It was as if he was working something out, something he hadn't seen before: and I'd no idea what it was. He continued to stare at me, then shut his eyes again.

"No! Don't go unconscious on me!" I shook him hard.

He opened his eyes, and looked at me. "Just leave me alone," he muttered, under his breath. "For the moment."

At least he was alive. I breathed another sigh of relief. "OK."

I sat back and waited. Then, just as it started to grow dark outside, a couple of cogs turned a few times in my head, but not enough. Time passed. The cogs turned again, only this time, something began to compute.

How many times had Joe said to me: "K*eep your mouth shut, don't ask questions, don't give opinions and don't talk about personal matters: the agent doesn't like it."*?

Joe had told me to go with the flow, and for the first time in my life, I'd actually obeyed one of his fucking orders.

I began to think hard.

What did Bentley really know about me?

In fact, how much did he know about my investigation into Stephen?

We'd certainly discussed plenty about the Nazis. We'd discussed the Dead Army and its ramifications, but the more I thought about it, the more I realised something didn't add up.

I crawled over to the window, and glared at the sky. A group of stars stared back, twinkling, as if laughing at me. Still the cogs turned, but I wasn't feeling any better. Something really wasn't right.

Then the fog in my head started to disperse, and a question took form: did Bentley know I *had* a brother?

Hell! Did he even *know* who Stephen was?

I scratched my head, and tried to think back. The only time Bentley had *nearly* seen me with Stephen, was when my brother had taken me out to dinner at Shepheard's. The day he'd taken me to the film studios. I'd come out alone, and clocked Bentley across the street. But Stephen had still been in the restaurant, settling the cheque. By the time he'd come out to join me, Bentley had already done an about-turn, and marched off in the opposite direction.

The cogs turned again.

Were we even singing off the same hymn sheet?

My mind went back to when we'd disembarked at Alexandria. Bentley had assumed I was going straight to the villa. Why did he think that? Joe must have told him. But why? Unless, of course, Bentley didn't know I had somewhere else to go.

The cogs turned again.

And how did Joe know that Farida would invite me to the villa? Unless she'd already told him.

The cogs turned again, only this time a bit more slowly. Something was going on, and I smelled a rat.

Suddenly there was a noise to my left. I turned my head. Bentley was getting to his feet. Then another noise, this time at the window. I turned back, just as a person, wearing a balaclava appeared, armed with a rifle, the length of a bazooka.

I jumped back in fright.

The figure smashed the glass, and beckoned us over. If this was some kind of joke, then it wasn't funny. I gaped like an idiot, as my mind went into overdrive. Either the person was there to get us out, or, worst-case scenario, he was there to kill us.

The figure – presumably some kind of soldier – eased itself through the window, and motioned for us to keep our mouths shut. Bentley remained behind me. I took a step forward, and looking out the window, saw a rope ladder dangling from the ledge to the ground below.

The soldier jumped back out the window, swinging from the ladder. He grabbed my hand, and we began our descent: the soldier, then me, and finally, Bentley.

The first clue that something was wrong, came about five rungs from the bottom. I was about to take another step, when a sense of misgiving stopped me.

Something else had clicked.

The soldier had cleared his descent, yet the ladder was beginning to sway. I realised that Bentley was preparing to jump and run. The realisation, and the fact that I didn't understand why, froze me. Then someone else guessed, or saw.

A single shot filled the air. I expected a burst of fusillade to follow, but it didn't. Bentley's body slumped heavily on mine, and we both tumbled from the ladder, landing on a pile of scrawny vegetation. His weight held me down, and I couldn't move. My nose was fixed to the ground, particles of dirt flying up my nostrils.

"Help!" I wheezed. "Help!"

My prayers were answered, up to a point. I felt myself being thrown over someone's shoulder, as if I were a piece of garbage. It was the soldier with the balaclava. My eyes misted up, my glasses fell off, and I heard the crunch of them breaking under his feet. Then, before I could stop myself, I was sick down his back.

The soldier walked on, my head banging against him. My eyes clocked five more balaclavas. So, he wasn't alone. They were all making funny gestures with their hands, so I decided to join in. They were communicating, but I was giving the world the finger.

How dumb was I?

Someone had hatched a plan, and not one hint had been dropped, only now my brain was focussing on one simple detail. Bentley had been caught in the line of fire, and it had taken one shot, and that was it.

But, more than that: what a fucking good shot!

55

British Military Hospital (BMH), Alexandria

Bette

Too good a shot, I thought, cynically.

I'd been transported to a hospital bed at the BMH in Alexandria. My brain was still in overdrive, and it was becoming abundantly clear that I wasn't dealing with particularly upright characters. As for the rest of the world, well that wasn't in much of a better state. Neville Chamberlain was on the wireless, announcing that Britain was declaring war on Nazi Germany.

At the start of my involvement, I'd taken it for granted that, at the very least, I'd be provided with the facts, but just about every bastard I'd met, had lied: and that might well include the hospital staff. I'd already been scrubbed and deodorised, but it appeared I was still concussed, so the army doctors refused to turf me out.

The consultant had been to see me, but I'd told

him where to go. Unfazed, he'd recited a screed of possible reasons for my behaviour. Then he'd gone, but now he was back.

"Strange psychological reactions can very often result from trauma," he said, listing a few. I suppose I could have explained myself, but would he have believed me? Fact was, I really couldn't be bothered.

"So, what now?" I asked.

"Stay where you are. You've sustained physical injuries and mental trauma, but hopefully you'll be stable in a couple of days. Then you can arrange to go back to Scotland."

Two days!

Fuck that for a game of soldiers!

I was being treated like one of life's rejects, and I didn't trust a living soul. I felt violated. If I returned to Scotland, I'd no doubt be lost in transit, and if I remained in hospital, I might well be X-rayed, overdosed, or end up with something stuck up my ass to check for thrush.

I wanted answers.

So, deciding I *was* medically fit, I found my clothes, discharged myself, and jumped on a train to Cairo.

56

Cairo, Egypt

Bette

I arrived at the railway station in Kamal Pasha Street, and jumped off the train. I was still sore from my ordeal, and the sun wasn't helping. My body was covered in so many bruises, I was beginning to look like a leopard skin.

But that wasn't what concerned me.

Something, or, somebody was tinkering with my sensibilities, and it didn't feel good. As I stumbled along, I began to realise that I might still be alive, but I'd also been well and truly screwed.

The sweat poured from my body, as I tried to unravel the series of events that made up the whole. Either I was undergoing some kind of transcendental experience of the subliminal kind, or, I was about to self-combust.

Whatever it was, something stank, and I felt that

nothing would ever compensate for what I'd just been put through.

I left the station.

Next stop, Shepheard's, I thought.

I found a bike that someone had abandoned. I grabbed it, and bumped along, trying to cycle through the traffic in a straight line. I veered with resolve, but without precision, my head down like a charging unicorn.

For most of the investigation, I'd had no inkling of what was really going on. I'd been dabbling in things I didn't understand, so it had been impossible to put things into proper perspective, even though my intuition had warned me, repeatedly, that something was desperately wrong.

Certain things had never quite added up, but the more I pedalled, the clearer it got, until suddenly, it hit me: the whole thing had been a ploy.

"Ruse! Ruse! Ruse!" I shouted, pedalling like a madwoman.

Getting nearer to the truth hadn't been a function of *my* hard work, but the result of a carefully laid plan, put together by somebody else.

The cobwebs continued to lift. I jutted my chin out with defiance, just as the bike hit a stone, and I flew off, and landed prostrate on the ground, my eyes glistening with badly suppressed tears.

"Fucking dodo!" I yelled. I got to my feet, kicked the bike, and in a bid to maintain some dignity, continued on foot.

I faltered for a second, not through tiredness, but to give myself a moment to redefine my thoughts, and orient myself. I'd been a dormant volcano, and now blessed with flowing ingenuity, I was about to erupt. Illogical nonsense was starting to become logical.

Somebody had been using me.

I reached Shepheard's, and made my way to Bentley's room on the fourth floor. The door was unlocked, so I waltzed in. A cough splintered the air. I turned to my right, and saw Joe sitting on a chair in the shadows to the far right. He looked surprised. I smirked. It was clear he wasn't expecting me. I opened my mouth to speak, then shut it again, in the knowledge that had I tried to, I'd have gobbled like a turkey. Instead, I glared at him. When he began to smile, my right hand twitched, and I felt an unprecedented urge to slap him hard across the face.

Angry?

You bet your sweet little ass I was angry!

Joe had duped me. On top of that, he'd made my hand twitch, and *that* made me fucking mad! I was prepared to take the whole of MPRS to task, demand new codes of conduct, and annihilate all current personnel.

But really?

What good would that have done?

Control, Bette, control.

"Hey, chrome-dome!" I finally managed. "Who killed Bentley? And why did you detail me to investigate my brother?"

Joe shrugged. "Ah! The truth," he sighed.

"Yeah, that would be nice!"

Joe squinted his piggy little eyes. "Well, my dear, if truth be told, we actually have two issues at hand here." He paused, and examined my face.

"Shoot!"

"If you insist." He smiled. "Let's see. First, we have the Dead Army, and then we have, or at least, we *had* your good friend Captain Bentley Ford-Jenkins."

I knew Joe was being facetious. "So?" I prompted him, my tone harsh.

"You'll remember how *we* met, of course? You and I?"

"Yup."

"Well, the magazine, *Amber St Claire* was actually created by MPRS, as a device to achieve another very important goal."

Why didn't that surprise me? "Spit it out, Joe! Spit it out!"

"All quite simple really, and all to do with the Dead Army." He smiled smugly. "Now where shall I start?"

"Just start, Joe!" My voice was weary. "Just fucking start!"

"Well, let's begin by saying that your father had connections with an occult movement during the last world war."

I recalled the memorial service at the villa. "The Thule Group or the Vrils?"

"To start with there was a connection to both, but the section I'm referring to, developed into what we now call the Dead Army."

I glared at Joe. "Go on."

"I've been following its trail since 1921. You see, I

was with the British Intelligence Corps back then, doing undercover work in Ireland at the tail end of their war of independence. That was how I came upon Omar O'Malley."

My ears pricked up. "O'Malley?"

Joe smiled. "We'd received intelligence about something, and O'Malley was a potential witness, so we brought him in for questioning, or at least, my men did. I watched the interview behind a one-way mirror, so he never actually saw me. He didn't have much to say, so we had to let him go." Joe paused.

"Go on!"

"There was just something about his accent that bothered me. It didn't sound right. Something told me he wasn't Irish."

"His accent? Fuck's sake Joe, surely his fucking name gave you a clue?"

"Not enough to arrest him, I'm afraid. So, I said nothing, and carried out my own private investigations. That's how I discovered that he wasn't Irish, he was German, and his real name was Heinrich von Kosch. He was of old German aristocracy, and until the end of the war, had owned a rubber plantation in Tanganyika, which had been part of German East Africa."

This was starting to sound like a spy story, and given Joe's track record of honesty, or lack of, I just couldn't decide if he was telling the truth. After a moment, I thought it best to give him the benefit of the doubt.

"You know, Joe," I muttered, "you really do have a prolific ability to talk gobbledygook, but on this occasion, I happen to believe you."

Joe shrugged, and went on to explain how Jim had worked in Africa as a foreign correspondent during the war. He'd met von Kosch, and got drawn into promises of a new way of life, and that had led to his involvement with the Dead Army.

"After the war," Joe continued, "von Kosch had to leave Tanganyika, so he moved to Egypt, where he procured the villa in the Hills, and also located a tomb, ideal for his purposes. He had your father and the Campbells in tow by then, but there was an incident, and Jim was kicked out the movement for disobeying orders. Von Kosch had him committed to a mental hospital in Scotland, and decided to lie low himself for a while. That's when he changed his identity, and went underground in Dublin."

"Why Dublin?"

"For starters, it was 1919, and the Irish had just started their war of independence, so this was another opportunity for von Kosch to attack the British."

"And secondly?"

"Richer pickings in Dublin for what he had in mind. Dublin has an abundance of industrial schools, where unwanted and neglected children are committed. Some survive, but others die. Von Kosch befriended a priest who ran one of these schools: a priest who claimed he could talk to the dead."

"I doubt that went down well in Dublin!"

"Didn't go down well with von Kosch either. Their association lasted a few years, but then the priest went missing, and his body was finally recovered by the Garda Síochána, floating down the River Dodder."

"And how did you link Jim to all this?"

"The British Intelligence Corps folded in 1929, but I'd collected enough information to set up another organisation: MPRS. With more agents on board, it became easier to follow the von Kosch-O'Malley trail backwards from Dublin to Cairo to Tanganyika. I eventually located Jim in a mental hospital in Scotland. He was a broken man by then. But the British Army got him out of there, and it wasn't difficult to recruit him to MPRS, and find out exactly what had happened; but more to the point, what was *going* to happen. That's why we got him to start secretly corresponding with Myra Campbell. They'd been lovers at one time, and she'd never got over him."

I rolled my eyes, and shuddered. "Jim wrote love letters?" I could scarcely believe it.

Joe shrugged, and delving into his jacket pocket, he produced his wallet. He opened it, and withdrew a photo. "Rothesay, I believe," he said, holding it out to me.

I took a step forward, and grabbed it. It was of me and Jim. I was eating an ice-cream, and Jim was scowling. I remembered the day. A very unusual day, a couple of years ago, when Jim, Stephen and I had jumped on a ferry to the Isle of Bute. Stephen had taken the photo.

"Where did you find that?" I whispered.

"It was found in amongst Myra Campbell's effects."

I looked up abruptly, in the knowledge that that could only mean one thing. "She knew who I was," I gulped, remembering how she'd stared at me when we'd met.

"Your father made a big mistake sending that."

"You didn't know he'd sent it?"

"No – and lucky for you, she didn't fire you in."

And, indeed, she had not. I didn't want to think of what might have happened, if she had. I shuddered, and tried to concentrate on the facts. "So, let me recap," I continued, "we're looking at Tanganyika to Cairo to Dublin and back again to Cairo?"

"That about sums it up," agreed Joe.

"But why did von Kosch decide to leave Dublin, and go back to Egypt?"

"It became safer for him to go back. He had a new identity, and he had unfinished business. The trials with the children in Dublin had failed, he'd bumped off the priest, so now it was time to achieve what he wanted on a much grander scale."

"And why get involved with the Egyptian cinema?"

"It let him blend in. He was a wealthy man, so he could get involved in just about anything he liked: and he was always the showman. Unfortunately for him, he just didn't quite get that accent right."

Things were starting to fall into place. "So, he returns to Cairo. New identity. New job. And time to really get down to business by opening up the tomb again. Would that be right?"

"Yes. It also presented an opportunity for him to attack the British again, this time at Suez, with the backing of the Egyptians and maybe the Nazis. You have to remember that Nazism has been taking hold of Germany since 1933."

"So, if the Nazis took over from the British at Suez, that would really clear the way for a German invasion."

"And not just using the national army, remember, Bette."

I shivered. "The Dead Army," I whispered.

"Indeed. When Himmler got wind of the Dead Army theory, well, that was right up his street. But now we've reached the point where it's time to show them all what MPRS is actually made of."

"And how are you going to do that?"

"Well, when Heinrich von Kosch, aka Omar O'Malley, and his sidekicks, Mr and Mrs Campbell, began to work more closely with the Nazis, we decided to put in two of our best agents."

"Agents?"

"Peter and Deborah Bellingham."

I took a step back. "You have to be kidding me!"

"I know you've met them."

"You bet your sweet little ass I've met them!"

Joe then told me that it was MPRS that had actually built the International Hospital for Sick Children, back in 1935, but that information was classified.

"Well, that explains the ambulances: all right-hand drive," I said. "But it doesn't explain the jeep at the villa," I added.

"I'll get to that," responded Joe. He went on to explain how the Bellinghams had been sent in, and had spent the last few years passing on duff information to the Nazis. They'd also infiltrated Omar O'Malley's circle, and had been accepted as loyal supporters of the Third Reich.

"So, that's why the Nazis are interested in the hospital. They see it as an ideal location for recruitment purposes," Joe concluded.

I shuddered. "Yeah. Dead or alive?"

Joe looked away. "The Nazis are still looking for ways to trap the mind," he said, not answering my question.

I didn't know whether to laugh, or cry. "And how the hell do they think they're going to do that?"

"Not sure about that one," admitted Joe. "But what I *am* sure of, is that now they've gone that one step further."

I wasn't sure I wanted to hear this, but I let Joe carry on.

"We've just learned that Berlin has issued orders telling the hospital to stop curing the patients, and if dead resources are still insufficient, they're to kill some of them."

I stared at Joe in stony silence. "And you're letting this happen?"

"Hasn't happened yet."

"But the kids who've already died? What about their ashes? I saw urns! I saw Nazis!"

"Dr Bellingham is using the ashes of burned logs."

My mouth flew open. "What? You mean to say, the Nazis are worshiping tree trunks?"

I'd have laughed out loud, if the whole thing wasn't so damned serious, besides which, my head had started to hurt, which reminded me of the attack in the tomb.

"And who the fuck hit me on the head?"

Joe looked smug. "One of our agents from MPRS, and don't take offence: it was done to protect you. All done with loving kindness, my dear."

"Fuck that!" I shivered. "And what about that bastard Witherspoon? I take it *he* wasn't one of your agents?"

Joe looked amused. "Believe it or not, you actually did us a favour."

Joe explained that Dr Witherspoon was supposed to be working for MPRS, but it turned out he was a double agent, and was working for the Nazis. I remembered Peter Bellingham's conversation with Willie Campbell about the double agent coordinating the construction of the arms factory in the desert. I was in no doubt now he'd meant Witherspoon.

"The jeep you mentioned," continued Joe, "originally belonged to Witherspoon. It was supplied by MPRS for his use, but he gifted it to O'Malley as a token of good will, and a sign he was a good Nazi."

The whole thing was a conundrum, which brought me back to Bentley. "And Bentley?"

"Ah, Bentley," sighed Joe. "Very sad. A good medium, but I'm afraid he developed a Nazi affiliation. It was all totally unexpected. Your brother, Stephen, of course, knew."

"Yeah! Stephen! Tell me about him, too!"

Joe went on to explain he'd had my brother transferred to the Canal Zone, where he'd purportedly left the regular army with a heart murmur, and taken up acting. His mission was to infiltrate O'Malley's circle of associates, which is exactly what he'd done.

"So," I declared, "what you mean, in plain English, is Stephen *never* left the army?"

"Quite."

"And that's why you assigned me to write an article on Egypt's film industry?"

"Needed to get you in."

"Why?"

But Joe had other things to say first. "Remember your article?"

How could I forget? "You mean the article Jim tore up?"

"Ah, that was unfortunate. I probably should have checked it first."

"You think?"

"Yes, well, this is where von Kosch, aka Omar O'Malley, and Farida come in."

"I know! The article was about them and Stephen!" And then it clicked. "So, what you're actually saying is, it didn't matter what I wrote, did it?"

"No, it didn't," admitted Joe. "But how was I to know you'd stuck a stupid damned photograph in it?" He shook his head. "What is it about your family and bloody photographs?"

That I didn't expect. "Farida gave me it," I spluttered.

"It was a keepsake, not for bloody publication!"

I narrowed my eyes. "How do *you* know that, Joe?"

He ignored my question, but continued with his

explanation. "Jim recognised von Kosch," he said.

I paused to consider this. "So, he blamed *you* for getting me and Stephen involved?" I concluded.

"Jim always had a habit of blaming everyone, but himself."

"That's why he got wasted, and fell down the stairs."

"Jim was a victim of circumstances, and we'll never really know if his death was an accident, or if he killed himself."

It was clear this didn't really matter to Joe. But that didn't explain Farida.

"Didn't Jim wonder who Farida was?"

"He didn't recognise her," replied Joe, cryptically.

"And why would he?"

"Because she's your sister. Well, half-sister to be exact. Jim never actually got to see her, not even as a baby."

My mouth flew open. "Whadda, ya mean?"

"Remember the incident I mentioned? Well, Farida was the result of an affair between your father and another woman, and the reason why your father was kicked out the movement in 1919."

I was about to ask what other woman, when something far more serious occurred to me. "Joe, how could you?"

"How could I what?"

"You encouraged an incestuous relationship!"

"No, no, no." Joe's tone was calm. "Farida knew who von Kosch was. We'd already recruited her as an agent for MPRS. Easy enough when we told her that it was von Kosch-O'Malley, who'd actually shot and mutilated her mother."

"What?"

"Our girl, Farida, was one of the lucky ones. O'Malley could have put her in an industrial school in Dublin, and bumped her off, whilst carrying out his experiments, but he changed his mind. Decided to educate her, and put her to better use. No real bond, anyway. Boarding school can do that to a child."

"Joe!" I gasped. "Did you just say von Kosch shot and mutilated her mother?"

"Long story, Bette. Tell you another time."

"Really? So, what was going on in Stephen's apartment that day? The day I met Farida for the first time?"

"Ah, that was unfortunate. We were having a meeting when you unexpectedly popped up."

"A meeting?"

"We panicked. Weren't expecting you so soon, and we certainly didn't want to be seen together."

I smiled, wryly. "That would have fucked up your plans, which *were*, incidentally?"

"To discuss ways to distract Bentley. Nothing puts a man off his work better than a niggling annoyance," continued Joe.

"A niggling annoyance?" I repeated.

"You helped take Bentley's mind off what was really going on. Only, we couldn't exactly tell you that. Unfortunately, you arrived a day early, and when we heard you getting out the taxi, well, I only just managed to grab my glass of champers, and retire to the cabinet on the landing."

"You left the front door open, Joe."

"Bugger!"

I started to laugh. "You left the door open *and* you booked the wrong date!"

Joe coughed. "My secretary booked the wrong date."

But the question of incest still bothered me. "Does Stephen know Farida's our sister?"

"Of course he does! It was a setup."

Well, that was good news, but it still didn't answer one fundamental question. "Then where the fuck *is* she?"

Joe looked at his watch. "Probably in the middle of pouring herself a cup of tea. She's in my flat in Pimlico, awaiting further instructions."

"She's in London?"

"We managed to get her away before she was arrested by the SS. I have to say, she made a grand job of that bastard von Kosch," he said, chuckling.

Well, that certainly solved *that* mystery. "Does Stephen know she's alive?"

"Of course he does. She's a fellow agent."

My mind went back to Bentley. There were still things that didn't make any sense. "If Bentley was cavorting with the Nazis, why did you need me to distract him? Why such an elaborate plan? Why not just fucking shoot him?"

Joe frowned. "I agree it's been something of a protracted enquiry, but the fact the stupid bastard broke his arm didn't help. That's why we had to give you extended leave."

"Yeah, I remember."

"What Bentley was about to do with the Nazis,

would have been classed as a grave dereliction of duty. He was about to become a double agent, and embark on a route that would have violated every ethic known to the medical profession. He became a security risk."

"Still doesn't answer my question. Why not just shoot him as a spy?"

"Ah, that's where it gets complicated. We couldn't do that because of his family. You see, the Ford-Jenkins family are a very rich Australian family. They own businesses all over the world, and send MPRS funds on a regular basis. So, you'll appreciate that anything we do to Bentley, affects our resources, which is especially important, now we've declared war on Nazi Germany."

"So, how did he break his arm?"

"Fell off a bloody horse in the desert!"

I shook my head. "Why not just leave him there to die?"

"Would have done, only he was found by soldiers from the British Army out on a training exercise."

The irony made me laugh. "So, whilst trying to eliminate him, you had to put him back together first. Didn't you find that a bit stupid?"

"We can't afford to take risks. Like I said, MPRS can't find itself under-resourced. If Bentley died a hero in crossfire, whilst destroying an evil operation, such as the Dead Army, his father, Sir Samuel Ford-Jenkins, would be in a position to show pride, and continue to finance our operations. Government here might even confer a posthumous knighthood for services rendered."

"So, what you're saying is, Bentley was a traitor, and you didn't want his family to lose face, because if they did, you wouldn't get any money?"

"That just about sums it up."

I was growing angrier by the minute. "So, what if I tell Sir Samuel what really happened?"

Unfortunately, Joe, as usual, was already one step ahead of me. "You forget, he's the one that supplies the money. He's, therefore, of great value in the fight against the Nazis. If you tell him, you may tip the balance. Tip the balance, and you promote Nazism. The choice is yours."

I stared at Joe. How dare he accuse me of trying to support the Nazis! I was mad, not just because of the position he'd put me in, but because something else had just occurred to me.

"If Bentley was so goddam dangerous, thank you very much for letting me work with him! Thank you very much for considering *my* welfare!"

"My pleasure!" replied Joe. "And don't take offence. I'm really not that bad. However, I'm afraid your feelings weren't relevant to the mission. Besides which, you didn't make too many mistakes."

Mistakes? Mistakes? As far as I was concerned, it was Bentley who'd made the one big fundamental mistake. The gifted psychic had achieved the impossible. He'd failed to foresee his own demise!

I took one more look at Joe.

He'd exploited me.

He'd cheated me.

I was upset.

I wanted to punch him, but knew that would land

me in the slammer.

I looked down at my hands, pleased that the fuckers weren't twitching. I turned back to Joe. Best to leave before I got physical.

57

The Spirit World

Bentley

Bastards! thought Bentley, as he relived the impact of the bullet, which had got him right between the goddam eyes.

Well, someone did a good job there. His physical body was well and truly defunct. As for his spirit body, that was still in a state of shock. His energy was soaring high, then plummeting with uncontrolled frequency, refusing to settle. He still couldn't believe he was dead, even though he really did know the score.

But why?

When he'd come to, as a spirit, that was, he'd found he no longer inhabited his physical body. His energy was no longer tied within the confines of flesh and bones, so he'd become as light as a physical feather, and although his human eyes were gone, he was still able to discern that someone in the physical world was putting his deceased physical body into a body bag.

So, this was it.

The connection between his spirit body and physical body was well and truly severed, one going one way, the other going another. It was his time. No footering around with a spot of astral travel. This time he really wouldn't be going back to that physical body.

And that was a bit of a bummer.

He hadn't finished the job.

Darling! projected a thought behind him. Bentley felt an intense swoosh, as the thought lunged towards him with the same intensity as the bullet that had just killed his physical body. When the oppressive presence of a familiar energy began to blend with his own energy, he realised what was going on. *Bentley, darling*, repeated the smothering spirit, *it's Mother!*

What the hell? It *was* Hell. All that talk about states of mind, and no actual places, well he begged to differ. This *was* Hell, and he was right *inside* it!

Sweetheart, I can read your thoughts. And it is a state of mind. You're home again. You're back in the world of spirits!

Bentley's energy became rigid, as he tried to remember the sequence of events. He recalled his spirit body being hauled towards a light, before stopping. All very precipitous, and all very different. He felt the force of his mother's vibration, and shivered. Mother never changed. Still the same old controlling energy, always recognisable. Bentley was consumed with emotion.

You sent me to jail!

His mother's spirit began to dissipate a little, and the impact reduced. She remained close, but no longer blended.

Now, that was a long time ago.

I was fifteen years old!

It was a learning curve.

Fifteen years old!

Now, let's not start being naughty about it.

Bentley felt his energy deflate. *State of mind,* he thought. *Happy thoughts! Happy thoughts! She might even go away!*

No darling, I won't go away! There's too much to do.

Hey, pal! projected another thought. It was coming from the opposite direction.

Bentley's spirit quivered, as he sensed a new and very different vibration. He relaxed, and absorbed the impact of a fast-travelling wave of highly-evolved intelligence, as it merged with his own.

Charlie MacTaggart! cried Bentley. *You bloody science freak!*

You freaking madman! returned Charlie, *I'd give you a hug, only I don't have any arms. Welcome back.*

Bentley's mind began to reflect. It was all coming back, not what had just happened, but what it was all about.

I always was a daft bastard! Always chose the worst missions.

All for the betterment of humanity and the soul,

though, interjected Charlie. *And don't forget, the harder the mission, the better you evolve, and I have to say, you've got guts!*

Not anymore, drawled Bentley, *not any more.*

Well, maybe not physically, agreed Charlie, *but in a manner of speaking.*

Suppose so, agreed Bentley, sensing the sudden closeness of his mother, as she began to tweak his energy. He projected himself further away from her, and revolved his mind back to Charlie.

So, anyway, what happened to that gorgeous little filly, Jessie? You know, your soul mate? What's she doing, these days?

Hey! shuddered Charlie's energy. *Less of the filly. She happens to be my grieving widow.*

Bentley was contrite. *Sorry mate. No harm meant.*

Charlie ballooned his energy. *Well, in that case, no offence taken. At the moment she's a WPC, out there on the earth.*

And does she have any recollection of the Spirit World?

None at all. Just blundering her way along her chosen path.

Bentley's energy dipped slightly. *I take it I'm back in the Healing Centre, getting rid of all those unwanted little particles you're always on about. Atomic and molecular reconstructions. Shedding and attracting. The Law of Conservation of Energy and all that.*

You mean Quantum Physics? laughed Charlie. *Very important. Something we never seem to get across. Energy cannot be created or destroyed, it can only change form, and that's exactly why you're still with us.* He paused. *I'm actually working on a project, but I'll get to that. Too many other things to discuss, first.*

Like modifications to my soul, suggested Bentley, *and changing my molecular structure?*

Rejuvenation, corrected Charlie, moving aside as another energy approached.

Bentley didn't move. He began to absorb the fluttering force of attractive vivacity. It was Jacqueline Brown. She stopped just outside his energy.

Nurse Brown, sighed Bentley.

How lovely to sense you again, she projected. *And can I just say, what a lot of particles you still have to shed, you terrible womaniser!* Jacqueline giggled. *I'm still getting treatment here. I'm not in the best of states, you know, a bullet through the head, and all that.*

Tell me about it! sighed Bentley, expanding his energy in an attempt to blend with hers.

Jacqueline moved back a little. *You do know, someone conned us, darling?*

Who?

If I knew that, I'd tell you!

Just don't tell me it was part of the mission.

Afraid it was, but we did agree.

Bentley wasn't surprised. *I did say I was a daft bastard.*

Yes, agreed Jacqueline, *and long before we blended with our physical bodies*.

Bentley felt his energy dip again. It seemed he had a long way to go. *So, what exactly happened?*

Well, continued Jacqueline*, we all agreed, as part of the mission, that we would tackle very difficult jobs.*

Mission? Mission? projected a sudden and very angry thought. It flew at top speed through the universal energy, still attached to an even angrier spirit. *I'll give you mission!* it bellowed, impacting first with Jacqueline, then Bentley.

Whoa! projected Bentley, sensing the throbbing pain of Myra Campbell's broken spirit.

Myra's energy undulated, bouncing in and out his own, reminding him that the poor woman's life in the physical world had been shit. But suicide? That was a memory that would remain with her for a very long time.

Myra, my girl, he soothed, *you have to calm down a bit.*

Lamb to the slaughter, I was!

No, interjected Charlie. *Your choice, and you still haven't learned.*

That bastard, Willie, nearly killed me!

Only, you got in first, reasoned Charlie.

Bentley sensed sudden panic in Myra's vibration.

Is he here? Is he dead? she demanded.

No, confirmed Charlie. *Willie Campbell is still languishing in jail, but you'd better get your act together, girl, because very soon, he'll be facing the gallows, and then he will be dead!*

I don't want him near me! whimpered Myra.

I understand, Myra, resumed Charlie, *but it was your choice. It was also Willie's choice.*

Choice? quivered Myra.

Well, I know he took quite a lot of wrong turns, granted Charlie.

Quite a lot? He took more wrong turns than a Glasgow cabbie!

I agree he went overboard, continued Charlie, *but that's something he'll have to deal with when he gets here.*

As for that bastard von Kosch, spat Myra, *well, I don't want either of them near me! Not Willie, not von Kosch, or Omar bloody O'Malley, whatever he wants to call himself!*

Don't worry, Charlie reassured her. *There's a special unit for them, so they'll be segregated for a long, long time. It functions on a totally different vibration. Shouldn't affect you lot.*

Charlie turned to Bentley. *You may have to get involved with that once you're back to health. Once a healer, always a healer. No getting away from it.*

Bentley felt himself grimace. *What did I say? Always was a daft bastard!*

At least you're working on it, smiled Charlie. *You're beginning to get the hang of it.*

It's a question of free will, projected a different and very powerful vibration.

Bentley hadn't noticed the arrival of the new spirit, but soon realised who it was. *Jim Kipper*, Bentley greeted him. *Pleased to meet you, dare I say, in the metaphorical flesh.*

Almost at once another more delicate energy joined them. It was Marisol: another *very* recognisable energy.

Bentley felt flustered. As he fought for self-control, he recalled the dreams, and the very intimate encounter between himself and Marisol that had resulted in the conception of a child.

Sorry, mate, Bentley finally managed.

Apology accepted, responded Jim, *but it wasn't actually your fault. The affair wasn't with you, just seemed that way.*

Bentley sensed Marisol's embarrassment, and watched her sidle into Jim's energy.

So, here we are again, declared Charlie. *One big happy group, ready to tackle what's ahead.*

And what's that? asked Bentley.

My new project for starters. It's something I've been working on, and the reason why you, Bentley, had all those dreams.

Bentley wasn't pleased. *So, what you're really saying is I've been nothing but an experiment?*

Me too! interjected Jacqueline, drawing her energy closer to Bentley's. *I only knew part of what was going on. They kept me in the dark as well.*

Yeah, about that, Charlie, said Bentley. *Do you happen to know why I was conned?*

Both of us, Bentley. Don't forget it was both of us! shimmered Jacqueline's vibration. *You more than me though.*

Suddenly something clicked. Bentley relaxed his energy, and drew away from Jacqueline. *You were involved too!* he accused. *You were the agent writing the report, only it wasn't about the Bellinghams, it was about me. You're MPRS!"*

You're not being fair, Bentley, admonished Charlie. *Jacqueline was following orders. She's realised her mistake, and is working on her guilty conscience.*

Joe told me you were working for the Nazis, whimpered Jacqueline. *The whole of MPRS thought you were working for the Nazis.*

That's a load of crock for starters, gasped Bentley.

Well, crock or not, Joe still believes it! retorted Jacqueline.

And that's why we need to get down to work, asserted Charlie.

I'm offended! bemoaned Bentley. *Offended! So, who else is MPRS?*

Charlie puffed out his energy. *Work first! Then we can cast recriminations. That is, if we still want to.*

Fine! spluttered Bentley.

Charlie relaxed. *To further things along, we're going to take another look at mental mediumship using dreams.*

Been there, done it! affirmed Bentley.

Yes, agreed Charlie, *and in your case, you became the communicating spirit.*

Yeah. Jim Kipper, murmured Bentley. *Jim? Where are you?*

Jim, who had been hovering in the background, allowed their energies to connect. *I'm here,* he affirmed.

And you're MPRS, too?

Afraid so.

Yes, yes, yes! intervened Charlie. *Work! Let's put things right. It's all part of the healing process. Now, back to dreams.*

So, what's the plan? asked Bentley. *I take it someone's going to become me?*

Before we get to that, let's just go over one or two points. If you remember, we're all here on our own personal path, and that, I might add, is a path not only of choice, but of learning. Charlie paused. *And there are still things you have to learn, Bentley.*

This wasn't sounding good. *Like what?*

You see, you've never really learned the skills of tolerance, or, indeed, the simple art of polite conversation.

What the hell does that mean?

Exactly what I've just said, sighed Charlie.

Listen mate! Bentley stopped short. Something else had just clicked. *Not Bette! Please, not Bette! Can't a man just die in peace?*

You're not a man, anymore, Bentley! stressed Charlie. *You're a spirit, and all we're asking of you, is to do your job, and complete the mission. The earth world is relying on it.*

But Bette? Isn't there anyone else?

Then just as Bentley thought his energy couldn't dip any further, Jim Kipper stepped in.

You do realise you're talking about my daughter? said Jim.

Bentley's energy took another dive. *Fuck me gently!*

You don't have the tools, sweetie, whispered Jacqueline, sidling nearer to him. *Not anymore.*

But Bentley wasn't listening. He'd just remembered the murder of Marisol. *Are you telling me that Bette's the child taken from the womb?*

No, no, no! Jim corrected him. *That was later.*

Bentley was confused. *You have other children?*

Two girls and a boy.

Bentley glanced at Marisol. *You?*

Only one of them is mine, she clarified. *They don't all belong to me.*

You know my son, said Jim. *Stephen Milligan. He's also an agent with MPRS.*

Bentley's energy began to quiver. He was in a state of shock. *Stephen is Bette's brother?* Bentley tried to calm himself. *Something else you didn't tell me, Joe.*

Come on, let's focus! ordered Charlie. *At the moment, Bette believes that you, Bentley, are a traitor.*

Things were going from bad to worse. *So, you want her to become me, like I became Jim?*

No, I think that would be virtually impossible, acknowledged Charlie. *Your assignment is to get into her mind, and restructure her thoughts.*

Bentley considered this. *So, what you're really looking for is a bloody miracle.*

You're there to make her understand the truth. When she's asleep and dreaming, that's when you infiltrate. You have to lay the seed of doubt, and guide her on. You have to make her understand that Joe is wrong. You have to make her realise that there are real traitors out there.

I repeat: fuck me gently!

We're dealing with dangerous people, doing dangerous things. Things that, if we're not careful, will destroy the physical world and all its inhabitants.

So, no pressure, muttered Bentley. *And what am I expected to do?*

You link with her mind when she sleeps. Blend with her. Become one with her. Guide her. Help her make the best decisions. Help her make a difference. Help her conquer those Nazi bastards.

Bentley cringed. *And when am I supposed to start?*

Right now, said Charlie. *She's in a bad frame of mind. Joe has just told her you're working for the Nazis. She's downed four double gins, and is lying comatose in a room at Shepheard's. It's an excellent opportunity!*

Bentley begged to differ. As far as he was concerned, the situation had just got worse. *Can't wait,* he mumbled.

Come on, Bentley! Let's take her back to when you were shot. Let's rejuvenate the circumstances. Tell it as it should be. Wire in there, boy! Wire in! Do it for Britain!

58

Two Worlds Combined

Bentley

As Bentley's mind delved further into the depths of Bette's drunken torpor, he hoped her brain cells wouldn't have a negative impact on the quality of his own ethereal constitution. His thoughts travelled deeper and deeper, in waves of subliminal energy, until slowing down, they finally connected with Bette's very receptive mind.

Good, muttered Charlie, who'd followed in close behind. *That's a start. Booze has made her very open to Spirit.*

So open, that Bentley was able to project an image right into the centre of Bette's third eye. For all intents and purposes, he'd created a screen for Bette's very own movie theatre of past events, not even in your typical old black and white, but in super movie Technicolor.

Nothing's moving, complained Bentley, as he zoomed in on the picture on the screen. It was a close-up of a face: his face, directly after the bullet had blasted him between the eyes. *And I'm not sure I like what's on the screen!*

Give it a minute, said Charlie. *We have to turn it into a retrospective movie. You need to fire it up!*

Bentley concentrated hard, and as he projected an intense wave of thought energy, the image began to move. *Got it,* he gasped.

Bentley watched, in horror, as his deceased physical body tumbled across Bette's prostrate form.

"Help! Help!" she wheezed, her nose fixed to the ground.

Then a boot hit Bentley's physical body. He anticipated pain, but there was none. He was already dead. The owner of the boot came into focus. It was a soldier: the one with the balaclava, who had climbed in the window.

Bastard! muttered Bentley, as he watched the soldier haul Bette over his shoulder. *Hey, careful, mate! She's the one destined to save the world, and you're throwing her around like a piece of garbage! And watch her glasses!*

Too late. They'd already fallen off. A crunch indicated they were well and truly broken. The soldier walked on, Bette's head bouncing against his back, until she was sick.

There, you've made her sick now! Give him the finger, Bette! Give him the goddam finger! Bette surprisingly complied.

Time then moved on.

Where are we now, Charlie? gasped Bentley, as he fought to maintain the link. It wasn't easy. *Damn it!* he spat. He'd just lost the picture again. After a moment, it returned.

We're linked to the deepest part of Bette's mind, responded Charlie. *Now, careful, we might have to fast-forward, or go back at some parts. Emotions are random, and can have devastating consequences. You have to remember, we're dealing with a human being, here.*

And that was the problem. Bentley knew he had to project maximum energy, but it didn't help that Bette's mind was fluttering all over the place.

I actually meant, where is she? Where is Bette? And where am I?

You're both at the BMH in Alexandria, replied Charlie. *You've been put in a body bag, and she's been taken to a ward on a stretcher.*

Bentley shivered. The movie had just jumped to the hospital mortuary. *They're shoving me into a fridge, Charlie!*

They're putting your physical body into a fridge. It's not attached to you anymore, so it doesn't matter. It's redundant to requirements. Your physical body is in the hospital mortuary, but you, the essential you, are here with me, delving into Bette's very complicated mind.

Like a lump of meat.

That's because your physical body is a lump of meat. Now, get on with the job. Control the movie!

Bentley concentrated harder. The screen jumped back to Bette. It was funny. Bentley no longer had his physical eyes, but by lowering the vibration of his energy, he was able to meld with Bette's physical eyes, and see like he used to, as a human being.

Bette lay very still in a hospital bed, until suddenly, with no warning, she sat up. "Ya fucking dodos!" she yelled.

A shock wave of energy flew into Bentley's consciousness. *Crickey, Bette! Cool it. Cool it.*

"Get me out this goddam hospital bed!"

You need to calm her down, said Charlie.

The screen had begun to quiver. Bentley almost lost the link, but fought back. There, the connection was reestablished. An image, albeit a still, appeared.

Boy, this was hard. When he'd begun his role as minder for Bette, he hadn't for one minute dreamed that that would continue into the hereafter.

Come on, gasped Bentley. *Let's get this show on the road!* He projected his thoughts at full capacity, and sighed with relief when the movie kicked back into motion. They were back in business.

"We're dealing with crooks!" hollered Bette.

Well, you got that right in one, thought Bentley.

"Crooks!" Bette's voice vibrated loudly within the confines of Bentley's consciousness. "The world is in a state of turmoil, and all you can do is lock me up in a hospital ward, out of the way!"

Can't say I blame them, though, reasoned Bentley.

The wireless was on, and Neville Chamberlain was telling the world that Britain was declaring war on Nazi Germany.

"You're all crooks! You're liars and cheats! And I want out!"

She's not making this very easy, began Bentley.

Focus, said Charlie. *Now, slowly, smoothly, tap in as if you're stroking the lobes of her human brain, then dissipate round her mind, touching every part, down to her toes.*

Bentley complied. *The things I have to do for Britain,* he thought.

Just at that moment, a doctor appeared, and began to examine Bette's face. "You know, my dear," he said, "psychological reactions can very often result from trauma."

"Fuck off!" hissed Bette.

Bentley's energy juddered, as Bette's truculent tone translated into an annoyingly sharp sound wave, that connected abruptly with his own controlled mind.

Can I suggest we fast-forward here? he said.

Keep your eye on the ball, said Charlie.

"We'll be arranging for you to go back to Scotland in a couple of days," resumed the doctor.

"Fuck that!" returned Bette.

They want her out the way, thought Bentley. He sensed that something was badly wrong. *Someone wants you out the way, girl! But we're not going to let that happen, are we?*

"Now, my dear, we're only trying to help," continued the doctor. "So, let's begin by checking out the old ticker."

"See that stethoscope round your neck," said Bette. "Would you like me to tell you what you can do with it?"

Attagirl, Bette! cried Bentley. *You tell him. You get*

out of there now! They've violated your integrity! You need answers! Get your clothes, discharge yourself, and get your ass back to Cairo!

As the train pulled into the station in Kamal Pasha Street, Bentley focussed harder.

They've been playing you, Bette! Playing you! Open your mind, and yes, you are undergoing a transcendental experience of the most subliminal kind! So, make the most of it!

"Something stinks!" hissed Bette.

Of course, something stinks! They all lied to you! But not just you. They lied to Joe, and look where that got us? We need to find out what's going on!

The movie screen jumped forward. Bette had stopped at an abandoned old pedal bike.

Don't take the bike! cried Bentley.

Waste of time. Bette bumped along, trying to cycle through the traffic in a straight line. She veered towards Shepheard's Hotel, her head down like a charging unicorn.

Bentley sensed a moment's compassion. He knew he hadn't been the best of partners to work with, but he had to get through to her. Bette continued to pedal like a lunatic, jutting out her chin with defiance, until the bike hit a stone. She flew off, landing prostrate on the ground.

I told you not to take the bike!

Bette got to her feet, and kicked it.

The movie fast-forwarded again. Now they were at Shepheard's Hotel. Bette was in the lobby.

Keep going, girl. I'm right behind you, shouted Bentley.

He watched as she took the stairs to the fourth floor, then marched into room 490.

I know I locked that door.

Concentrate, Bentley, ordered Charlie.

They were now in Bentley's room, but it wasn't making sense. Then someone coughed. It was Joe. He was seated in a corner, and seemed surprised to see Bette.

What the hell's Joe doing in my room?

Shut up and focus, returned Charlie.

Bette took a step nearer Joe. "So, who killed Bentley?" she demanded.

Yeah, who killed me? That's something I'd really like to know?

"And why was I detailed to investigate my brother?" she added.

Stephen? mused Bentley. *You never told me that, Joe.*

Joe can't hear you, Charlie reminded Bentley.

The movie suddenly fast-forwarded. *Whoa!* cried Bentley, *let's not miss anything!*

It stopped. Joe was speaking. "We have two issues at hand here," he said. "The Dead Army and Bentley Ford-Jenkins."

What? Bentley was bemused. *Me? Why me?*

Concentrate, said Charlie.

Joe smiled as he spoke to Bette. "*Amber St Claire*, was created by MPRS, as a device to achieve another goal, which went into action when the Nazis started to become a threat. We also put in two of our best agents: Peter and Deborah Bellingham."

Bentley couldn't believe what he was hearing. *Why didn't you tell me that, Joe? Why didn't you tell me?*

"The Nazis are particularly interested in the mind," continued Joe. "They're trying to find ways to trap consciousness."

Bentley turned to Charlie. *And you know as well as I do that that's impossible. You can't put consciousness into a bloody box!*

I think we'll fast-forward here, said Charlie.

Bentley didn't argue. He watched the screen move forward and stop at a very worried-looking Bette.

"So, where does Bentley fit into all of this?" she asked.

Yeah, what about me? What about me, Joe? What else didn't you tell me?

"Ah, Bentley," sighed Joe. "Very sad. He was actually a very good medium, but I'm afraid he developed a Nazi affiliation."

Crock of shit! Tell her, Charlie!

Tell her, yourself, Bentley. You're the one in charge.

The movie continued to run through previous events. It was elucidating, particularly when it started to highlight true identities, and explain what certain individuals were really up to.

So, let me get this right, Charlie. Stephen, who's Bette's brother, was investigating me?

Afraid so, old chap, replied Charlie.

Bette was sent in to distract me?

Charlie seemed embarrassed. *Yup.*

And Omar O'Malley was really Baron Heinrich von Kosch?

Right again, confirmed Charlie.

And 'pièce de bloody résistance': Farida O'Malley, whom I never actually met, isn't O'Malley's real daughter, she's Jim's daughter, and therefore the half-sister of Bette and Stephen. She's also an agent with MPRS, and was investigating me, and now she's hiding in London to stop the Nazis arresting her. What's going on, Charlie?

It is rather a lot of information to absorb in one go, responded Charlie. *Maybe we should fast-forward for a bit?*

Hell no! cried Bentley. *Not when it's getting this interesting!*

Bentley focussed harder, and his mind zoomed back on to the screen, where Bette and Joe were talking about him.

"You know, Joe," said Bette, "there are still things I don't really understand. Why did you need me to distract Bentley? Why such an elaborate plan for him? Why not just shoot him?"

Oh yeah, Bette. Just shoot me! Hey wait a minute: someone did shoot me!

"I agree it's been something of a protracted enquiry," said Joe, "but the fact the stupid bastard broke his arm didn't help."

Stupid bastard? Did you hear that, Charlie? No wait a minute, I am a stupid bastard. Fell into the net, hook, line and sinker!

"That's why you got extended leave, Bette,"

continued Joe. "What Bentley was about to do with the Nazis, would have been classed as a grave dereliction of duty."

Bentley felt his emotions run even higher. *I wasn't going to do anything with the Nazis!*

"Bentley was about to become a double agent, Bette."

You lying piece of crap! sneered Bentley.

"He was a security risk," said Joe.

Bentley's vibrational energy reached explosion point. *Security risk, my arse!*

"But that couldn't be made known to his family," continued Joe.

You bet your bottom dollar you couldn't have said that! My father would have had you kicked out the army. Discharged for bloody stupidity!

"Why not?" asked Bette.

"Very simple," replied Joe. "They're rich, and Bentley's father sends MPRS funds on a regular basis."

You bastard!

"So, you'll appreciate that anything we do to Bentley, affects our resources. Especially important, now we've declared war on Nazi Germany."

Bentley was about to hit orbit.

Don't listen to him, Bette.

Concentrate! ordered Charlie. *You need to keep that vibration lowered to maintain contact! Remember, we're dealing with a human being!*

Bentley counted to five, then gently lowered his vibration. He *had* nearly lost the link, and this certainly wasn't the time to do that.

He zoomed in again, and found that Joe's face was still on the screen, his voice booming out explanations.

"If Bentley died a hero in crossfire, whilst destroying an evil operation, such as the Dead Army, his family would be in a position to show pride, and continue to finance our operations."

You had it so well planned, Joe.

"British Government might well confer a posthumous knighthood for services rendered."

Well, you know where they can stuff that!

"And what if I tell Sir Samuel what really happened?" said Bette.

You do that, Bette! Just go ahead and do it! Tell the old man!

"You forget," said Joe. "He's the one that supplies the money. He's, therefore, of great value in the fight against the Nazis. If you tell him, you may tip the balance. Tip the balance, and you promote Nazism. The choice is yours."

I've seen enough! cried Bentley. Bette's anger was shaking his consciousness. He tried to sever the connection, but he couldn't.

"You exploited me, Joe," said Bette.

He played us both! shouted Bentley, his own emotions taking over.

"You know, Joe," said Bette, her voice remarkably calm. "I'm just going to leave. I've got a lot to think about, and I'm going to leave right now, because I know if I don't, I'm going to get physical!"

But Bentley wasn't finished. *Stiffen him, Bette! Stiffen him!*

Bentley! Charlie's voice was sharp.
OK. Good decision, Bette. Good decision.

59

Shepheard's Hotel, Cairo

Bette

Should have stopped after the third gin. Twelve hours sleep, and nothing to show for it, except a mindful of dreams, which I couldn't remember properly, and a very sore head.

Never again!

It was late morning, and I was sitting on the veranda at the front of Shepheard's sipping strong coffee, feeling very sorry for myself.

"This is for you," said a male voice, which was clear and gentle with an unmistakable Scottish lilt.

I looked up and saw Stephen. "Scottie's back," he smiled.

"Thank fuck for that," I mumbled.

Stephen was in British military uniform. In his left hand was an attaché case, in his right was a necklace. Not just any necklace, but Farida's necklace, minus the swastika. "She wants you to have it. Her way of saying sorry."

"Yeah! Yeah! Yeah! All in the name of national security," I responded, taking it from him.

"She feels bad," said Stephen, pulling out a chair and sitting down. He placed the attaché case at his feet.

I forced a smile. "Good. That must mean she has a conscience. Not too many of those floating around."

Stephen shrugged. "You could be right."

"Anyway, what happened to the Jerry badge?"

"The swastika?"

"Yeah, that thing that was supposed to have been found during an excavation."

"Not strictly true," admitted Stephen.

"So where is it now?"

"Let's just say, if they ever exhume the body of Heinrich von Kosch, or, Omar O'Malley, as you knew him, someone will find it lodged in a place where the sun doesn't tend to shine."

"Farida did that?"

"He murdered her mother."

"And guess what? It seems I murdered our father!"

Stephen winced. "The photo? Don't take it to heart, Bette. Farida feels bad about that too. She really did mean it as a keepsake, and certainly not for our father's eyes."

"Well, tell her to be a bit more specific in future."

"I think the old man was ready to go, anyway."

"That's no excuse, and you know it!"

"Possibly." A waiter appeared. "Double whisky my

good man," said Stephen. He turned to me. "Another coffee?"

I nodded. "You know something, Stephen, I think we have to be very careful here."

"What do you mean?"

"Well, there are things in my head, things that don't add up."

Stephen grinned. "And that's new?"

"Shut up! It's important."

"What things?"

"I don't know, but I woke up this morning with one hell of a muddled head. You see, Joe told me about the real mission, you know, Bentley and all that."

"Very sad, but necessary."

"Really? Was it really?"

Stephen's face became grim. "He would have passed on secrets to the Nazis."

"You think so?"

"Yes, Bette, I do."

"Well, I don't. I don't think it was Bentley that was the traitor. I think someone played him."

Stephen was about to speak, but the waiter returned with the whisky and coffee. "Surely you don't mean Joe?" he said when the waiter left. He took a gulp of whisky.

I stirred sugar into my coffee. "No. I think Joe's been conned as well."

Stephen took another gulp. "Then who?"

I paused, and took a sip of coffee. "You know Stephen, I really don't know, but I'd like to know."

"Then you'll have one hell of a time trying to find

out."

I pursed my lips. "Yes, I will."

Stephen leaned forward. "You seriously think Bentley was innocent?"

"Yes, I do."

"Then you'd better tell Joe."

I scratched my head. "Like that would go down well. No. Leave it between the two of us for the moment."

"OK. By the way," said Stephen, picking up his attaché case and opening it. "I nearly forgot. This is for you. A lost friend."

My eyes lit up. "Ginny-Hooker? Where did you find her?" I asked, taking the doll from him.

"It's a 'she', is it?"

"Yup."

"She just turned up."

"Like a bad penny?"

"Like a bad penny," agreed Stephen, swallowing the final dregs of his drink. "Want to go back to the villa? MPRS have requisitioned it, so it's there any time we need it."

"Yeah, the villa," I said. "Wonder what they'll decide to do with it?" I finished my coffee.

"By the way," said Stephen, "we have transport."

I followed his gaze to an automobile: Farida's V8, which was parked across the street. "Does it still actually go?"

"Like the wind, so I'll drive."

We crossed Kamal Pasha Street, and as we walked, loud barking blasted from within the vehicle. Pressed against one of the windows, were two muzzles. The Doberman and the mongrel. Their eyes glowed, and they howled like a couple of out-of-tune guitars.

Great! I thought. *We've just inherited two monsters from Hell.*

"I think they like you," said Stephen.

The dogs continued to bark in unison, their teeth shining like white ceramic tiles. They looked hungry, and I guessed if we didn't feed them soon, we might be dealing with a pair of hungry crocodiles.

"What's going to happen to the world, Stephen?"

"There's going to be a fight for control," he replied.

"But why do the Nazis want so much control?"

Stephen shrugged. "All we know is they've created their own set of rules, and given their own interpretation of what's right. They've rescinded human values, and flouted everything dear to normal civilisation. And it's very unfortunate that it's taken until now for other countries to actually try and stop them."

"And what about us?" I asked. "What's going to happen to us?"

"We're going to have to face a horrible war, Bette. Horrible. There'll be millions of deaths, and that's a conservative guess."

I shivered. "Not good then?"

Stephen looked grim. "Time to go," he said. He opened the front passenger door, and I climbed in.

No, it wasn't good. What's more, something else had just occurred to me. The dogs might be safe, but what about the budgie and the goldfish back in

Glasgow? There would be food shortages in Britain, so I had to rescue them, before someone cooked them, and served them up with fries for dinner.

But how the hell would I do *that*?

Then there was Bentley.

I *had* to prove his innocence, but how the hell would I do *that*?

And then a more pressing consideration.

How the fuck was Stephen going to get the automobile up the Muqattam Hills?

60

International Hospital for Sick Children

Deborah Bellingham

Deborah Bellingham had many facets to her personality. She was radical, she was creative, but best of all, she was not afraid to take a chance.

She admired her face in the bedroom mirror. Her expression manifested disinterest, but her gut said otherwise. In her left hand was a ring. She held it up to the light, and examined the sapphire, her face now sullen, as she imagined her husband's eyes looking tenderly into those of Jacqueline Brown's.

Deborah's dog sat obediently by her side, and rested its head on her lap. She teased its fur and began to review her life.

Deborah's mind had been moving into the realms of fantasy for some time now, and the more she achieved, the more she wanted. She'd met adversity in every shape and form, and each time, had dealt with it in her own inimitable way. It was as if she were a practitioner of magic, but most important of all, her profession had given her a special licence to kill.

She held the ring back up to the light, and examined the initials on the shank: PB and JB. She felt herself flush. She stamped her foot and kicked the dog, causing it to whimper and run out of the room. Her husband had never had any true regard for her feelings. It was all just pretence. He'd got engaged to another woman, whilst still married to her. He'd even got the woman pregnant.

Deborah was consumed with jealousy. How she'd hated Jacqueline Brown. But then Deborah had finally managed to get the upper hand.

Jacqueline Brown had been an easy target, and eliminating her had been a delight. No one had suspected Deborah's actions, not even Joe Bannerman. Andrew Witherspoon had got the blame for that one. Extremely convenient, since he'd been blown to pieces, and couldn't defend himself. Furthermore, although his identity as a Nazi agent, had been revealed, his death meant he could never disclose hers.

MPRS had taught her to shoot, and she'd become an excellent sniper, which was of particular use, now that she'd turned and become a double agent. She knew she was smarter than Witherspoon. No one would discover her Nazi association, least of all her unfaithful husband.

Her mind shifted to Captain Bentley Ford-Jenkins. Like her, he'd been trained as a doctor and a soldier.

They hadn't known one another, although she'd seen him eyeing her up in the Long Bar at Shepheard's. Now, that had amused her. It had also confirmed a fact: Bentley was like putty in the hands of a beautiful woman. And she, Deborah, was that beautiful woman.

So, back to the plan.

The Nazis were intent on finding ways to control the mind after death, but their methods were primitive. Then there were the dark energies out there, drifting in the spheres of the Spirit World. These energies had to be managed and controlled. But it was all so haphazard. What was needed were proper leaders, both here and in the Spirit World.

Deborah had decided a long time ago that it was her duty to reign over planet Earth. But she needed a consort. A proper consort to rule from the Spirit World. When she'd been transferred to MPRS, her choice had become clear: Captain Bentley Ford-Jenkins.

She savoured the thought of slipping into his mind. She would do what she was best at, and seduce him into submission. However, for that to be, Bentley in the physical state, had had to go.

Deborah smiled. It had been so easy. Men were always the same. They succumbed to the wiles of women. Joe Bannerman was another fool. She'd told him she had used the ashes of burned logs, but of course she hadn't. She'd quite happily handed over the ashes of dead children, just to see what would happen.

The funny thing was, everything had fallen neatly

into place. She'd built up a file of disinformation on Bentley. All lies, but feasible lies. Lies that Joe had believed, because *she* was his greatest soldier. Joe had even selected her to shoot Bentley, and that was exactly what she'd done. She'd hit him straight between the eyes.

Exciting times lay ahead.

Deborah was thankful for the short sightedness of MPRS, and rejoiced in the fact their tactics were about to backfire. She would soon learn how to *really* control the mind. She would find ways to manipulate it. She would determine how to control Bentley Ford-Jenkins, and teach him how to overturn the laws of nature and physics, and open the portal to start again.

By doing this, she could admit her own retinue of neophytes, crones, dissidents and untouchables, and by counting on their unstinting support and unswerving loyalty, she could build her own special team, and create new beginnings for a functional Dead Army.

61

Central Police Office, Glasgow

DI MacLeod

MacLeod almost jumped out of his seat. "Sweet Jesus!" he gasped, under his breath, gripping the newspaper in his hand, as if not to do so would cause it to flutter away.

He'd been right all along.

Well, he couldn't prove he was completely right, but at least he might have *damning* evidence. Unfortunately, the *damned* evidence was still insufficient, but at least it was a start.

MacLeod's annoying younger brother had just returned from another business trip to America, and had paid MacLeod a visit at the police office to boast about the success of a number of his business transactions. He'd stayed an hour, and when he'd left, had tossed a copy of the *New York Times* into MacLeod's bin.

MacLeod, sorely jealous, and very disturbed by the cheek of his arrogant sibling, had retrieved the paper with a view to flinging it out of the window. That was until the front headline grabbed his attention.

"Six bullets to the chest and stomach bring Amityville hoodlum down," he read aloud. The rest he read to himself, savouring each and every word.

'The true identity of Long Island foster parents, Paddy and Shauna Milligan, has been revealed, following a shootout at the Church of the Immaculate Conception of the Blessed Virgin Mary.

'Irish immigrants, the Milligans came to New York in 1914, and since then have been posing as foster parents. Paddy (known to his associates as Gripper Milligan) and Shauna have 'cared' for over four-hundred kids, but during this time, have been actively involved in organised crime, including kidnappings and murder.

'The district attorney's office is now faced with the additional problem: were all the kids 'in their care' taken legally, or was something far more sinister going on?'

MacLeod didn't need to read any further. Bette Milligan had been fostered out to a Mr and Mrs Milligan in the very same town. She had to have been one of those children. So, was she an 'innocent', or was she a programmed gangster? Had she been sent to Scotland for a particular purpose: to pose as a juvenile delinquent, then purportedly redeem herself, all the while gathering intelligence for a far more serious purpose?

It really was just too much of a coincidence.

As for that little besom, MacTaggart, her behaviour had been most uncharacteristic. No doubt the influence of Bette Milligan. Yes, that had to be the case. Not only was Bette Milligan a gangster, she was a witch practising black magic, and that really did go against the grain.

MacLeod shivered. Two weeks' suspension, without pay, would certainly teach MacTaggart to think twice before disobeying orders again. As for Bette Milligan, that remained to be seen.

62

Greenock Prison, Scotland

Jessie

Jessie examined the face of the sleeping woman. Mrs Fairbairn was completely out of it. Probably on morphine to dull the pain, and she had to be in pain. There were about half a dozen burn marks on her face, some of them weeping. Jessie leaned forward, and stroked her hand, but Mrs Fairbairn didn't stir. Jessie sat back and sighed.

"What have they done to you? What have they done?" Still no response.

Jessie raised her eyes. She knew in her heart that they'd got it all wrong. Well, at least DI MacLeod had got it all wrong, but the problem was she had no idea what to do to make it right.

"What's going on, Charlie?' she whispered. "What's going on?" She stared at the burns on Mrs Fairbairn's face. "Come on Charlie. A bit of help wouldn't go amiss."

Still, she stared, until very gently, the burn marks seemed to melt into the woman's cheeks. Jessie frowned and rubbed her eyes. The marks had returned. Was this what stress did to you? Too much stress?

"Time to relax, Charlie," she sighed. "Time to relax."

Maybe it *had* all been too much. Maybe what she'd seen at the Spiritualist Church had never really happened. The mind could play terrible tricks, but when the marks on Mrs Fairbairn's cheeks started to disappear again, and her face altered in shape, Jessie knew that relaxation was *not* going to be part of the course.

"Charlie?" she whispered, as his familiar face began to take form. "Charlie?"

"Hello Jessie!" It was Charlie's voice, this time emerging from Mrs Fairbairn's right shoulder.

Jessie smiled. "I see your students have changed the position of their voice box."

"A work in progress," replied Charlie.

Jessie shook her head. "Just tell me this, Charlie. Am I *really* seeing and hearing you, or, am I going off my head?"

"It's real, darling," returned Charlie. "It's me, and I'm here to tell you you've still got lots of work to do. They've got it all wrong, and you need to act."

Jessie shook her head again. It seemed crazy that whatever was out there couldn't intervene. "Why can't *you* do something, Charlie?"

"It's not up to me. I'm only here to guide. I can't

do it for you. You see, it's a human thing."

Jessie began to laugh. "I've only got two weeks, Charlie, *and* there's a war on. What on earth can I do in two weeks?"

"You have a life time, Jessie, and the choice is yours. Wherever you take yourself, and whatever you do. It's *your* life and *your* decision."

"So, help me out, Charlie. What would *you* do?"

"Well, I'd probably start with the Hills. The Muqattam Hills in Egypt."

"I've never heard of them."

"Then I'd look up Bette Milligan."

"Well, I've certainly heard of Bette."

"Then I'd take a look at an organisation called MPRS."

Now that *was* familiar. MacLeod had obsessed about it. He'd also referred to a military contact, someone who was close to the Chief Constable. Joe Banebridge? No. It was Bannerman. Joe Bannerman.

"Then what would you do, Charlie?"

"'Not my job to say, Jessie. But a trip to a villa in the Muqattam Hills, where you'll encounter Bette Milligan would probably be most advisable."

Charlie's face began to disappear.

"Charlie!" cried Jessie, leaning forward and grabbing Mrs Fairbairn's hand. But Charlie's face had gone, and was replaced by weeping sores on Mrs Fairbairn's cheeks. "Charlie! Charlie!" But it was no use. Jessie sensed Mrs Fairbairn stir, and tightened her grip on the woman's hand.

Mrs Fairbairn opened her eyes. "Your work is in Egypt," she whispered in her own voice. "Go to

Egypt. Find the truth. Don't let me die for nothing."

The significance of Mrs Fairbairn's words suddenly struck Jessie. She stared into the woman's eyes. They remained open, but their glazed expression suggested death.

"Nurse!" cried Jessie. "Somebody! Somebody! I need help here!"

63

Villa, Muqattam Hills

Bette

Well, Stephen did get the automobile up the hills. Not that I had anything to do with it. I shut my eyes from start to finish, sensing the vehicle negotiate parts I didn't even want to see. As for getting it down again, well that was something I'd suggest to Stephen he wouldn't even try.

I followed Stephen into the kitchen. The cooking range was on, and it was stiflingly hot. Joe was sitting in the corner, his hand gripping a bottle of whisky.

"Lamb and vegetables are in the larder," he said. "And try and have dinner ready for seven. We have a celebration. That bastard Campbell went to the gallows this morning, and we have a visitor."

"Pay no attention to him," said a familiar voice behind me.

I turned abruptly. "Farida!"

"Got a bit fed up with the afternoon tea in England," she said, raising her right hand, which was holding a bottle of champagne. "Had to get back to Egypt for a spot of the high life, so they flew me back in secret."

I began to grin, and was about to throw my arms around her, when I remembered she was one of the ones who'd conned me. Hugging could take place at a later date. I still had a point to make. I tried to look mean, but my delight that she was safe far outweighed my annoyance. In any case, she was my little sister.

What the hell!

I pulled her tightly towards me. "Remind me not to get on your wrong side," I murmured, as she gently pushed me away.

"You mean, like O'Malley?" she said.

"O'Malley," I agreed, still not sure which was worse: getting stabbed, or having a swastika pushed up your ass.

No doubt about it, though, Farida had done a first-class job. I looked at the clock on the wall. Five o'clock.

"You know, Joe," I said, turning back to him, "if I didn't know any better, I'd be thinking you had the same bottle of whisky permanently glued to your fingers."

"That's as may be," smirked Joe, "but I'm here to celebrate."

"Well, whoopee fucking dee!"

"Come on Bette," interjected Stephen. "Let's put our differences aside, and do as the man says."

But I wasn't interested. I didn't want to party. As far as I was concerned, there was nothing to celebrate. I'd been conned, and I certainly wasn't going to drink to that.

"I'm having a coffee," I said, my eyes turning to the copper kettle, perched on the cooking range. "Anyone else want one?"

"I'll have one," said Farida. "Then we can open the bubbly."

"I think Stephen and I will retire to the dining room,' said Joe, "and make a start on this little bugger here." He raised the bottle of whisky. "We've a lot to discuss." He paused for a moment, then turned towards me. "Wouldn't go near the living room, though, Bette. The bulb's just gone. Have to be careful of the ghosts: boo!"

"Splitting my sides laughing!" I growled.

Joe turned back to Stephen. "First things first. Angel's going to have to take a dive. I'm afraid he and his dicky little ticker will have to leave, never to return."

Stephen grinned. "You're breaking my heart," he said, following Joe out of the room.

"You, my good man, are getting posted to a secret location here in North Africa. There, you'll join a special unit." Joe's voice grew faint.

"Asshole!" I muttered.

"I agree," laughed Farida, "but he *does* get the job done."

"Does he? I'll take your word for it."

"Don't be sore," said Farida, stepping forward and patting me on the back. "Anyway, I'm away to powder my nose. If those two are going to the dining room, I suggest we *do* go to the living room. Let's defy Joe and have our own little party by candlelight! There are candles in my room. I'll go and get them." She turned and left the room.

Typical. Hadn't even thought of ghosts till Joe had mentioned them. Fucking dodo!

I waited for the kettle to boil, and as I did so, began to reflect on events. Then just as I was about to put myself into an irreversible state of depression, the kettle whistled, and my sanity was restored.

I made two mugs of coffee, and taking a sip of mine, headed in the direction of the living room. On the way, I passed the dining room. The door had been pushed over, but I could still hear the muffled sound of faint laughter.

Bastards! They were probably talking about me.

I continued towards the living room. The door was open wide, allowing in some light from the hall, but all I could make out was the grey shape of furniture. I was about to step into the room, when I recalled what had happened the last time. Quite memorable in fact, since I'd tripped over the very dead body of Omar O'Malley.

I shivered. "Fuck's sake, Bette! Get a grip!"

I wanted to blame Joe. But who was I kidding? The ghosts and ghouls of the past number of weeks had already become well implanted in my brain. I couldn't move. Shit! The sweat was pouring off me.

More faint laughter came from the dining room. *Should have joined them,* I thought. A couple of scotches, and I'd be challenging the spooks to come out and show themselves. But no way was I going to give in to what Joe wanted. I'd made one or two allowances for Farida, but Joe was something else.

So, what the hell was I frightened of?

Ghosts didn't really exist, did they?

But what if they did?

I took a step into the room and the floor creaked. "Jesus!" I rasped. "It's a fucking floorboard!" Another step in, and a different floorboard creaked, casting an air of derision in my direction. Four strides later, I was in the middle of the room, next to the couch: the exact spot I'd found O'Malley.

Beside it was a small table, where I plonked the mugs, before sitting down. I looked across at the shadowed shapes in the room, and squinted as I tried to make them out. The drapes across the window were shut, but I was still able to discern the large bookcase that covered the best part of two walls, and could almost see the marble fireplace.

When my eyes hit the outline of a lamp in one of the corners, I decided to get wise. Fuck the candles. I got up, and reaching the lamp, felt for the switch. There was a click, a brief flash of light, followed by a pop, then no more light.

"Shit!"

My heart was racing.

More laughter emanated from the dining room.

"Yeah! Just you two go on drinking! Never mind me. Never mind the fact I nearly got electrocuted and the fucking lights don't work."

Time to investigate, but best first to unplug the fucker.

I got down on all fours, and searched for the socket. My hand hit the plug. "Got you!" I exclaimed pulling it out. It was then that something briefly grabbed my ass.

"What the fuck?" Whatever it was, grabbed it again. "Fuck's sake, Joe! Not funny!" I spun round, but even in the dim light of the room I could see that no one was there. Or, more to the point, no one human was there. When the invisible thing grabbed my ass a third time, I was ready to flip.

"Stephen!" I shouted. "Farida!"

This time the thing grasped my hair, and yanked my head backwards. I opened my mouth to scream, but nothing came out.

"Always did like a feisty little redhead!" rasped a voice in my left ear, which took me back to my adventure with Willie Campbell in the jeep.

"No way! Not possible!" I stuttered. It couldn't be. It didn't make sense. Someone was playing a trick. "Not funny, asshole!" I yelled to no one in particular. Not difficult, of course, because there was no one to yell at.

And then a different voice, this time in my right ear. "This is *my* home!" it hissed, its Irish intonations sending a shiver up my back.

"I don't *believe* in ghosts!" I screamed. My head was tugged further back. Time to change tactics. "I'm not *afraid* of ghosts!"

But who was I kidding?

The hold on my head was suddenly released. I turned abruptly to examine the room, but there was no one there. Not even an outline of a person amongst the shapes that adorned the unlit room.

No image.

No sound.

Simply the echo of that menacing voice, resonating in my ear, as it whispered: "This is *my* home!"

64

The Spirit World

Bentley

Poltergeist activity! Poltergeist activity!

Charlie's shrill warning reverberated through the ether, attacking Bentley's spirit with unearthly force.

Bentley pulled himself back. *Easy! Easy!*

Suddenly there was a swoosh of energy, and a third being, which Bentley didn't recognise, emerged from seemingly nowhere, with the force of champagne toppling out of a freshly uncorked bottle.

Hello chaps, said the energy, drawing near.

Who's this? asked Bentley.

It's William, replied Charlie.

Bentley was confused. *William?* It certainly wasn't Willie Campbell.

So, what's the problem, Charles? asked William.

Charles? repeated Bentley. The posh bastard was using Charlie's Sunday name.

It's mayhem! bemoaned Charlie.

Bentley didn't understand. *Would somebody like to tell me what's going on?* he demanded.

Charlie was growing impatient. *We have a situation, Bentley. I called William here because we need all the help we can muster.*

Bentley's energy relaxed. He was certain that Charlie's kind of situation would be tantamount to little more than the wrong answer to one of his sums.

And thank goodness you're here, William, gasped Charlie. *It's those bounders*: *Willie Campbell and Omar O'Malley. You know, the one that used to be von Kosch. They've slipped the net and buggered off!*

Bentley was growing even more confused. *So, William, who are you? A bounty hunter?*

Not exactly, said William.

It's really very worrying, continued Charlie. *Word in the ether is that they've joined forces with Andrew Witherspoon and a newcomer, one Paddy Milligan, also known to his friends as Gripper Milligan, a newly-deceased New York gangster.*

Ah, roaming spirits, sighed William.

Charlie was now panicking. *Yes, and out to wreak havoc. What's more, they've already started to pursue the target!*

Bentley was perplexed. *Target?*

Charlie seemed ready to explode. *Bette Milligan, of course!*

Bentley shuddered. *Strewth! What do they want with her?*

Do I have to explain everything? Charlie lamented.

It would help, responded Bentley.

Paddy Milligan was one of Bette's foster parents. She was sent to him by von Kosch. Joe Bannerman managed to rescue her before any great damage was done, but now Paddy wants her back!

Bentley remembered Joe telling him Bette was from an unfortunate background, but he hadn't mentioned anything about a gangster connection.

So, if Milligan's dead, why does he want her back?

To do what he tried to do before he was bumped off, exclaimed Charlie. *Groom her, get into her mind and turn her into a Nazi!*

He'll not manage that! derided Bentley.

We can't take the chance, stressed Charlie. *This is war. War of the minds, and that's where you come in, Bentley.*

Bentley felt his strength plummet. *Again?* he said.

You're the only one who can get into her head safely.

This was rapidly turning into another case of déjà-vu. *What about him?* suggested Bentley, turning to William.

Not possible. Too much to do, said William.

This annoyed Bentley.

So, if you're not a bounty hunter, and you're not a minder, who are you, and why are you here? And why won't anyone just let me die in peace?

William pushed his energy out, until it towered up into the ether, connecting with every spirit in the universe.

My name is William Thomson. I'm also known as Lord Kelvin. And the reason, my dear chap, you will never rest in peace, is quite simple: it's because of the

Laws of Thermodynamics. The first Law relates to the conservation of energy, and dictates quite clearly that energy cannot be created or destroyed, it can only change form. And you, sir, are a perfect example.

END
Or, is it...?

ABOUT THE AUTHOR

Caroline was born in Glasgow, but was brought up in Kent. She studied languages, then moved to France to work as a secretary, first with Campanile, then with Interpol. When she returned to the UK, she joined Strathclyde Police (now Police Scotland). On retiring from the police, she studied creative writing at Glasgow University and pursued an interest in Spiritualism and Psychical Research. She is now President of the Glasgow Association of Spiritualists. 'Enemy on the Other Side' is Caroline's first novel.

Printed in Great Britain
by Amazon